Curiosity of Laura Stone

Laura Stone Mysteries

Michael J Spanhanks

BOGGY CREEK PUBLISHING

MICHAEL J SPANHANKS

Publisher: Boggy Creek Press
For more information or to book an event, contact:
http://www.michaelspanhanksbooks.com
ISBN: 979-8-9853968-7-4

Cover Design by Innovative Presentations
Editing by Michael Bush

PeriodImages.com
VJ Dunraven Productions, Mary Chronis, Period Images, Pi Creative Lab
Photo ID - 2015-01-07_02.36.18
Photo ID - 2016-02-16_16.34.07-2

123rf Images
Photo ID: 100340529
Contributor: scottff72

Shutter Stock images
Photo ID:460209283
Contributor: Romashka2

Bible References
Job 14:1 KJV
Nahum 1:7 KJV
Philippians 2:3
Hebrews 4:12
Genesis 2:24
Romans 10:9
Matthew 19:5-6

MICHAEL J SPANHANKS

The Bible suggests that curiosity, the desire to learn and acquire greater wisdom, to gain insight and understanding is to be part of our life. Luke 2:52 tells us that even Jesus grew in wisdom.

‡

He taught me also, and said unto me, Let thine heart retain my words: keep my commandments, and live. Get wisdom, get understanding: forget it not; neither decline from the words of my mouth.
Proverbs 4:4-5

The Return

Chapter 1

*L*aura Stone withdrew the letter from her handbag and studied it once more. Growing up, her father Horace Stone had been as sturdy as an ox, never sick a day, and gave her strength at her mom's death.

The year before she left for college, Laura opted to stay and help around the ranch, but Horace pleaded against it, saying she must go to Boston and fulfill her mom Naomi's dream of acquiring a proper education. But now that her father had passed, she must be the resilient one.

Nine days before, she had left Boston by Transcontinental Rail. A few days into the trip, she realized that sleeping in the seat was no luxury—her neck throbbed from lying against the back. She could have opted for a hotel during a stop and caught the train a week later, but she felt it prudent to hasten to Santa Fe and settle matters regarding her father.

A big man on the train with menacing eyes caused her to feel uneasy. She noticed he wore a gray tweed suit and vest and smoked a nauseating cigar, permeating the air with the most undesirable aroma. Throughout the entire trip, he seemed fixated on her. Though he appeared once to have something to say, his only utterance came as a passing remark heading towards the privy.

The ticket master strode through the door. "Folks, we are about an hour from Santa Fe. If your travel ends there, please collect your luggage from the overhead repository and prepare to exit the coach."

After receiving the instructions, folks gathered their belongings. Others took the opportunity to stretch and move around. For some, Santa Fe was an interruption in the lengthy course to San Francisco.

"I will require a week in bed to mend from this trip," said a woman behind Laura.

A man countered, "Ma'am, just be thankful you did not travel by stage. Took me over a month once in that vivacious cubicle."

Laura grasped her suitcases and a bundle of journals bound in leather from the overhead storage. Despite her intention to peruse them along the way, her thoughts stayed on her father's passing. The attorney's letter suggested that the sheriff was suspicious regarding the cause of death, which made the affair quite curious.

The whistle blared, signaling the passengers to their culmination point. From several miles away, the brakes squealed, decelerating the heavy segments of steel until the train movement's termination.

Laura snatched up her bags and followed the other passengers down the aisle.

The gentleman exhibiting the peculiar behavior lingered at his seat. "Ma'am, I could carry those for you."

Hoping to avoid a lengthy conversation, Laura turned and said, "I can handle them. Thank you."

"I'm getting off here too," he continued. "Got a business matter to deal with in Santa Fe."

"Maybe I'll see you around."

"That would be my pleasure, though I did not catch your name."

She sighed and peered out the windows before offering it, relieved to feel safe by the surroundings. "It's Laura."

"Mine is Thomas Fletcher. Maybe we will run into each other around town."

"Yes, maybe so."

She marched from the train to the boarding dock and set her bags down, gazing at the town.

A fellow preparing to board saw her confusion. "Ma'am, are you new to Santa Fe?"

"Yes. Can you advise me which way to the sheriff's office?"

"You'll find it straight ahead on this street and to the right."

"Thank you, sir. Have a delightful journey." She gathered her bags and set a pace on the boardwalk.

The placards nailed to the outside wall made the sheriff's office simple to identify. She delayed examining them.

"Some bad ones come through these parts," came an utterance. The voice behind her belonged to a balding man about sixty years old, who had on a soiled white apron.

"The name's Gordon Andrews. I own the mercantile across the way."

"I'm pleased to meet you, Mr. Andrews. My name is Laura Stone."

"Stone? Like in Horace Stone?"

"Yes. He was my father."

"Was so unfortunate to hear of his passing. Horace was vibrant and full of energy."

"Yes, he was. Sadly, I must run, Mr. Andrews, but I will require supplies soon."

"So, are you sticking around?"

"I've settled nothing yet."

"Come on in when you get ready. We'll fix you right up."

He walked away as Laura fidgeted with the doorknob. She set down one of her bags and reached again.

Before her hand found it, the door opened abruptly, and a fellow with a mustache wearing a black hat, a striped shirt, and a vest, with a gun on his hip, stood before her. "I didn't know anybody was out there. Can I help you?"

"So, are you the sheriff?" Laura asked.

"Yes, John Ellison is my name." He took her bags inside and motioned for her to follow.

"Sheriff, I'm Laura Stone. You sent a telegraph to attorney George Walsh in Boston addressed to me?"

"Yes I did, and I'm sorry for your loss, Miss Stone, but I'm glad you're here. Horace was a good friend, always peaceful, and would give you the coat off his back."

"Thank you, Sheriff. Um, in the wire, you suggested my father's death was suspicious. What did you mean?"

"When I first saw Horace's body, I agreed with the doc's statement that his heart may have given out. But a few days later, resting at the desk, I thought about all those folks showing up on his land. I shouldn't have said it was suspicious, though."

"What folks? Who was coming onto my father's land?"

"Those miners. You didn't know?"

"I'm afraid I'm in the dark."

"Ralph Floyd got over on your father's land digging for gold and hit a modest load. Next thing you know, miners are climbing those hills hoping for treasure. Oh, Horace ran them off, and he even came for my help. We both struggled to make them leave."

"Are you thinking that one of the minors may have killed my father, Sheriff?"

"Now, don't go saying that, Miss Stone, or believing it either, because I don't know. I only speculated in my mind that there was a possibility."

"You mentioned that the doc—"

"Yeah, Doc Simms. He said it looked like Horace's heart had given out. But you see, there was a dreadful place on his head, like he may have fainted and fallen on some rocks."

"And that gave you second thoughts about the doc's theory?"

"Yes and no. I know Doc Simms is excellent at what he does, but the way that wound looked, in my mind, was more than a heart condition, and the fact that I knew your pa was as healthy as they come. That's when I started thinking it could have been that other fellow who done it."

"*What* other fellow?"

Sheriff Ellison rose from his chair and stared at Laura. "He declares he was helping Horace control the miners, but I don't know. I can tell you this. I expected there'd be scads of those miners turning up there after Horace passed, but I saw no one, though I haven't been back in a while."

Laura's jaw tightened. "Sheriff, you've had all this time and haven't discovered anything more?" She paused, waiting for his response. "Well, since you've had so much difficulty investigating my father's death, *I* will help you uncover the truth."

The sheriff's eyes pierced her. "Now, Miss Stone, it's best you stay out of it and let me deal with matters of the law! And for your information, I'm still looking into it. It's just that a lot has happened around here."

Laura could not shake the feeling that something was indeed amiss about her father's passing, and the sheriff's excuses only made her angry, piercing her blue irises to the core. "You should have already completed your investigation. You knew something was wrong when you stated in the letter that his death was suspicious."

"Now, Miss Stone, there are other complications to consider when probing around about your father's death, and it takes time."

She knew she should leave it there, though the sheriff's explanations annoyed her. "Sheriff, I require a horse and a buggy to take me to the ranch."

"Your father has a couple of horses. The reddish one was his favorite, though they aren't here now."

"The reddish one is Copper."

"I'll have Elijah Ellison help get you there. Elijah is my cousin and works as a deputy. I'll see to it he takes you home in the buckboard. Your father should still have a buckboard, and those horses of his will draw it."

"Thank you, Sheriff."

As the sheriff hunted for Deputy Elijah, Laura reflected on their conversation. Horace only wanted to raise his cattle and live his life in peace. But could someone have killed him over gold? *I will find out what happened.*

Chapter 2

*A*s the buckboard pulled into the ranch, Laura noticed the place looked almost exactly as it did the last time she was home. To the right of the property stood the barn, with two spacious corrals attached. Near the house, Naomi had dedicated countless hours tending the flower garden, and they looked beautiful—a stunning display of blanket flowers, cherry sage salvia, pansies, and her favorite, coral bells.

Her head turned noticeably to a shutter hanging to one side of the window. *Needs some repairs.*

"Horace wasn't much for upkeep these last years," Elijah said. "Spent most of his time with those cows."

"He doesn't have to worry about it anymore."

"You mean about the cows?"

She smiled and reached for her bags. "Thank you for the ride. I'll see you in town, I suppose."

"Yes, ma'am, I'm sure you will."

As Elijah and the team drew away, Laura turned her attention toward the house as she stopped on the porch. She peered across the field, searching for the cattle, but there were none. *Hmm, I wonder where they are?*

She dropped her bags and strolled toward the barn, catching the familiar aroma of horse droppings—a sign she was home. *Shew!*

"Copper, where are you, boy? Star! Copper! Come on, boys! Whoop, whoop!"

Moments later, two geldings, a sorrel, and a gray horse, trotted through the corral's open gate.

"Hey there, boys. Good to see you. I'm glad you are okay."

The gray horse wandered close and nudged her on the arm. "Star, did you miss me? I know you must have missed Father, and I'm sorry he's not here for you."

She reached across the hallway, grasped a bridle, and slipped it onto Copper. "Let's go for a ride."

Before leading the sorrel through the doorway to saddle him, she tossed hay out for Star. Then she mounted and rode toward the field to search for the cattle. *I hope someone hasn't helped themselves as they did for the gold.*

A half-hour later, she came upon a place known to her family as the old pond, expecting to find the herd, but a deer sprang through the woods. As she paused the horse, a couple of fish stirred ripples on the water but nothing of the cattle. Remembering her father's grumblings about having to ride into the hillsides hunting for lost calves, she set her sights on the bluffs.

After riding along the ridge for a while, a stench caught her attention. On the ground lay the corpse of a newborn calf. Dismounting, she examined it. "What did this, Copper?"

Something passed in her peripheral vision startling her. As far as she knew, her father only had two horses, and she was sure she saw another. She mounted Copper and spotted it again, a black horse and rider. Then she booted her horse into a run. "Come on, Copper. Let's catch them."

Copper ran hard, skirting the trees and jumping crevices

made by heavy rains. Now forty feet ahead, the rider seemed in no hurry but slowed when he heard her behind him.

"Hey, you! Stop there!" Laura shouted.

At the comment, the rider reined up his mount and looked back. "May I help you?"

She guessed the man was in his mid-thirties. He wore a black hat, a plaid shirt beneath a brown vest, and leather chaps. Behind the sad eyes and dark mustache, he was rather good-looking. And though he offered no hint of hostility, he wore a six-shooter on his right hip.

Laura gazed at him with a needle stare. "What are you doing here?"

His brows raised as he wrestled away a smile. "Well, ma'am, I don't know that it's any business of yours, but I ride through here most days."

She pushed up straight against the stirrups, honing her stare. "I'm making it my business because *I own* this land."

The stranger shook his head. "No, ma'am, this land belongs to Horace Stone. So I might ask, what do *you* want?"

Setting her hands to her hips, she said, "I am Horace's daughter. And you'll please cease with the ma'am."

He smiled and shoved back his hat. "I would if I knew your name."

She turned her somewhat reddened face away and then back. "I'm sorry, mine's Laura Stone."

"I've heard of you."

Reining her horse to adjust the sun from her view, she examined the man once more. "Just tell me what you're doing on my property? Never mind, I know the answer. You're one of those who've been stealing my father's gold."

"No, ma'am. Horace was my friend."

She huffed out a sigh. "Seems everybody has become a friend of my father's since someone found gold on his place."

Again, he shook his head. "No, it's not like that at all. Your father ran into trouble managing those miners, so I offered my help, and we pretty much had them shooed away before he passed. And after his death, I figured they'd turn up here again, so I camped out in the bluffs watching for them."

"What's your name, mister, and where do you live?"

"My name is Kenneth Barlow, and I stay with my folks south of Santa Fe when not working a cattle drive or breaking horses."

"Maybe I should turn you into the authorities."

"Then, by all means, if you feel it's your duty."

She half-grinned. "How do I know you're not just after the gold for yourself?"

"Well, first, I don't believe this ground holds much gold. Second, I think maybe Ralph Floyd got the best part, and the others wasted their time."

"Yet, they kept coming back," Laura replied.

"That's the way it is with gold strikes. The news travels like wildfire, and everybody wants a piece of the pie."

Her chest rose, and a muscle convulsed in her throat. "They can stay away. And Mr. Barlow, since I don't know you, I suggest *you* keep off my father's land. The sheriff will take care of those prospectors."

Barlow shifted his hat. "Are you speaking of Sheriff Ellison?" He laughed. "Don't count on him, Miss Stone. Your father pleaded for Ellison's help and got none. He came here a few times to make a good show. Then after your father passed, someone told me they spotted him lurking nearby one evening with a pick and a pan. I assume they meant he was panning for gold."

"Are you positive? He sounded competent to me."

"Maybe competent at poker and whiskey, but serving folks? He talks a big talk, is all."

"Is there not any law in these parts?"

"Sure. You might go to Albuquerque and speak to the U.S.

Marshal, though I doubt he'd help. The Texas Rangers might, but they don't get out this way much."

Laura sighed and gazed at the ground. How was it so complicated in a simple place like Santa Fe?

"Miss Stone, I've enjoyed chatting with you, but I have a fellow expecting my help with a horse. I better mosey along." He tipped his hat to bid her goodbye, kicked his horse into a gait, and rode away.

"I don't know what to think about this country, Copper."

Chapter 3

*L*aura found several jars of canned food in the cupboard. She knew her father must have bought them because her mom had been the one who loved to grow things in a garden. Wherever they came from, Laura appreciated the green beans for supper and the peaches for breakfast.

As the sun came up, she sat drinking coffee, hearing a sound from outside. She rose and rushed to the door, noticing her father's cows had drifted home. *I hope there is enough grass and water. But what do I know? Father always took care of them.* Laura had helped Horace herd them to a pasture or to a corral for branding, but he never required her to take a significant role in ranching. He had his dogs for that.

The dogs? Where are the dogs? Horace always had a couple around to work the cattle. Someone indeed must have taken them, she thought, or they found a new home.

She stood at the door, gazing at her mom's flower garden as they glistened in the early sunlight. Their sweet fragrances saturated the morning air. Then she was reminded, as she peered at the barn, that she must hitch the wagon and go to Santa Fe for supplies. And along the way, she would stop at her parents' gravesites.

"I'm so sorry, Father," she said. "I wasn't here when you needed me. But I promise that if something unspeakable has happened, I won't rest until those involved pay the price."

She found the harnesses where Horace always stored them and led the horses into the hall space where the wagon sat. They backed into place as if knowing work lay ahead. In a short while, she was on the road to Santa Fe.

* * *

A blacksmith pounded a horseshoe into shape as Laura guided the team through town. Lively folks walked along the streets as she traveled by. The Transcontinental train roared from the far end of town, signaling a near departure time.

Laura had navigated the wagon beside Andrews Mercantile when a gentleman dressed in a dark suit and tie moved toward her. She suspected he was studying her, so she rushed down from the wagon in hopes of eluding him. But the gentleman perceived her strategy and hurried her way.

"I don't believe we've met?" he announced upon approach.

Laura spun to his enthusiastic smile and saw that he bore a brown hat melding with his fine suit and tie. Then with surprising behavior, she stared into his fine-looking face and radiant blue eyes. Instinctively, she drew in a deep breath and brushed the wind-blown hair from her face. "I...I'm sorry. The name is Laura Stone."

He removed his hat and held it in one hand. "I've heard about you. My name is Pastor West, or Steven if you like."

She half-shrugged, offering a kind smile. "I suppose the entire town knows of my arrival."

"Maybe not everyone, but that's a good thing."

She turned to look away, but his handsomeness lured her gaze. "I'm happy to meet you, Mr. West."

Her gorgeous complexion and light hair captured his attention. "Um, the pleasure is mine, but while you're staying, I hope you'll visit our little church."

Laura sensed her face reddening as he watched her and peered to the ground, hoping she might avoid sending the wrong message. "Maybe I will, sir." *And maybe I'll come to show off my Eastern dresses because I doubt much has changed since childhood.*

"That would be splendid, Miss Stone," he said, maintaining his gaze until he sensed an uneasiness and watched as she turned away. "Um, I have folks I must visit, so I'll leave you to your interests." Putting his hat on, he strode away.

Hmm. He is quite nice-looking but very forward.

She spotted Mr. Andrews through the mercantile entrance putting away canned peaches, and marched toward him. "Mr. Andrews, who prepares the peaches for you? I ate some this morning. Father had them in the cupboard, and they were delicious."

"Good morning, Miss Stone. Um, that would be May Adams. Your father purchased them all the time."

"Thank you. I must have some."

"Well, I have plenty."

Laura snooped around the store, seeing what else Mr. Andrews carried. Santa Fe wasn't Boston, but she must survive until the time came to leave.

"Can I help you with anything else, Miss Stone?"

"Please call me Laura."

"Well, then you call me Gordon. That's what most people around here call me, though some use other names, especially when I'm out of what they're looking for."

"Oh, I'm sorry."

14

"They mean well. Folks don't understand the mercantile business and how painstaking it is bringing in supplies."

"Maybe you will have the things I require, which are beans, flour, bacon if you have it, several jars of those peaches, and cornmeal. Oh, and do you sell hog fat?"

"I do, and got some in today."

"Father always had a hog to kill growing up, but I didn't find any around the place."

"No, I suspect your father stayed busy watching those cows and running folks off his place. So, you're staying in Santa Fe for a while?"

Laura jerked her head around. "Do you know those folks Father ran off?"

Gordon brushed the whiskers on his chin, studying her request, and then looked around at the other customers. "I expect I can tell you what I've heard," he whispered. "But not here in the front. When we have you loaded, follow me to the rear of the store, and I'll share what I know."

"I'm indeed grateful."

After loading her supplies, Gordon led Laura to the back of the store and the names of the men who spoke of her father's gold. There were so many that she considered hiring an investigator, though finding one in Santa Fe might not be as straightforward as in Boston. So where would she look?

She scribbled some names down in her notepad and placed it in her pocket, then headed for the wagon pausing when she recognized the man standing near the mercantile entrance. *Oh no. Thomas Fletcher.*

He grinned and started her way. "I speculated if we might meet again."

"Ah, Mr. Fletcher. And I wondered if you had returned home after your business doings at Santa Fe."

"Well, sadly, my business is still pending. Now, might I purchase your dinner sometime, Miss Stone, at the Hotel restaurant, of course?"

A notion struck her. "Um, Mr. Fletcher, I don't mean to pry, but would you mind if I inquire what kind of work you do?"

"Not at all. I work at a bank in New York. However, these duties often bring me to other banks across the country. My job is to investigate the validity of contracts acquired by banks from citizens. Now, I cannot delve into specifics for reasons of privacy. But it's all boring stuff, I assure you. Then I also work as an investigator."

"I had a belief you might."

"Is there something I might assist you with?"

"Yes. Um, is that petition for dinner still on?"

"It is."

"Could we do it now so I can get my supplies home?"

"Yes, of course."

* * *

When they were seated, Laura revealed to Thomas Fletcher that she doubted heart failure caused her father's death. At first, Fletcher was skeptical of her theory until Laura told him about Horace's physical condition and about the men who came to his place for the gold.

Fletcher leaned casually back in his chair, trusting he was not exposing his disinterest in her quest. "So you *are* sure someone has discovered gold on the property?"

She offered a listless shrug of her shoulders. "I only know what they talked about, though I lived on Father's ranch for almost twenty years growing up and never knew of any. Only Father would have known with certainty."

Fletcher peered down at the table, considering what to say. "Perhaps, but we know folks have gone there to dig."

Laura instantly bristled. He still did not realize her intentions. "Mr. Fletcher, my interest is not whether there's gold on Father's land. My objective is to find out if someone murdered him for it."

He lifted his elbows to the table, rubbing his hands together, pondering her entreaty. "Oh, call me Thomas, please." He paused a moment. "Yes, I can look into it, though I can't guarantee the answer you're looking for. First, I'll call on the sheriff about your story, then visit the doctor for confirmation. After that, I'll reveal my findings."

"And what about those names I gave you?"

"Ah, yes, in time. But I hope you realize those names are gossip, pure hearsay, which may or may not lead us somewhere. I prefer we *not* begin there."

Her heart sank at his lack of interest in her leads. But why was his attention on her if not to help? "Well, Thomas, I must leave so I can tend to the horses."

"Yes, yes, I'm sure," Fletcher said, then opened his mouth as if to speak again but held back.

"Is there something more, Mr. Fletcher?"

"Er, no. I will get moving with what I have."

Laura rose from the table. "Thank you for dinner and for agreeing to help."

"You're welcome."

She stepped from the restaurant and climbed into the wagon, pondering if Fletcher was a waste of her time, then started home.

Chapter 4

L aura woke the following day, intending to check the cows early. She rummaged through an old trunk of her mom's for clothes to wear. After changing, she saddled Copper and rode toward the herd.

She noticed as she rode along how the trees and bushes had grown taller than before, and the piles of branches and tree stumps indicated that Horace had labored hard to clear the meadows.

The letter she received said there were around forty-five heads of cows on her father's ranch, including the calves. She came upon their tracks moving away from the creek. Then through an opening in the woods, she saw them bunched. *Why are they here?*

Then a sudden smell of smoke struck fear in her. She forced Copper forward, pushing their way through the herd. Just beyond the woods lay another large clearing. When she reached the outer edge of the trees, she saw a man standing near a fire, grasping a yearling. Another pressed the branding iron to its hip.

"You better not be changing brands," Laura declared. "These are my cattle!"

A man with a dark hat and a patch over one eye turned, dropping his arm to his hip. "What are you doing here?"

A rifle cocked from behind the wood line and drew their attention. "I'd leave those cows alone if I were you. And if you get on your horses, you can ride out of here right now."

Laura lifted her chin, her pulse throbbing. "No they can't! They are branding my cattle with intentions to steal them."

"And we stopped them," replied the man as the thieves rushed to mount their horses.

"You're letting them get away?"

The thieves rode out, sending dust into the air.

A fellow on a black horse rode from behind a thicket and started toward her.

"It's you! I thought I told you to stay off my property."

"Kenneth."

"What?"

"My name is Kenneth."

"The point is, Kenneth, you are here again, and I've asked you not to come."

He grinned, shaking his head. "Well, ma'am, I'm not sure you'd be alive right now if I hadn't."

"I can take care of myself."

"Oh, yeah. One of those men was reaching for a gun, and I bet you don't have one."

"I didn't feel the need since I'm on my property."

"If you're going to work cattle, you need one. How will you take out a mountain lion if they attack your herd? Not far from here, I saw the remains of a dead calf. Gold wasn't the only reason your father attended the herd so much. He'd killed three cats before I came to help."

Laura shifted uneasily in the saddle and gazed around the

field.

"He heard they had moved in on a herd of cattle west of here before they went to market. He said it must have been their feasting ground until the owner herded them away to market. Once the cattle were gone, the cats came to his place. Horace figured they needed a new place to feed."

"Father said nothing about mountain lions in his letters to me, or that he had a weak heart."

"Laura, maybe he hid it so you wouldn't come. And don't ever think your father had a weak heart. On the contrary, Horace was the toughest man I've ever met."

She leaned forward in the saddle, sobbing.

Kenneth bounced from his horse and ran to her. "Are you alright?"

"I don't know."

"Come down for a moment?"

She stepped from the saddle, her face wet with tears. "This is harder than I imagined. I thought to stay only a few days to tend to Father's things, and then I learned people had been stealing gold from his land. And this morning, I find men rebranding Father's cattle. What am I supposed to do, Kenneth?" She reached out and hugged him.

He drew his hat from his head as she held him. "Everything will work out, Laura. This is the first I knew of men stealing his cattle, though I'm not surprised."

Laura peered into his face. "You said a moment ago that Father didn't have a weak heart. What did you mean?"

"The doc blamed Horace's death on his heart, but I believe something else went on. I was the one who found your father on the backside of his place. His wagon was there, and some tools lay on the ground. It looked like he was there to mend a fence.

"I found Horace at the bottom of the gully. There was a terrible wound on the back of his head. The doctor declared your father hit his head, which he thought stirred up a weak heart. They looked no further after that."

"Even with all those people coming here, that's what they settled on?"

"That's right. Laura, I studied the barbed wire. That wire didn't break—someone cut it. I believe whoever did it was coming through the backside of his land for a good reason and maybe to hide who they were."

"You're saying those after Father's gold didn't want to be exposed? Then why not just wear a bandana over their face like an outlaw?"

"That only works if no one recognizes your horse. Around here, people identify you by your horse and saddle."

Laura thought about it for a moment. "Then that might also mean that it's someone in an important position, even someone Father knew, who was after the gold. And might be the person who killed him."

"This is only a theory, Laura, and I can't prove any of it."

"Doesn't mean you're wrong."

"After Doc Simms told me he felt Horace's death was a heart problem, I saw Sheriff Ellison. He said Doc Simms was the professional and stood by him."

"So he never investigated?"

"No. I pushed the sheriff to examine the barbed wire, but Ellison protested, still siding with the doc."

"Kenneth, why would he not consider what you told him? Sheriff Ellison claimed he was a close acquaintance of my father's. You don't suppose he was the one slipping in digging for gold, do you?"

"Sheriff Ellison was no acquaintance to your father. When Horace told him of the miners, he did nothing. The sheriff's reluctance to help perturbed him."

"Then the sheriff lied to me. He made it to sound as if he and Father had been friends."

"Maybe they were once and something changed, but I

know this. Gold changes a man. Jesus spoke about greed in the Bible. He said, *Take heed and beware of covetousness, for one's life does not consist in the abundance of the things he possesses.*"

Laura was not one to read the scriptures, but knew those who did were decent folks. This side of Kenneth was unexpected. "So what can I do?"

"What I told you about watching for the miners was true. Since I found the cut wire, I've been observing those who might have done it."

"But I need proof."

"Maybe I can help with that. Unlike the sheriff, I was your father's friend."

"Kenneth, I misjudged you, and I'm sorry."

"Then make it up to me. There's a dance tonight in town. Go with me. There's someone who'll be there that I want you to meet."

"Alright, I will. Might be a good time to get to know folks."

"Good. I'll pick you up around five in a buggy."

"I'll be ready."

Chapter 5

*B*uggies and buckboards occupied the livery's outskirts as Kenneth and Laura arrived. Kenneth guided the buggy beside another and parked it, and then walked around to assist Laura.

"I wish there were better light for you," Kenneth said.

"It's fine."

He reached for Laura's arm and escorted her inside. Folks watched with curiosity as Kenneth led her to a table.

"Feels strange with so many eyes on us," Laura declared. "Living in Boston, I knew everyone at the events. Once, I did here, but so much has changed."

"Several new folks have moved in. Some because of the gold, not at your father's place. Others for jobs with the railroad or the new stockyards."

A band started playing a song as they walked inside, and folks began dancing on the dirt floor.

Kenneth turned to Laura. "Would you care for some punch?"

"Yes, please."

As he stepped away, Laura recalled several dances her parents had brought her to. She would laugh as she watched them twirl and turn to the music. *Those were great times.*

Kenneth returned to the table with another fellow. "Laura, I'd like to present a friend. This is Pastor Steven West."

Pastor West removed his hat and reached for Laura's hand. "We met before at the mercantile. I must say, you are a beauty. Of course, I shouldn't speak such, even though I am stating a fact."

Laura blushed at the words.

Kenneth sensing an awkwardness said, "Laura, Pastor West is my friend as well as my pastor. I attend his church, and so do several here."

"Oh, I didn't realize."

"I wanted you to meet him and hoped you might join us Sunday."

"Yes, that would be wonderful, Miss Stone," Pastor West responded. "I know you will find our people welcoming."

Church? I don't know about that. "I'm sure they are wonderful. Thank you both for appealing to me. I must take it to heart."

Laura could not help but notice Pastor West's striking appearance, and a thought came to her. But she brushed it away, for it would only produce suffering knowing the time would come when she must leave for Boston.

"Laura, there's a buddy at the dance I must see," Kenneth declared. "Do you mind?"

"Not at all."

"Then I'll leave you in the excellent hands of the pastor."

"We will be fine."

They sat quietly, peering at the musicians and dancers.

West's blue-eyed gaze drifted to her. "I'd suggest a dance, but I've not procured that exercise."

Laura glanced around the room. "That's okay. I'll enjoy your company as we watch the others."

"Yes. Then may I ask how matters are progressing at your father's place? I know how challenging it is when a family member passes."

"My time at home has been unexpected. Yesterday, Kenneth and I rode upon some men branding father's cattle."

"You mean they were going to take them?"

"Yes."

"That's awful. Have you told Sheriff Ellison?"

"Haven't found the moment."

"He's here at the dance. I can bring him to you."

"Don't trouble yourself." Since Kenneth told her about the sheriff, Laura lacked the confidence that Ellison would serve her well. If he had robbed her father's gold, cattle theft would be nothing.

"Would you know their faces if you saw them?"

"I think so, and I'm concerned they may show up again."

"I'm sorry for your trouble. What can I do to help?"

She turned her head back to the dance floor. "I'm sure you have enough to do with your congregation without involving yourself in my trouble."

He reached and touched her arm. "I'm here for you. I could also put you up at the church until the matter's settled."

She pulled her arm away. "No, that would look improper. Besides, I should be at the ranch watching for those fellows."

"That's mighty risky by yourself, Miss Stone."

"Just Laura, please."

"Laura has nothing to fear, Pastor," Kenneth remarked, stepping up behind them. "I'll watch over the herd until those men get what's coming to them."

Laura spun in her chair. "By getting what's coming to them, you mean captured?"

"Yes, of course," Kenneth said as he took a seat beside

them. "But they might not go easily."

"I prefer not to see anyone hurt."

"And what if it's the same fellows who killed your father?"

Pastor West's eyebrows raised as he peered at Laura. "What did you say...killed your father? I thought Horace died of heart complications. Kenneth, that is how he died, right?"

"That's difficult to know for sure. The fence Horace was there to mend wasn't down because of the cows, as supposed. Someone cut it."

"What does that mean?"

"I guess it means those after the gold found a way in. Horace may have stumbled onto them and got himself killed."

"May have? Kenneth, that's conjecture."

"I'm not so sure anymore. There were tracks around where Horace died that didn't belong to his horses. I looked them over and put them to memory."

Laura aimed a sharp look at Kenneth. "You didn't tell me that."

"I'm sorry. You had enough on your mind, and I figured to inform you later."

Laura gazed around the dance floor. "Has anyone seen Doc Simms tonight?"

"I believe he had a patient to see, Mrs. Roxie Giles," Pastor West replied.

Laura turned to Kenneth. "I'd like to speak with him. Will you show me where his office is?"

Kenneth stood from his chair. "Yes. We can go together."

"Laura, if you don't mind," uttered Pastor West, "I'd like to tag along and hear this."

Laura rose from the chair. "Then let's go."

* * *

When they entered the doctor's office, Simms was in an

examination room with a woman and her child. Laura wandered around the waiting room, peering at the various items. She thought it fascinating that a physician would have dime novels of gunmen killing folks lying on a small table. On a nearby wall hung tattered placards of surgical methods and procedures. A vase with a lovely bouquet of blanket flowers and moonshine yarrow sat on a table beside her.

The door opened, and Doctor Simms trailed behind a woman in her early thirties and a young girl about six. "I'll be right with you folks," Turning to his patient, he said, "Just watch her, Roxie. If you see any changes, bring her to the office."

"Thank you, Doctor," Roxie said.

Doc Simms turned to the others. "Hello, Pastor, Kenneth. What brings you two to my office tonight? Shouldn't you be at the dance?"

"We were, Doc," Pastor West replied. "The young lady with us wants to visit with you."

He gazed at Laura. "Hello, Miss. What's wrong with you?"

"Oh, I'm fine, but I'd like to ask you about my father, Horace Stone."

Doctor Simms' eyes widened. "You're his daughter, aren't you?"

"Yes, I arrived a few days ago."

"Well, it's nice to meet you. Horace was an honorable man. Now, what did you want to ask me?"

"I spoke with Sheriff Ellison, and he told me you had said Father died of a weak heart. Is this correct?"

"I'm sorry for your loss. About your father, you must know there were gashes in one area on his head. I said I thought he may have had a weakened heart that caused the fall. We believe he died on impact after he struck those rocks below. There's just no way of knowing for sure. Back East, there are forensic specialists for such things. They examine the bodies in a unique way for a more specific manner of death, though not yet advanced enough for all cases. And I'm indeed not qualified for such and must base my judgment on what I see."

"Doctor Simms, could the wound have resulted by force from a blunt object, like a hammer or something similar?" Kenneth asked.

"Of course. Anything with such impact as a fall would do it. What are you suggesting?"

"We know Horace was there to mend the fence when the accident occurred. I found the barbed wire cut, so we know his cattle didn't break through the fence. Someone did this purposefully, making his death both convenient and suspicious."

Doc Simms cast them a wary look. "I've given my conclusion based on my examination. Maybe you should speak with the sheriff if there's more."

Laura stepped closer to the doctor. "I've spoken to him, Doctor. The sheriff confirmed what you told him."

"I wish I could offer more, but that's not part of my training."

Doctor Simms gazed at Kenneth and then Laura. "I'm pleased you two found each other."

"What do you mean?" Laura asked.

"A brother and sister finding each other, of course. I figured you'd learn of this one day."

Kenneth bit back a chuckle. "How can you suggest that Laura and I are siblings?"

"You didn't know? Um, yes, you are half-siblings."

"That can't be right, Doctor. Nancy and Eugene are my parents."

"I wish your mom would have told you, Kenneth. I regret I'm the one who opened this door."

"Then Doctor, I demand to know what you know, and so does Laura."

"Oh well. Horace is a father to you both. Before Horace married Naomi, he and Nancy were close, and everybody expected they would wed. I don't know what went on, but they broke it off. Months after that, Nancy came to me pregnant. I'm not sure if Horace ever knew it. Nancy withheld the pregnancy from everyone, remaining out of sight most of the time. I often carried her food before Eugene came along."

"Before he came along?"

"Eugene is one of my best friends. We met when I was in medical school in St. Louis. He came here hoping to start a freight business at the same time as your mom's pregnancy. Eugene took food to her several times when I could not, and they became close friends and soon agreed to marry. Eugene thought that if they wed in secret, they could conceal the baby's arrival—and it worked. Turned out, everyone has believed Eugene was your father."

"He *is* my father—to me. He's all I ever knew."

"Your mother will kill me when she finds out I told you."

"But now I have a brother I didn't have before," Laura stated.

"Eugene asked me to keep it to myself, and I promised I would. But when I saw you two together, I assumed you knew. I suppose this says my promise meant little."

"I've learned a lot since being here," Laura said. "If only I could find out what happened to Father."

Pastor West standing nearby listening, said, "Laura, maybe some things should stay where they are. So often, these things lead to more harm than good."

"But if someone killed Father, they could do it again. I can't let this go."

"I agree with Laura," Kenneth said. "We must find the truth."

"But maybe, for now, we should head back to the dance," Pastor West suggested.

"Yes, I suppose you're right," Laura said.

MICHAEL J SPANHANKS

Chapter 6

*L*aura awoke, the conversation with Doctor Simms saturating her mind. She wondered if her father had known. Or did it embarrass him to mention her half-brother? Nancy Barlow's life would not have been the same had others learned of her unwed pregnancy. And did Mom know about Kenneth? She wished she had asked the doctor.

Her mind shot to the handsome Pastor West, wondering what life would be like married to a minister. Then what about her life in Boston? Her father had hoped for her to return home when she finished college, but she had remained and accepted a journalist position at a newspaper. Her ambition had always been to become a writer. Becoming a pastor's wife might indeed change the course of her career.

Oh, why am I dwelling on this? Mr. West has yet to ask for a rendezvous.

She got up from the bed and put on her clothes, with plans to ride to the cattle. If anything else happened to those cows, she would feel awful.

Copper spotted Laura coming his way and ran to the fence. "Hello, boy. I see you are ready."

When she had the horse saddled, she mounted him and set off towards the cattle. As she rode through the meadow, she came to a deep gorge where her father once found a crippled cow. Unable to find the herd, she rode on.

Copper carried her through the section of woods where they had before caught the cattle thieves branding yearlings. There were at least two dozen cows and calves scattered about. Then she spotted a black horse. *Kenneth. Wonder what he's up to.*

"Hello, brother," Laura said, beaming as she came to him.

"Hi there. That brother thing might take a second to get used to."

"I know. Did you speak with your mom about it?"

He dusted off his hat and returned it to his head. "I tried, but Mom didn't want to admit anything and said she'd have words with Doc Simms for opening his mouth."

"That you are my half-brother doesn't bother me at all. I hope you feel the same."

"Oh, Laura, I do, but I wish they had enlightened me before I was half-grown."

"I get it. But I have no one to discuss this with. Both parents are now gone."

"You're right. I shouldn't be so childish."

Laura dismounted. "Kenneth, I saw you studying the ground. What were you doing?"

He slipped from the saddle and laid the reins across the horn, allowing his horse to graze. "Well, it's been dry, so most tracks are hard to spot. And animals covered some, though not all. You see, I spotted some tracks in town I thought looked like some I'd seen at your father's place and figured I'd ride out and confirm them."

"Are you saying you might know who was here?"

"I believe that two men who were part of the gold-digging are the same ones involved in the cattle rustling."

"The sheriff won't listen, will he?"

"He may not, and that's why I'm here. I wanted to tell you I'm going after the U.S. Marshal in Albuquerque."

"I thought you said he wouldn't come."

"He might not, but I have to try. If our sheriff is involved, I hope that's enough to persuade him. I'll pray about this as I head that way."

"Speaking of prayer, what do you think of Pastor West?"

"Pastor West? There's not any better around here. He's wonderful with people, and everybody loves him. You like him, don't you?"

"Maybe, but I'm still figuring things out."

"Well, I could tell you impressed Pastor West. That's why I left him with you at the dance. He told me he had met you already, but I introduced you to him anyway."

"Kenneth, if he cares for me, why hasn't he asked me for a date or dinner?"

"Pastor won't rush things because he's a gentleman. You may have to show a fondness toward him first. He's a preacher and doesn't want folks to think he's forward."

"I see—but enough of that. Come and help me find the rest of the herd."

"They are on the other side of the pond."

"Can we ride over there?"

"Sure, follow me."

They came upon the cattle about a half-mile away. A bull was in the mix with them. Several cows had young calves. They found the yearlings scarred from the branding iron.

"Laura, look at those brands. Your father used an S for his brand, with a line through it. They branded over his and turned it into a J. There's only one man I know who fits this brand. His name is Stewart Jiles."

33

"But he can't be alone in this."

"I didn't get a look at the faces of the rustlers the day we ran them away, but I know the ones that Stewart runs with. I'm betting they are the same."

"Kenneth, Father said he had forty-five heads of cattle in the last letter I got. I counted eighteen at the creek. So there should be twenty-seven here."

Kenneth pushed up on the stirrups to get a headcount. "I only count twenty."

"That means they stole seven of Father's herd."

"This could be the evidence needed, at least for the rustling. I know where Stewart lives. So before I ride for the marshal, I'll head to Stewart's and find where he's hiding them. Maybe he hasn't already found a buyer. If they are there, we'll have the evidence they stole your cattle and more to convince the marshal."

"Is there anything I can do while you're gone?"

"I'm sure Pastor West would love a visit. There's a church service in the morning at eleven o'clock."

She grinned. "I feel prayer coming on."

"Good. Now, are you ready to head back, Laura?"

"I suppose, 'cause now I must decide what to wear tomorrow."

"You will surprise him, for sure."

Chapter 7

Santa Fe buzzed with people as Laura guided the team through town. She steered them near the trees at the church and stepped down from the wagon.

Several families reached the doorway, pausing to shake hands with neighbors and friends.

Laura stroked her hair, checking if any of her blonde strands had wandered out of place, and then started for the entrance.

The people stirred about as she stepped inside, smiling and shaking hands with Pastor West, who stood a few feet away.

He turned to Laura as she walked closer, a huge grin on his face. "I'm so pleased to see you, Miss Stone."

"Oh, call me Laura. I'm glad to be here." She wondered if she should have fibbed like that, for she wasn't glad to be there. She had sat in this sanctuary years before with her childhood friend Rachel and never sensed a closeness to God.

"We are about to start, so I must find my place."

An older gentleman started the service by leading a song as a woman played along on a pump organ. The crowd sang through three selections until the moment for Pastor West to speak.

Pastor West stepped into the pulpit. "Did you know you woke to something special this morning? The Scripture tells us that each day there is mercy awaiting us. We were each lost in sin, shut up in its prison. But Jesus paid the price tag for our sins on the cross. We should have been the ones they crucified, yet the Father in Heaven made a way for us through his Son, Jesus."

Someone said amen.

Laura marveled. He did that for me?

After a while, Pastor West came to his closing. "The message of the cross is simple. Jesus died for each of us. To receive his gift of salvation, we must confess our sins. Romans chapter ten and verse nine says, *for with the heart man believeth unto righteousness; and with the mouth confession is made unto salvation.* So this morning, our altars are open to anyone who wishes salvation."

Laura sat weeping. She had heard the message before but had never received Jesus. So many situations in life had happened until she thought God was dead. But today, after hearing this powerful sermon, her heart burst for more.

Pastor West called for heads to bow and a show of hands for those desiring salvation. Laura was the first of several to lift a hand. He then called for them to the altar to pray with him.

There was no hesitancy as Laura stepped forward, unconcerned that tears streamed down her face or if kneeling might crumple her pressed dress.

Those who came forward remained until Pastor West had taken a moment to pray with them. When they arose, he requested they turn toward the congregation.

"I wouldn't embarrass any of these who came forward

today, but I'd like to make a point. Right now, heaven rejoices because they surrendered their hearts to the Lord. They have joined those everywhere who serve him. They are children in the Lord who may not comprehend the word of God. Now we can pray for them and stand available to disciple them."

After the service ended, Pastor West came to Laura. "I'm pleased you found the Lord."

"Why do I feel so peculiar?"

"That's the way it is when God lifts our sin. All that weight gone from our lives."

"Must have been a lot of sin."

"Yes, for us all. May I ask if you are leaving for home right away?"

"I was, but do you have something in mind?"

"Well, the café will provide an excellent meal today. It would please me if you'd accompany me for lunch—my treat, of course."

"Yes, I would love that."

* * *

As they ate their lunch, Laura shared with Pastor West what she and Kenneth had discovered about the cattle, except for the names of the men they spoke about.

"So, how are you receiving this new revelation about a brother?" Pastor West asked.

"Well, it's different, though I think it's harder for Kenneth since his mother is living."

"I can only imagine how that discussion went. Where is Kenneth? I thought he would be here today."

"He's gone after the U.S. Marshal," she whispered.

"This is getting serious, then. I suppose I'm not surprised since cattle rustlers and gold thieves are part of the Western way of life."

"But this time, it's all on my land."

"I'm sorry for that, Laura. Your situation is way more than any young woman should face."

"I'm going to be alright. Maybe someday I'll sell that place."

"And I presume you'll return to Boston?"

"I haven't determined that yet. Life has taken some curious deviations, and I want to know what else might turn up before deciding to return."

"That seems a prudent approach."

"Maybe and maybe not. Back in Boston, I have a job as a journalist, though I don't know how long I can remain gone and hold it."

"You know there is a newspaper here."

The waitress stepped up with their lunch.

"Thank you, Gloria."

Laura unfolded the napkin and laid it on her lap. "I've enjoyed writing for the *Boston Press*, but my heart is in writing books. That's why I went to school."

"I'm fascinated. That's quite an ambition."

"Thank you. I have recorded several fictional stories and poems I could organize for a book."

"That is remarkable. You must publish your stories."

"Well, that's the hard part. I plan to contact an editor friend to help with publishing."

As she took the first bites of lunch, Laura peered across the room, spotting Mr. Fletcher at a table a short distance away. His eyes met hers, and he rose from his chair and strolled her way.

Pastor West noticed the change in her expression. "Is something wrong?"

Her lips tugged into a frown of discomfort. "I know that fellow, and I must speak with him."

"Would you like for me to leave you two here?"

"No, please stay."

"Hi there, Laura," Thomas Fletcher said when he reached their table. "I'm sorry I've missed you since our arrangement."

"No, I've only been to Santa Fe a few times since coming home," Laura said. "Oh, please have a seat, Mr. Fletcher."

"Call me Thomas."

Laura pointed across the table. "This is Pastor West. Pastor, meet Thomas Fletcher. We met on the train."

Fletcher pulled out a chair and sat down. "Pleased to meet you, Pastor."

"Yes, same here, sir."

"Well, I guess you'd like an update," Fletcher said.

"Yes, please."

"I had a visit with the sheriff, and I hate to say this. He should keep away from the bottle. But it seems his visit with Doctor Simms has settled in his mind regarding your father. The doctor told the sheriff that your father most likely died from a weak heart."

"Yes, he mentioned it."

"The sheriff is bent on staying with the doctor's deduction."

"But what about the gold thieves?" Laura asked.

"You know, I figured one of the best ways to collect information like that was to show up where a fellow who steals gold might appear. And that's the saloon. Sorry, Pastor. I love Blackjack, and I've played a lot of it. When I'm into my game, I pick up on talk of all subjects. So I sat and listened to story after story. If any man was in that saloon and knew about gold on your father's place, he never talked about it."

"I'm sorry to hear that."

"Laura, I'll be wrapping up my business in a few days and must leave for New York. But I wanted to inquire if you might sell your father's place—all of it, house, barn, and the cattle. Maybe this is too soon, though I know your home is in Boston and I thought you'd want to return soon. So if your ranch is too much, I'd love to purchase it from you."

"But Mr. Fletcher, *your* home is in New York. How would *you* run a ranch here?"

"I was considering hiring a foreman for that duty. The cattle would be another source of revenue for me. I visited the land office to make sure everything was clear on your place, and it was. There's enough land there to add several hundred more heads of cattle. So let me ease your mind of cattle rustlers and gold thieves."

"I told someone only today there's a possibility I'd sell. But I need time to think it over, sir."

Fletcher grinned and raised straight in his chair. "I'm sure two to three days will be sufficient now that I've made my offer."

Laura drilled him with a sharpened stare. "I'll think about it and pray on it."

He cleared his voice several times and tapped his fingers on the table. "Praying sounds like a fine idea, and I hope the Lord prompts you to make the correct decision because it would be regrettable if I had no place to turn to when I grew old."

Pastor West zeroed in on Fletcher with a hard squint. "I'm sure Laura *will* make the right decision."

Fletcher seemingly ignored the pastor's comment. "Ma'am, I desire that property."

Wary of Fletcher's brazenness, Laura said, "Mr. Fletcher, I said I would pray and think about it!"

Fletcher's face reddened, and he stood, knowing he had pressed too hard. "I'm sorry, just getting worried in my old age. Laura, you take all the time you need." He tipped his hat and returned to his table.

A faint smile shadowed Pastor West's face. "That was uncalled for."

Laura sat shaking her head. "I felt like a target."

The pastor's blue eyes pierced hers with a bit of alarm. "You *may* be a target. That fellow scares me."

Laura watched Fletcher calmly eating across the room. "Steven, could there be another reason Fletcher wants Father's land?"

"I suppose that's possible. You know, I hadn't realized the trouble you are dealing with until now. Think about this. Your father dies, and they don't foresee you coming home, but here you are. I don't know what the law is about these things, but I'm assuming there's some decree Fletcher might use to offer a legal bid for your place should you not sell. Maybe the law has determined it's still in your father's name until some paper, some form, is signed and forwarded to you. Maybe through the land agency or someone higher up. Also, Fletcher may be friends with the governor or some senator."

Laura's eyes widened as she heard him speak. "Could that happen?"

West shrugged. "There's no way to know, though I speculate that if Fletcher was already eyeing that land, your presence here put a kink in things. And now he doesn't know what to do. What concerns me is it could trigger troubling circumstances for you."

"Oh, my."

He reached and touched her arm, staring into her eyes. "Laura, please don't go home today. I'll find someone you can stay with."

"But I must tend to the cattle."

"Then allow me to ride with you. I'll sleep in the barn and help you with those cows tomorrow."

She was already having trouble curtailing feelings about her father's death, and now this. "You're scaring me, Pastor."

"I don't mean to, but I feel your situation is grave."

"Alright Steven, only for a couple of days, though. Do you have a gun?"

"Yes, and I can shoot some."

She shook her head. "Where's the law when you need them?"

"Maybe Kenneth will help with that."

Chapter 8

$\mathcal{P}$ astor West rose from the wooden cot. He stretched and then stepped to the doorway of the barn. *That cot is nothing like my bed.*

Wandering toward the house, he peered at the beautiful flowers, hoping he wasn't up too early for Laura.

The front door opened, and Laura stood in a night robe, staring out.

"I'm sorry," Pastor West said, turning his back to her. "I was waiting until I knew you were awake."

"Would you like some coffee?"

"That I would love."

"Then come in, there's plenty. And don't worry about me wearing this old robe."

As they relaxed at the kitchen table, Pastor West stared across at her. "I hope you don't think me too eager, but I'd like to say how lovely you are."

"I admire your honesty, and in truth, I thought you were eager at first. And while we're being honest, I've watched you since I arrived. I'm generally modest, but there's something about you that I very much appreciate."

"Now you're about to make me blush."

"Oh, I find it hard to believe that you, being a Pastor who socializes with people, might become embarrassed."

"Maybe because you inspire certain emotions, which makes me question what is right for a man of God."

"But aren't ministers allowed relationships?"

"Yes, but there's been no woman I was comfortable around."

"You can't know unless you pursue it?"

Steven peered into her blue eyes. He yearned to take her in his arms and kiss her, but it seemed too soon after her father's death. "I should saddle our horses." He rose and started for the door.

"And I will cook some bacon and eggs while you do. Come inside when you're finished."

He nodded. "Sounds like a treat."

* * *

After breakfast, Pastor West brought the horses to the porch, and Laura stood waiting, her blue eyes glistening in the morning sunlight, her golden hair dancing in the gentle breeze. Without hesitation, he drew her close and kissed her.

"What took you so long?" Laura said as they separated.

He smiled. "I wanted to be sure of my feelings."

"And now are you?"

He leaned forward and kissed her once more for a short moment. "Yes, now I am. But if I want more of these?"

"There are plenty, except we've got to find that herd."

"You're right, and I apologize."

"Don't apologize. You're a man and allowed a life involving a woman."

"But I must be careful. Some in the congregation prefer I remain unaccompanied and with my heart only encouraged by the things of God."

"Do you think God expects that of you?"

"I used to, but through much prayer and digging into God's word, I realize some men need a relationship."

"Steven, God will let you know what is best for you."

"Yes, he will. Well, let's find those cows."

* * *

When they reached the gully, Laura spotted the cattle. "Look down there."

"Is that all of them?"

"Maybe. Let's ride closer."

As they came upon them, she knew with a glance they had split up again. "Some are missing but perhaps bunched elsewhere."

"Then let's find them."

An hour later, they came upon the rest of the herd on the other side of the largest field.

Pastor West raised his hand. "Hold up, Laura. I thought I saw smoke beyond the trees."

Laura looked above the trees and spotted it. "They are branding my cattle again. We have to get over there."

"Wait! Is there a way to reach the backside where they can't see us?"

"Yes. We can ride back, catch the gully, and follow it around."

"Just remember, they might have a lookout, so we must watch for them and keep quiet."

Reaching the gully, they urged the horses downward on the rough terrain. Large boulders had fallen during the storms presenting a challenge, but they worked around them until they came near the smoke.

"Hold here," West said. "I'll search out our options."

He had climbed the side of the gully near a batch of pines when he spotted one fellow holding a calf. Another prodded it with the branding iron. A third man sat on his horse, surveying the field.

West turned and hurried back to where Laura waited. "There are three of them. I'll move around and take the one on the horse. The other two are at the fire. Hopefully, you can see me from across the opening. I need to get close enough to catch him off guard before you call out. Find some cover, and if they pull their weapons, shoot."

"Let's hope they lay down their guns," Laura said.

He paused, staring at the ground.

"What's wrong, Steven?"

"You shouldn't be going against these rustlers, Laura. That's what the law is for."

"But if we don't, they will get away with stealing my cows."

"I know, but this really scares me."

"Can't you shoot a gun?"

He nodded. "I can shoot plenty good, but *you* will have two to handle."

"Steven, don't worry about me. My father taught me how to shoot when I was ten years old. I'm a little rusty, but I'll be fine."

He peered at her in awe, sensing there was more to her than he realized. "Okay then, give me time to get around there."

"I'll be watching for you." Laura dropped from the saddle, grabbed her rifle, and started up the side of the gully.

As West reached the other side, the man on the horse sat cutting tobacco with a knife. West eased behind a large tree, peering across the opening. Laura waved back at him.

When she knew Pastor West was in place, Laura cocked

the rifle and pointed it at the fellow with the branding iron. "Put it down!"

Both men turned and stood still when they heard her voice.

"Take off your gun belts and drop them to the ground with your opposite hand."

The man holding the branding iron dropped it and reached to loosen his, but the other fellow paused.

"I'm not asking again. I better see those gun belts on the ground, or you'll get a bullet."

Across the way, Pastor West had forced the lookout from his horse and tied his hands behind him. There was nothing he could do to help with the other two men.

Laura waited for the second man to comply, but he went for his gun, firing several rounds at her before running for cover behind the nearby trees. His buddy rushed in behind him.

"No, don't make this so hard," Laura said.

She fired three rounds at the rustlers as they settled behind the trees. After twenty minutes and both firing bullets, the two men remained dug in.

Then another round of shots echoed beyond them.

"Hold up, Laura," came a voice from the woods.

The outlaws stepped out into the opening with their hands high. Kenneth rode out behind them, along with a man wearing a badge.

"Your timing was perfect," Laura said.

"We saw the smoke and figured someone was branding your cattle. I can't believe you went up against them by yourself."

"She wasn't alone," Pastor West said, walking up behind them. "Who do you have with you, Kenneth?"

"This is U.S. Marshal Chester Walsh."

"I'm pleased you're here, Marshal," Laura said. "We've got

a lot to tell you."

"I've heard," Marshal Walsh said.

"I'm sure you have," uttered Pastor West. "We can add to what Kenneth shared."

"Then why don't we gather these men and get them on their horses," Marshal Walsh replied. "You can help me take them to Santa Fe so we can lock them in jail. Then we'll talk about that other problem."

"Yes, sir," Laura said.

Chapter 9

After locking the thieves in jail, Marshal Walsh gathered with the others at the café, promising to stick around and investigate.

"Marshal, those tracks led back to Santa Fe," Kenneth said. "One set belongs to a man I know. So I went to his house the night before I rode to you and saw Laura's cows in his corral."

"Does this man have a name?"

"Stewart Jiles. He's trouble around these parts, though I've never known him to steal cattle."

"Marshal, these people stealing gold from Father's land, do you think they're related to the cattle theft?" Laura asked.

"I don't know. And you say this man Fletcher had pressured you to buy your place?"

"That's right."

"I have to wonder if he's purchased any property next to you, Miss Stone."

"The land office will have records," Kenneth said, rising from the table. "I can check."

"Purchasing land is not a crime. We need to know how he got it. Did Fletcher coerce anyone into selling?"

"We should speak to the landowners?"

The marshal took a sip of tea, pondering the situation. "There may be holdouts. So Kenneth, find out who may have sold property attached to Miss Stone. While you're doing that, I'll visit the doctor. I need to hear his account of your father's death, Miss Stone."

"Marshal, do you think any of this will lead to finding out who killed my father?" Laura asked.

"Right now, we don't know anyone did."

"He went to those hills to fix the fence that someone cut."

"But who's to know why that fence got cut? True, it could have been to get to your father's gold. Or maybe the cattle rustlers took advantage. I know either of those things could be a motive for murder, but we have nothing that'll hold up in a court of law. Hopefully, Kenneth will find a lead at the land office."

"I understand."

Laura started crying as Kenneth and Marshal Walsh left the café. "I wish this was over."

Pastor West reached a hand to hers. "I will pray the marshal figures something out soon."

Laura peered at him, teary-eyed. "And what about Sheriff Ellison?"

"I have doubts regarding Sheriff Ellison's involvement in the gold-digging. I've known him for some time. Ellison is fond of his job and wouldn't risk it for dishonest work."

"I hope you're right."

Kenneth returned from the land office. "Hey, folks. Fletcher did purchase some other land and is trying to buy another piece of property joining Laura's. The owner of one piece of property died mysteriously. His family has moved on from Santa Fe."

"What about the land Fletcher's after now? Are those folks living at their place?" Laura asked.

"I don't know, but we should find out. I'll tell the marshal."

As they stepped from the café, Marshal Walsh exited the doctor's office. They disclosed what Kenneth had learned, and he agreed they should speak to the owner.

* * *

An hour later, they came upon a place deep in a wooded area only five miles from Laura's land. Cattle foraged in the field beside the road as they rode toward the house.

Kenneth dismounted and walked to the porch.

But as he reached to knock, an elderly man pushed it open and bolted out, aiming a double-barrel shotgun. "I'm not sellin'! I already told that man."

Kenneth held up his hands. "Whoa! We're not here to buy anything, only to speak with you."

He shoved the shotgun toward Kenneth. "I'm tired of talking about it. Now get off my property!"

"Hold on now, Mr. Sharp," Kenneth said, waving his arms. "We're investigating the man who wants to buy your land."

Marshal Walsh then stepped near the porch. "Herbert Sharp, I'm U.S. Marshal Chester Walsh. We came to ask you some questions about a man named Fletcher. Now put down the shotgun."

Herbert lowered the weapon and leaned it against the outer wall of the porch. "I'm sorry. I thought you wuz those men trying to force me to sell my property."

"No, sir. We'd only want information, mainly about Thomas Fletcher."

"That man's a swindler!" Herbert said. "He came here the first time, all nice and asked to buy my property. And that's without riding around and even looking it over. That by itself, told me something wasn't right. He came again the day after, offering a little more money but not enough for me to sell. Then Fletcher started harrying me, not physical like but with words, saying cattle might die or something might happen to me."

Laura dismounted and walked to them. "Mr. Sharp, did you know my father, Horace Stone?"

"Yes, we watched over each other's cattle if they crossed into each of our lands. If I found some of his, I'd drive them back to his property, and he'd do the same. That was before we put up the barbed wire. The wire solved most of our problems. What happened to him was tragic, though I don't believe he died of natural causes."

"Mr. Sharp, there are two other properties close by that Fletcher bought. Did you know the owners?" asked Marshal Walsh.

"Knew them both. Ann and George sold and moved back to Texas, though he wasn't happy about it. He told me Fletcher came to his place the second day with a bunch of men and guns. Scared George that they might start killing. So he went to town the next day and signed papers at the lawyer's office. They moved out right after that."

"What about the other family?" Laura asked.

"You haven't heard? Moore is their name. Eli Moore fell to his death in the canyon that runs through his place. Eli been there all his life. He knew how dangerous that canyon was. Bessie came by to warn us about Fletcher the day she left with her brother. She said he came to their place hassling them to sell. Told me the whole story."

"That's sad," Laura said.

"Marshal, Eli didn't fall in that canyon," Herbert said. "Those men pushed him into it. They killed Horace too, and I can prove it."

"How Mr. Sharp?" Marshal Walsh asked.

"There was a witness."

Everyone stared as Herbert scratched at his beard. "I'm

just wondering if I should say. Two men have died already."

"There's only one way to stop the killing. That's by telling me the name of the witness. If he agrees to testify, I can arrest those who did it. But you informing me is only hearsay and will not stand in a court of law."

"Okay, but I ain't certain he *will* testify. You'll have to talk with him, and that won't be easy."

"Okay, but who is it?"

"He's called Big Jeremiah. Never heard a last name or even if he has one. His pa raised him in the mountains. After his pa passed, Big Jeremiah stayed there because that's all he knew. He traps for pelts along the creeks through these lands."

"I met him when I was a young girl," Laura remembered. "Once, my father brought him inside the house for coffee. They talked for hours that day."

"So, how do we locate Big Jeremiah?" asked the marshal.

"Follow the creek at the backside of my property. That's the same one that goes through Horace's place. If Big Jeremiah ain't on the mountain, he'll be trapping in the creek. Now that creek falls into the river farther on down. He traps there too."

"I'll ride after him," Kenneth said.

"Kenneth, I'll need to go along," Marshal Walsh declared. "If Big Jeremiah doesn't come, at least he can state what he knows to me, and you can witness it."

Kenneth suggested they get supplies.

Herbert walked toward the front door. "Come in here. Elva will help me put together whatever you need."

"Thank you, Mr. Sharp," Marshal Walsh replied.

"You may find him by following that creek. But it's best to set up a camp when nightfall comes. Big Jeremiah will see it and come to you."

"You reckon he will?"

"He'll know it's a friendly camp."

"Alright then, we better gather those things and get on the

trail."

"Marshal, we're going on home," Laura said. "Come by and tell us what this man says."

"Might be tomorrow late or the following morning. You folks watch out for others coming to your places. I don't want to see anyone else hurt or killed."

"I'll stick around at Laura's place and help her until this is over," Pastor West said.

Kenneth grinned at Laura. "That's a great idea, Pastor."

Laura and Pastor West headed home as Kenneth and Marshal Walsh rode to find Big Jeremiah.

Chapter 10

L aura peered through the doorway of the barn as Pastor West lay sleeping on the cot. "Pastor West, would you like some coffee?"

He turned his head toward her. "Wow, I slept well last night. But maybe I shouldn't have slept so long."

"Why? It's not late, and I was about to start breakfast and thought you might enjoy a cup of coffee." As he sat up, she handed him the steaming cup.

He took a sip. "You make great coffee."

"I learned how from my father."

"Wish I could have spent more time with him."

"Did he ever go to church?"

"Yes, he was at church often until he had trouble with those folks coming onto his land. He and Kenneth missed a few services, watching over things here. Kenneth was the one who got your father started at church."

"He said nothing about it."

"Kenneth is modest and wouldn't. But you know, I see

many of the same traits in him as in you. He's curious about things like you are. I can see why you are writing for a paper. Most journalists make brilliant investigators."

"Kenneth has been helpful to me. While we're speaking of him, I'd like to ask if you think I should offer Kenneth part of the ranch. He *is* Father's other child."

"I can see why you'd think you should. But that determination should only be yours."

"I thought maybe he should be the one to run things here when I leave for Boston."

"Are you going to leave us soon?" Pastor West walked closer to her. "I hoped you'd stay."

"My home and job are in Boston, though. I'm sure Kenneth will do well running things here." She peered, whispering, "I must have a good reason to stick around."

"Would marrying me be a good enough reason?"

She stared at him. "Are you serious? You're asking me to marry you?"

"I am."

Laura grew breathless. She had always imagined marrying a man in politics or a wealthy businessman from Boston, but found herself now considering this unexpected offer. Her ranch sat in the backwoods of Santa Fe, Texas, and the pastor of the only church in town had propositioned her. Despite her surprise, she couldn't help but feel excited at the prospect.

"Laura, are you alright?

"Um, yes."

"Yes, you'll marry me, or yes, you're fine?"

"Yes...to both."

They laughed and kissed for a spell.

"I couldn't tell if you enjoyed my company or were tolerating my presence," Pastor West said.

"Nonsense. I've enjoyed your presence from that day at the mercantile; only I was nervous. The most handsome man ever walked up to me and introduced himself. I suppose the word I'm looking for is giddy."

"I'm pleased when I'm with you, Laura."

"So I suppose I have some decisions to make. I have a home in Boston that I must sell and then also do something with my furnishings. Marshal Walsh can wrap things up here."

"What if he can't find evidence your father's death was murder?"

"That would make me unhappy, knowing what we know. But not enough to return home for good."

"Good," Pastor West said. "Now that it's settled, we should eat breakfast and check on those cows."

"Alright, breakfast it is for my husband-to-be."

* * *

Laura pressed Copper through the trees, herding the cattle to better grass. Pastor West rode ahead of her, working a momma cow and her calf back to the others.

He peered across the field, spotting a rider. "Hey, Laura, a black horse on the other side."

"That's Kenneth," Laura replied.

They rode in a hurry to him.

"Hey, brother. Did you find that man?" Laura asked.

"We did. Follow me to your house. Marshal Walsh is waiting with Big Jeremiah."

Thirty minutes later, they came to Laura's house and dismounted. Marshal Walsh and Big Jeremiah sat on an old bench near the porch.

"So, let's hear what you found, Marshal," Pastor West uttered.

"Jeremiah saw the whole thing when they pushed Eli Moore into the canyon. Laura, he also saw them murder your father. There were four of them, and one *was* Thomas

Fletcher."

Laura turned to Big Jeremiah. "Which one killed Father?"

"The one in the fancy suit. He done it," replied Big Jeremiah. "I saw him pull a shotgun from your father's wagon. One man distracted Horace a minute, and your father turned away. That's when the man in the suit hit him over the head with the gun butt."

"Big Jeremiah has identified the man in the suit as Fletcher. So if Fletcher's in Santa Fe, I'll arrest him and those other men, too, for murder. Big Jeremiah is coming along to point them out."

"What about the gold thieves and the cattle rustlers? And was Sheriff Ellison involved in any of it?" Laura inquired.

"Sheriff Ellison is an old cowboy looking for an easy way," Marshal Walsh said. "He may have dug for a little gold, but he had nothing to do with Fletcher."

"There have only been a couple of old codgers searching for gold on your place," Big Jeremiah said. "Horace then ran off. Then because that other fellow found a little is why that man Fletcher wanted your land. But all he had to do was ask me. There's not much gold left in the dirt in these parts. This ground got mined out sixty years ago."

"So, who cut the fence?" Pastor West asked.

"The man in the suit told one of his boys to cut it. I heard him say he wanted the sheriff or anyone who paid attention to think the miners or the cattle thieves were behind the murder. I don't know it for certain, but I believe that man in the suit hired those cattle rustlers and may have hired the miners."

"So is that it, Marshal?" Laura asked. "You'll arrest Fletcher and his men, and it's over?"

"Yes ma'am, except for the trial. But It looks like we got them—because of you and Kenneth's help."

"So I guess you will head back to Boston, Laura?" Kenneth asked.

"As soon as I complete my other business."

"What other business?"

Laura walked to Pastor West and reached for his hand. "We are getting married."

"I knew it, and you won't find a better man than Pastor West."

"You're right, Kenneth. But I still have a problem."

"What's that?"

"I need someone to run the ranch. And since you're my brother—"

"Half-brother."

Laura grinned. "Since you're my half-brother, I thought I should offer you half of the ranch, and maybe, somewhere in the future, you could buy the other half from me."

Kenneth marched to her. "I would, sis. You are the best sister I've ever had. Well, you are the *only* sister I've ever had." He hugged her and then pulled away, smiling. "God put Horace and me together. And now I have the opportunity to continue his work."

Marshal Walsh rose and walked beside them. "Well, while you folks are planning weddings and sorting out land and cattle, Big Jeremiah and I are heading to Santa Fe."

"Thank you so much, Marshal," Laura said.

Big Jeremiah turned to face her before mounting. "I knew your pop. He was a fine man."

"I remember you coming by and drinking coffee with him. The two of you talked and laughed for hours that day."

"Until he had to go check on those cows." Tears came to his eyes.

Laura reached and touched his shoulder. "That's right. He loved those cows."

Marshal Walsh and Big Jeremiah mounted and rode toward Santa Fe.

"So, when is this wedding?" Kenneth asked.

Laura turned to Pastor West. "Steven, what about Sunday after the church service?"

"Do I still have to preach?"

"Well, I do need preaching."

"Then I suppose it is Sunday."

"Yippee!"

Pastor West peered into Laura's eyes. "I love you."

"I love you, too, Steven. And soon, I'll call you husband."

"And I'll call you wife." Then he kissed her for a long while.

"Hey, folks," Kenneth replied. "Don't you have cattle to look after?"

They laughed and started for their horses.

False Accusation

Chapter 11

Orland Flack entered the Santa Fe Journal and made his way to his office. He gazed at the article before him and shook his head. "Ms. Stone, please come in here."

Laura glanced at him through the window. *What this time?* She laid down her pencil and moseyed into Orland's office. "Yes, Mr. Flack."

"This is not Boston, Laura. We cannot print stories that probe into people's lives like this, or soon we won't sell newspapers."

"That's not probing. I'm stating the facts. Everyone knows Russell Little is a gambler. People saw him cheating, and I have witnesses."

Orland pushed the article at her. "But you state someone anonymous saw him."

"Yes, I'm trying to protect the witness."

"That's not protecting Russell."

"Why would I want to protect a card shark?"

"Now Laura, you will refrain from that sort of

terminology here in Santa Fe regarding the local folks. That's a good way to make enemies. What happened with the lady's pie sale at church? I asked you to give me a story regarding that."

"I have it done, Mr. Flack, but those things are boring. I need the freedom to write about topics such as court cases or cattle rustling—"

"Stop, stop! I sent a telegraph about your work from Boston before hiring you, Laura. You wrote about dangerous the most people there, and I'm surprised you didn't offend some after those stories hit the press."

"But Mr. Flack, that is real journalism. People in Boston crave tough-to-get stories. You may not realize this, but newspaper sales always increase when these kinds go to print."

Flack stared at her, shaking his head. He understood the fascination Laura had because there was a time he had written about some men sentenced to hang, which angered his readers. They argued it was not the newspaper's place to publish these narratives. He backed away from such stories when they threatened to stop purchasing the paper.

Hearing something unusual, Flack turned to see a young woman standing in the doorway wearing a fashionable dress with a flouncing skirt edged with narrow frills. She had on a modern, matching shallow-crowned velvet hat with a narrow brim. "May I help you, Miss?"

"Hi, they told me this was the place of employment for Laura Stone."

"Why, yes. Laura's right here." He pointed to an arca behind the printing press.

Laura stepped out from behind the press with interest. "Olivia? What are you doing here?"

"I've missed my dear friend."

"I've missed you too. Mr. Flack, please meet my best friend, Olivia Bunney."

Orland, in the meantime, had drawn closer. He reached

and took Olivia's hand. "We are glad you're here, Olivia. I hope you find us friendly in Santa Fe."

"I'm sure I will."

"Olivia is a doctor, and a mighty good one, which is why I'm curious that you're here," Laura said, turning again to her.

Flack frowned at the statement. "Doctor, huh?" he whispered.

"It's a long story," Olivia stated. "I took a room at the hotel. If you'd like to come by, we can chat."

"Mr. Flack, do you mind if I have the rest of the day off?" Laura asked.

"Sure. I see you two have much to catch up on. Just grab that story and clean it up a bit."

She craned her neck and peered at his office. "Alright, I'll alter a few words and make you happy."

* * *

The Queen Hotel housed a restaurant where they sat at a table to chat.

The waitress stepped up beside them. "Can I get you something?"

"Do you have hot tea?" Olivia asked.

"Only cold, but I can make it hot for you."

Olivia shook her head. "No, cold tea will be fine. Bring a glass for us both."

"Yes, ma'am."

Laura leaned forward against the table. "Okay, you must tell me what you're doing here?"

Olivia shrugged and smiled. "No great reason, except when you wrote and told me about this place, it fascinated me, and the time felt right to get away."

"What about your patients?"

"When I decided to come, I began stretching my

appointments until only a few needed attention before leaving. I handed those to a colleague I trust. But what about you? In the letter, you said you were getting married. So, I suppose it's Mrs. Laura—"

"That did not pan out," Laura said, shaking her head.

"I'm sorry."

Expelling a silent breath, Laura offered a leveled smile. "It's fine. I don't think I would have been the best wife."

"You said he pastored a church?"

"Yes, the only one around for miles."

"You don't want to be a pastor's wife because that's quite an undertaking, from what I hear."

Laura shook her head. "That's not it. Steven and I saw the role of a wife so differently. He wants a woman who will stay home and fulfill what he calls a woman's duties and someone who will help tend to the women in the church. I'm just not cut out for that person. And then, when I mentioned working at the newspaper, everything changed. Steven comes from a conservative background and would not give in to my desire to continue my career. We still talk to each other."

"I sure thought when I came here, you'd be married, though it now sounds like it's for the best you didn't."

"I think so."

A loud eruption of bangs sounded outside as several men on horseback rode by the window.

Olivia peered through the windows. "Is there a parade?"

"No. Those are cowboys riding in from one of the large ranches. They sometimes come for whiskey and women and always on Saturday."

"I will keep that in mind. So, are you still part-owner of a farm?" Olivia asked.

Laura tilted her head toward a table alongside them, hearing some men talking. Of the two chatting, one seemed in charge as he spoke in a soft, rough voice, "We'll hit the bank tomorrow night. Can't wait any longer. It will be Sunday night, and everyone will be home."

"Laura, are you alright?" Olivia asked, noticing her disorientation.

"Yes, I'm sorry. I am a part-owner. I know little about ranching, so I asked Kenneth to work it. If I lost my job at the Journal, I'd have a backup plan."

"What does that mean?"

The man across from the other spoke. "But Coy, we can't just go in at the front door. People will see us."

"Harbin, they bolt the back door from the inside. We got to go in at the front."

Olivia waved a hand in Laura's face. "Hey, hey! You seem preoccupied. Are you alright?"

Laura grinned. "Yes, I am. I'll explain some other time. Regarding your question, my boss, Orland Flack, doesn't want to turn me loose. Seems like he's afraid to print the truth."

The waitress set down their glasses of tea.

Olivia, still thirsty from the journey, reached for a glass. "Thank you."

Laura peered at the waitress. "Yes, thank you, Gloria."

Olivia took several swallows of tea and sat it down. "That is so good. Now Laura, you mentioned your boss is afraid to print the truth. But journalism is about the truth."

Laura threw a hand into the air and shrugged. "I know. Something must have spooked him in the past. He's worked for other newspapers and is knowledgeable about the industry."

"Maybe he's concerned for you. It sounds like he wants to protect you, Laura."

"I don't need protecting."

"Maybe you do and don't know it. You know, if things don't work out, you can always return to Boston."

"I think I'm here for a long while."

"I know."

"Well, I have other things to do," Laura said. "I'm staying at Esta Dowd's boarding house two blocks down if you need me."

"I think I'll go to my room and rest for a while. I had thought I might sleep on the train, but it was mighty rough."

Laura rose and pulled money from her pocket.

"No, no, Laura, I've got this."

"Well, thank you. Maybe tomorrow you can come to the church. That's where I'll be for the morning service."

Olivia wrinkled her forehead. "I don't know, but I'll think about it."

Chapter 12

*L*aura's mind whirled after hearing the two men talking about robbing the bank. The sheriff seemed uninspired when Father needed his help. Would sharing with him what I heard do any good?

The sheriff stood outside his office, speaking with a cowboy as she arrived. "I'll be with you in a moment, Miss Stone."

Laura sat on the porch in one of the rocking chairs, waiting.

After several moments, the cowboy walked away, and Sheriff Ellison turned to her. "What can I help you with, ma'am?"

"Sheriff, I was at the Queen Hotel restaurant drinking tea with a friend when I overheard something strange."

"What might that be?"

"Two men sitting next to us were discussing plans to rob the bank tomorrow night."

"You heard them say that?"

"Yes, Sheriff. They spoke softly, but I could hear them."

"Hmm, bank job. Do you know these men?"

"I've never seen them before, but I haven't been here long."

"What'd they look like?"

"The one in charge wore a black hat with those medallion things around it. He had a mustache and a deep voice. The other was sandy-haired with a brown hat. His back was to me, so I didn't get a good look. His voice was higher."

"They don't sound like anyone from around here."

"I wonder if they are staying at the hotel."

"I can't arrest them on hearsay. But you say these men plan to rob the bank tomorrow night?"

"The man said everyone will be home because it's Sunday night."

"Well, thank you, Miss Stone. I don't want you to worry about this. I'll take it from here."

"Sheriff, I'd like to be there when you go after them for a story."

Sheriff Ellison thought about her comment. "No."

"I will not be in the way. I promise."

The sheriff removed his hat, scratched a place on his head, and returned it. "Miss Stone, you'll stay out of sight in case there's a gunfight?"

"Yes, sir, I will."

"Did he mention a time?"

"No, but he told his partner they would use the front door because the back door locks from the inside."

"Hmm. Sounds like they've done their homework."

"Sheriff, I must go back to work, but I'll see you tomorrow night."

As Laura turned to leave, she spotted two riders coming into town. The one in front she knew as Big Jeremiah. "Sheriff, that's Big Jeremiah, and the man behind him has a shotgun on him."

"What is Walter Teele up to?"

Teele reined to a stop near the sheriff and stepped from his saddle. "Sheriff, I caught a murderer. Thought it best I bring him on in to you."

"Walter, this is Big Jeremiah. You're saying *he* murdered someone?"

"Not just one, Sheriff. Three! He butchered the entire Wheeler family with a knife!"

Folks in town started gathering around Walter to hear the story.

"I killed no one," Big Jeremiah insisted. "I told this vermin I came along and found them dead."

"The blood on his knife tells it differently."

"Coons. I just skinned out two coons. They are at my cabin, hanging high. I would have smoked 'em when I got back, but I needed to check another trap."

"Sheriff, I saw him hovered over little Luella," Teele replied.

Laura came closer. "Sheriff Ellison, everyone knows Big Jeremiah is a fur trapper and only trying to survive in those hills. He's not a murderer."

"Miss Stone, I've got to put him in jail. Judge Morley will decide how to proceed. But I'm figuring those dead bodies will determine if he needs to stand trial."

Laura peered at Big Jeremiah, his gray beard and animal skin hat, his sad eyes signifying the mess he found himself in.

The sheriff instructed him to dismount.

Laura followed behind as they made their way to the jail. "I'll find out what happened to the Wheelers and get you an attorney."

"Don't bother," Big Jeremiah replied. "I can tell these folks need someone to pin it on. I told Teele I thought it might be Indians, but he didn't listen."

"Why do you think it was Indians?"

"Saw the hoof prints in the road. Unshod ponies. Teele never looked at those tracks."

"Where is the Wheeler farm?"

"That place is about five miles east. You take the road to a pond and turn left. Teele had me bury the bodies in the field before we came."

Laura stepped from the cell and turned to the sheriff. "You can't hold a man responsible when there is no evidence. Where are the bodies? You have no legal right to put him in jail without proof."

"Yes, I do. I have Teele's word. I've known him for years and trust what he's telling me."

"Then you have to allow me to exhume those bodies and let a doctor examine them."

"Exhume them? That's out of the question. Digging them up would be disrespectful. No!"

"If you don't allow this, you may see an innocent man hang. Do you want that on your conscience?"

Sheriff Ellison stared at the floor, visibly concerned at her words. "Who will help you perform this abomination? Doc Simms will not, I am sure. He was Ocie's doctor when she had Luella. Doc's known the Wheelers for years."

"I have a friend, a doctor, who just arrived from Boston. Maybe I can persuade her to do the autopsies."

"You said her. A *woman* doctor?"

"Olivia is a skilled surgeon. Kenneth will help me after church tomorrow to dig the bodies up and bring them back."

"What makes you think doing this will give us any more information than we already have?"

"Sheriff, I don't, but I'd rather have the facts than let an innocent man take the fall. New forensics are happening in other places. You need to trust me on this. Olivia can determine if Big Jeremiah's knife was the murder weapon."

71

"That may be, but then you must persuade Judge R.T. Morley or a jury that Big Jeremiah did not use his knife."

"One step at a time, Sheriff."

"Alright, but I'll have to find you a place in town to perform this inhumane barbarism, and right now, I have a bank robbery to intercept. So I must find a few good men to help."

"I'll go to the farm and speak with Kenneth. Maybe he can help after we dig up the bodies. Pastor West is also good with a gun."

"You know this how?"

Laura smiled. "Just trust me." Then she walked out of his office.

* * *

The door opened, and sleepy Olivia stood staring at Laura.

"I'm sorry, Olivia. I should have known you were resting."

"No. I slept longer than I wanted to. Come in."

"Olivia, I still can't believe you are here. When I first saw you in the office, I thought you were a dream."

"No dream, Laura, and the urge to come here surprised even me. I suppose I had to see how the West captivated you so. I knew you were from Santa Fe, but then you spent so much time in Boston that I never thought you would return to stay."

Laura sat in a chair. "I'm a country girl at heart. I should have come home sooner, if nothing else, to visit my father before he passed. But time has a way of drifting by, like a sailboat on an ocean."

"Stated with the elegance of a journalist."

"Olivia, I must explain what happened at the restaurant earlier."

"You seemed quite distracted."

"I overheard something from those men sitting beside us."

"What?"

"Let's just say they plan to break the law. I wanted to hear enough so I could tell the sheriff."

"You always did live dangerously."

Laura peered at her friend. "Olivia, I have a request you may not care to do. If not, I will understand."

"A request? You know I like requests. Will *we* break the law?"

Laura grinned from one side of her face. "Nothing like that, though you may not like my request."

"Okay, let's have it."

Laura explained how the sheriff had arrested Big Jeremiah for murder, and the necessity to exhume the bodies.

"That is quite a request," Olivia said from her sitting place on the bed. "And I suppose you have a good reason to exhume these bodies?"

"Do you remember when I wrote about the problems I ran into when trying to find out what happened to Father?"

"Yes."

"The man they've arrested, Big Jeremiah, witnessed Fletcher tossing a man into the canyon when he wouldn't sell his land. And I know Father wouldn't have sold to him, so that may have been why Fletcher killed him."

"I'm glad that you've settled your father's death."

"Yes, me too."

"Okay, when do we exhume the bodies?"

"After church service in the morning, we'll eat at the hotel before heading out."

"Sure. Where do we examine them?"

"The sheriff said he will find a place."

"I'm glad I brought my bag."

"So, will I see you at church in the morning?"

"I don't know, Laura. I'm pretty tired."

"Think about it. But I'll find you in the restaurant if I don't see you at church."

"Okay."

Chapter 13

*L*aura stayed in the spare bedroom at the ranch rather than riding back to town at night.

The following day, Copper fought her when the time came to leave. She pushed him to make it to the church service on time.

Kenneth rode beside her on his black gelding called Ace. "Just hard to believe those men spoke openly about robbing the bank. It makes me wonder if they told it so you could hear. Maybe this is all a distraction for something bigger."

"For what? What else could there be?" Laura asked.

"I can think of two possibilities. Maybe the train is bringing in a prisoner, some member of a gang whose men would rather see free."

"That's a long shot, if you ask me. So what's the other possibility?"

"The freight office. A lot of money goes through that place, and on the weekend, even more. Verner Givens would need to deposit money in the bank come Monday. What if this is a diversion to pull attention from the freight office before Verner can take the money to the bank?"

"So, do you suppose these men knew I worked for the Journal?"

"Were they seated when you got to the table, or did they come later?"

The look on Laura's face told him it was the latter.

"Then we have to plan for both. I'll tell Sheriff Ellison about the freight office," Kenneth said. "He'll need to cover both."

"I can't believe I'm party to a robbery."

"A robbery hasn't occurred, sister. More importantly, it's not your fault. Still, we know there are wicked men around these parts who'd rather steal than work for a living."

"Maybe they figured the bank was too risky and decided to strike the freight company. Maybe one of them knew how much money Mr. Givens takes in."

"Those kinds lurk around towns like Santa Fe, looking for easy money."

"Speaking of easy money, how's the ranch going, Kenneth?"

"Not so easy, for sure."

"I'll help if you need me."

"No, I've got Diedrick Simms to help. He's a good hand with the cattle. Diedrick will meet us after lunch to help dig."

"I can help dig."

"Laura, stick to writing and leave the difficult things to your brother."

"Half-brother."

"Oh, is that how you feel?"

Laura laughed. "No, I don't think of you as half, but *you* always say it."

"Maybe I shouldn't. So, let's settle it then," Kenneth said. "I want us to make a pact that we always use the term full siblings."

"I agree. We are forever full siblings," Laura replied.

"So if I get in trouble with the ranch and need money, you'll lend the business some, right?"

"Oh, that's why you wanted to be full siblings."

Kenneth laughed. "No, no. I'm only kidding. As the foreman of the ranch, I take full responsibility."

"Okay then."

* * *

As they came into town, Laura decided she should find Olivia. Kenneth rode a block further and dismounted at the sheriff's office.

Sheriff Ellison spotted him. "Has Miss Stone been to see you?"

Kenneth sat in one of the rocking chairs outside the office. "Yes, I'll help with the robbery if you need me. But the thing is, Sheriff, I'm not sure it's the bank they're after."

Kenneth took Sheriff Ellison through what he and Laura had discussed.

"I hadn't thought of the freight office," Ellison said as he sat down beside Kenneth. "Though I have wondered why the robbers would allow those women to hear them plan a bank robbery."

"I know what you mean."

"I still got to cover the bank. The town council would fire me if it got hit, and I knew about it and didn't stop it."

"How many men do you have, Sheriff?"

"My brother Elijah will help, and I'll speak with Pastor West after the service."

"He'll be a good help. I know a couple of bronc-busting friends."

"Sure, if you think they're trustworthy."

"They can use a gun just fine. Diedrick Simms is riding from the ranch around noon to help dig up the graves. He can stay over and help us later in town."

"I know nothing about him."

"I don't know a lot. Deidrick rode in, needing work a few months back and has been a great help. He seems the quiet sort. But I found him practicing with his gun one day. Never go up against him, Sheriff. Trust me."

"That good, huh? Maybe I should see if there's a paper on him." Sheriff Ellison moved forward in his chair.

"Hold up," Kenneth said. "I looked through those at your desk one day when you weren't in the office and found nothing on him."

"That's good, but I have a larger stack inside the desk drawer."

"Sure, but can we get past the robbery first?"

"Alright."

Kenneth rose from the rocker. "What time do we set up for them?"

"Right after dark. I want everyone out of sight. I picked up a key to the bank and will get one for the freight office. Maybe you should take some men and cover it, Kenneth. There's no way I can be at both places, and I want someone there I can trust."

"I'll do it, but I want Pastor West and those bronc-busters with me. You can use your brother and Diedrick. Diedrick will come in handy if one of those robbers is quick with a gun."

"Okay, but will you have time after digging up graves to find those boys?"

"No problem, it's on the way."

Sheriff Ellison nodded.

Kenneth started for his horse, then stopped and turned back. "Teele's wrong about Big Jeremiah. That old man's hurt no one."

"I can only go by what Teele told me. Maybe that doctor friend of Laura's can come up with something."

"Maybe so. I'll meet you here before dark."

✳ ✳ ✳

"So, Laura, you're going with those guys tonight?" Olivia asked.

"Sheriff Ellison doesn't want me to, but I have to see it to get the story right. Me as a witness will make for a better report."

Olivia sat staring at her friend. "Laura, you are so brave. I don't think I could do it."

"You are the brave one, Olivia. People's lives are in your hands each time you operate on them."

"I guess I've gotten used to it, or maybe it's the years of training. Being involved in some major surgeries, I was fortunate."

"Why is that?"

"Oh, you know how it is. Folks don't trust a woman to cut on them."

"You mean the men don't?"

"Those male doctors put up roadblocks for all the women doctors, even though we've undergone the same training."

"That is so wrong."

"Laura..." Olivia paused and looked away.

"What is it?"

"There's something I must explain. The doctors have pretty much pushed me out of Boston."

"What? Why would they?"

"Because they want to. Can I be honest with you? I came to Santa Fe wondering if a move was in order. I hoped this town might be desperate for a doctor."

"But will you find it any better here?"

"Nothing can compare to what I've gone through in Boston. My dear friend Jackson was so upset when I wanted to come."

"Jackson?"

"Jackson Ellinger and I were seeing each other off and on. He too is a surgeon. I had believed that after our acquaintance commenced, the surgeons would ease up on me. I was wrong. They were worse. They badgered Jackson and didn't mind me knowing it. He wanted me to believe their actions didn't bother him, but I know it grew heavy."

Laura shook her head, hearing the difficulties Olivia had faced.

"So, Laura, is there a need for a doctor in Santa Fe?"

"I wish I could say yes. Doc Simms has been here for some time."

"I thought I would ask."

"He doesn't do autopsies, though. So maybe there is room for you in that line of work. Have you had any training in forensics?"

"Yes, some, though not extensive."

"Maybe forensics is a way to ease you in and help folks get to know you. Then, when Doc Simms retires, the town can hire you."

"I don't know. Let's see how these autopsies work out first."

Chapter 14

The church service ended, and everyone shook hands. Pastor Steven West made his way to Laura.

"I'm sorry we were late this morning, Pastor," Laura said. "You know, it takes us women longer to dress than men."

Pastor West winked and permitted a hint of a smile. "Yes, I'm sure."

Laura perceived his teasing gesture and grinned back at him. "I want you to meet my friend Olivia from Boston."

Pastor West's smile enlarged as he pivoted toward the guest and reached for her hand. "I'm pleased to meet you, Olivia. How long are you staying with us?"

Olivia nodded and took his hand. "My situation is undetermined."

"Oh?"

"Olivia is considering moving here," Laura said. "She is a doctor, but we already have one."

"You know, Doc Simms might allow you to work alongside him. Sometimes he can't keep up, and the town is growing."

"We'll see," Olivia replied.

Pastor West turned to Laura and whispered, "I heard something about digging up bodies?"

"Yes, you heard about the Wheelers."

He nodded. "Sheriff Ellison mentioned it."

"I've asked Laura to do some autopsies on them to see if it was Big Jeremiah's knife used in their murders."

He peered at Olivia. "You can do that?"

"Well, yes, if there's a measurable difference in width and length of the wounds."

"Amazing. Laura, I'm available to help dig those bodies up if you need me."

"We have enough help, but thank you, Pastor, for offering."

"Sure."

"We have to go, Pastor West. Kenneth is meeting us at the café for lunch before we leave."

"Oh, sure. It's great to see you. Olivia, I'll pray you find direction for what's next in your life."

"Thank you."

Olivia turned to Laura as they walked. "I can see why you liked him so much. My, my, such a handsome man. It's clear how he dotes over you, and I'm sure he's heartbroken you turned him down."

"He'll get over it."

"Do you think there's any way he'll come around to seeing things as you do?"

"I explained to Steven that times are changing and women need more independence. But he believes a woman's place is in the home."

"Such a shame. A man like that must turn a lot of eyes."

"That's not everything."

They made their way to the café, where Kenneth waited.

"How was the service?"

"Wonderful. Pastor West preached about faithfulness. Folks said they missed you. What happened?"

"I went early to talk with my bronc-buster friends, Cooper Tillman and Reeves Fincher. They will help tonight with the sheriff."

"Will that be enough?" Laura asked.

"With my ranch hand, Diedrick Simms, Pastor West, and Sheriff's brother Elijah, yes, I think so."

"I hope everyone comes through this."

"Anything is possible when banks and freight offices get robbed."

"Please be careful, Kenneth. I don't want to lose the only brother I've ever had."

"It will take more than a couple of bank robbers."

After lunch, they found Diedrick and headed to where Teele had buried the Wheelers. They located the graves behind the house, as Big Jeremiah had told them.

"I don't feel good about this, Laura," Kenneth said. "Are you sure?"

"We have to know if Big Jeremiah did it. Without evidence, there's no way of proving his innocence. I'll find him an attorney tomorrow. He'll need to know what we learn."

"Well, Diedrick, guess we better dig," Kenneth said.

They dug until they had all the bodies free from the soil. Kenneth and Diedrick lifted them into the wagon.

"So, what happens when Olivia's finished with the autopsies?" Kenneth asked.

"I want to have a memorial service and rebury them," Laura said. "Pastor West can help with that."

"Yeah, why Teele didn't think about that."

"That is something to ponder. Maybe Teele had a reason for burying the bodies as he did?"

"What are you thinking, Laura?"

"Only that Big Jeremiah may be right."

* * *

People gathered around the wagon when they brought it to a stop at the sheriff's office.

Sheriff Ellison stepped from the porch. "I asked around town, but no one would volunteer their home to do autopsies. So, take them to the old boarding house at the end of the street. There's no one living there."

"That will be fine, Sheriff," Laura said.

"I can't believe you'd dig up their bodies," cried Lurline Willcock. "This is just not done."

Laura stood up in the front of the wagon. "We just want justice, folks. We can't let an innocent man hang if he didn't do it. We're hoping Olivia can tell us if the weapon used was Big Jeremiah's."

"Sheriff, why are you allowing this hideous experiment to happen in our town?" Burney Cutts asked.

"No, the murder of three people is hideous," Sheriff Ellison said. "And as long as I'm Sheriff, we'll do what's right and only charge and convict the guilty."

Gordon Andrews, the mercantile owner, had walked over to them. "I know we want the truth, but a thing like this will spread, Ellison. Folks in other counties will hear about it and think there's a cult at Santa Fe. They'll call us grave robbers."

"So be it, Gordon. All the folks around here know Big Jeremiah as a trapper and fur trader. He's harmed no person we know of. Even so, he'll stand trial. But we want the truth concerning these murders, not hearsay. Teele will get his chance to testify. The doctor will administer an autopsy to help find facts that will come out in the trial. Doctor Bunney has trained for this. They do them in the East. It's called forensics."

The people walked away, shaking their heads and

murmuring.

Kenneth reined the wagon forward. Soon they reached the old boarding house.

Olivia gandered at the tattered house with shutters missing and paint faded. "Wow. So your town can only provide this dilapidated old building? Well, we can make it work, but I will need oil lamps to see by and water to clean my hands."

"We'll get all that from my place," Laura replied.

"Are you sure the bodies will be alright until morning?" Kenneth asked.

"Yes, but they already stink," Laura said as she peered at Diedrick, who held his nose. "Diedrick, are you alright?"

"I'm not sure I can do this."

"Use your bandana," Kenneth said, chuckling. "Tie it over your mouth and nose. You know, like a thief."

"What did you call me?"

"I'm kidding. Just get it on so we can get these bodies inside."

Olivia found an old table inside to use for her work. Diedrick and Kenneth carried each body in and laid them down.

Olivia examined Grief Wheeler's body first. "The knife cut appears narrow. But I'll know more tomorrow when I measure the depth. We should visit the sheriff's office and examine the weapon. I'll need its measurements."

"We can do that on the way to my place," Laura said.

Kenneth stepped into the wagon. "I'll take the wagon and horses to the livery stable. Diedrick and I must prepare for the robbery."

"Olivia and I will be along soon."

"No, Olivia is going to her hotel room," Olivia said.

"You don't want to watch the robbery with me?"

"I don't care to be around guns and evil men. So please

don't ask me to."

"I just thought you'd want to go."

"I'd rather not."

Laura turned to Kenneth. "We are heading back to Olivia's room. I'll meet you at the sheriff's office in a while."

"I may not be there long. The sheriff is sending me to the freight office."

"I should hurry, then. Take us in the wagon to the hotel."

"Alright. Load up."

Chapter 15

$\mathcal{L}$ aura, Pastor West, Kenneth, and his two bronc buster friends sat inside Verner Givens' office, waiting. Givens boasted a successful week, bringing in over two thousand dollars from ranches purchasing large quantities of goods the train would not transport. The money was in his safe, locked up.

"Kenneth, which door do you think they'll hit?" asked Reeves Fincher.

"Who knows? I suppose you need the mind of a thief?" Kenneth replied.

"Are you sure the freight company is their plan?" Cooper Tillman asked.

"No, Coop, but this is why we're covering them both. Let's try to keep our talking down. When these boys come through those doors, we must be alert. So, don't let your mind wander."

"Sure."

"How about Reeves and myself move to the other door?" Cooper asked.

"Yeah, if you can find a place to sit, but away from those windows."

Pastor West moved beside Laura after Reeves and Copper left the office. "Laura, how have you been?"

"The Journal keeps me busy writing stories."

"I know. Read them all. Card Game Gone Bad. Another stood out to me. City Council Votes Yes For County Fair."

Hearing Pastor West taking an interest in her stories made her wonder if his feelings had changed. "So you can see what good I can do as a journalist, right?"

"Oh, sure. I believe you are an excellent writer."

"But still not allowed if married to Steven West."

Kenneth peered at his sister, wondering why she grilled Pastor West. He had already told her his feelings.

"I'm trying to understand your way, Laura, but things like this take time."

Steven had never been open to her working if they married, so his needing more time was at least a step in the right direction. "I can give you time, but I won't wait forever, Steven. If someone comes along that suits me, time may run short. And I'm not getting any younger."

"I know, and I'm praying about it."

"Good."

Kenneth had heard enough. "You two should stop talking now so we can hear the thieves."

"I'm sorry," Laura said.

* * *

Sheriff Ellison observed Diedrick Simms as he leaned in his chair. *I should have looked through my papers for this one.* "Diedrick, have you ever been in trouble with the law?"

"I ran with some bad men years ago but left them when they talked of rustling cattle."

"That's good. Did they ever do the rustling?"

"Yes, and hanged for it."

"Too bad. Lots of boys think rustling and stealing other people's stuff's an easy way to make money."

"Lazy men do."

Elijah laughed. "I'm plain lazy myself, though I ain't about to rob banks or rustle cattle. Seems like hard work to me."

"Oh, hush, Elijah," Sheriff Ellison said. "I gave you the robbery *because* you're lazy."

Elijah laughed again. "Well, I am, and I can't help it."

"I know."

"Diedrick, Kenneth said you were a pretty good worker at his ranch. Where'd you learn to punch cattle?"

"I worked some drives from Texas to Kansas. Now that's hard work and dirty too. Not much bathing on the trail."

The thought of Diedrick coming from Texas and Kansas worried the sheriff. Lots of gunhands came out of those places. "So, what brings you to Santa Fe?"

"Just needed a change, and a friend told me this was a great place."

"Hmm. You sure found it at Santa Fe."

Diedrick smiled. "I think so." He reached for his weapon and turned it to Ellison. "Drop the gun, Sheriff, and come closer. I can tell where your curiosity is leading."

Should have looked at those papers. "I bet there's a paper on you from Texas," Sheriff Ellison uttered.

Diedrick ignored him and turned to the deputy. "Elijah, take off your gun belt and lay it on the table."

"You can't get money out of the bank safe," Ellison said. "They have one of the latest and tested it against dynamite."

"I'm not going to blow it."

"Then what?"

"Deputy, you're going after the bank owner. Bring him here in a hurry, or Sheriff Ellison will get a bullet."

89

"Sheriff, what do you want me to do?" Elijah asked.

"You do as he says, Elijah. I don't believe this man's kidding."

"You're smart, Sheriff, 'cause Santa Fe will need a new lawman if he doesn't return in fifteen minutes."

The sheriff instructed Elijah to go out the back way.

Diedrick stepped forward and shoved the gun in Elijah's face. "If anyone besides the banker man comes, your days will shorten, Sheriff."

"Alright, I got it," Elijah replied. "I'm going now."

Elijah opened the back door and peered into the street before closing it behind him.

"I should have looked through my papers," Sheriff Ellison stated. "Bet there's a poster on you."

Diedrick snickered. "My bet is you won't find anything."

"Maybe not, but I'll still look through them when this is over."

"If you live." He peered at the clock on the wall. "If your deputy doesn't make it back in thirteen minutes, well—you know."

* * *

Concerned that the thieves had backed out, Kenneth walked to the window and cracked the curtains. Peering out, he spotted Elijah running down the street. *What is going on?*

"See anything, Kenneth?" Laura asked.

Kenneth kept his eyes on Elijah until he spotted three men advancing toward the freight company. "I think they're coming our way."

He looked again and saw Elijah walking back toward the bank with someone else. *The banker. No.*

"We have a problem, folks. I think they're robbing both."

"The sheriff will take care of the bank," Pastor West said.

As he returned to his place, Kenneth replied, "I think they already have the bank."

"But how?" Laura asked.

"Don't know. I saw Elijah heading toward the bank with the bank owner."

"That doesn't sound good," said Pastor West.

"Let's just do our part and let the sheriff do his."

Pastor West nodded. "Right."

The side door to the freight company flew open when a thief kicked it. Three men walked into the dark building and headed for the office, only to meet with guns staring at them as candlelight brightened the room.

"There's no need trying anything," Kenneth said. "We have you covered. Drop those pistols on the floor. Now!"

One man shook his head. "Boys, they got us."

"But Coy, we can take 'em."

"No we can't, Harbin. They got us." He tossed his gun to the floor.

"Laura, get their guns," Kenneth said. "You men turn around and put your hands behind your back."

"How did you know we'd try for the freight office, mister?" Coy Buttrom asked.

"When you let the women in the restaurant overhear your plan, we figured it was a distraction. The only two places in town with money worth robbing were the bank and the freight office."

"We didn't want the bank," Coy said.

"Yeah sure, that's what we thought, though we know your men are there now?"

"Don't know anything about that."

Kenneth turned to Pastor West. "Diedrick, it has to be."

"We better get these to the jail and help them," Laura said.

"And right away." Kenneth shoved Coy toward the door. "Move it, fellows."

Chapter 16

*P*astor West pushed open the door to the sheriff's office. Sheriff Ellison sat at his desk, looking through some papers.

"We have three needing a cell," said Pastor West.

"There's the key." Ellison pointed to the wall behind him. "Put them in the last one."

Kenneth peered at Elijah, who sat nearby. "I can't believe you left the bank instead of waiting things out."

"He had good reason," Sheriff Ellison said.

"What do you mean?"

"We got robbed."

"More men?"

"Nope. Only your good ranch hand."

"Diedrick?"

"Caught me by surprise. He made Elijah go after the bank owner while he held a gun on me."

"And you let him?"

"Um, he promised to put a bullet in me if the banker didn't show up in fifteen minutes."

"Sheriff, how much did he get?" Laura asked.

"All of it."

"You're going to get up a posse, right?"

"You bet, Miss Stone. But I don't think our town folk would appreciate it if I woke them this late at night."

"They won't mind, Sheriff. That's their money he took off with."

"Not all of it. Emory said some belonged to the bank and was not easy to replace."

After locking the thieves inside a cell, Kenneth returned to the office. "We need to get the people up and build a posse."

"We have six here, and I don't want just anyone."

"Sheriff, I'll get Gus Hewett and Morton Ackerman to help," Pastor West said. "They're both excellent with a gun."

"Ask those two first. If they don't, we'll get the word out that we need more. And I suppose you can tell a few around town about the robbery, though they will not enjoy hearing it. But please allow *me* to tell the councilmen and the mayor."

* * *

Laura felt her lack of sleep when morning came. She had waited on the sheriff and Kenneth as they readied a posse for dawn. The sheriff had come across a poster of a man believed to be Diedrick Simms, though his real name was Cullen Adkinson. Along with two accomplices, Adkinson had committed bank robberies in Kansas.

She sat at her desk, pencil in hand, attempting to craft a narrative about the attempted robbery of the freight office and the subsequent events that transpired at the bank. It was imperative that she conveyed the truth about the events, ensuring that the sheriff was not to blame.

Hearing outside noises, she arose from her chair. The

posse rode out as she approached the window.

She imagined the wave of fury directed from the town at Sheriff Ellison. Though not a great fan of hers, he didn't deserve the blame. The city council must know that keeping him on was more important than any negativity the incident brought.

She sat again and wrote three stories before Orland Flack reached the office.

One story was about the Wheeler murders. If Orland allowed her version, she would write Big Jeremiah as innocent until proven guilty. But would her boss allow it? *Orland has a strange way of looking at things.* She had omitted the grave digging, fearing most folks would hate that part and might even turn against her.

The other two stories were about the bank robbery and the attempted freight robbery. The town would think they were living in hell, she thought, with so many dreadful events brought to their attention. But I've written the truth.

The coffee finished making, and Laura sat drinking a cup, waiting for Orland and hoping he appreciated what she had written.

Thirty minutes passed, and Orland walked through the door. "You're here early, Laura."

"Yes, I've been here for a while writing stories."

"Don't tell me. You wrote about that mountain man. What's his name?"

"Big Jeremiah."

"Ah, yes."

"Well, that's *one* story. But a man robbed the bank last night, and some others attempted to rob the freight office."

"A man robbed the bank? Oh, dear."

Orland sat down hard, appearing ill.

"Are you alright, Mr. Flack?"

"I had my money in the bank. That's my life's savings."

"Don't worry. A posse rode out after him."

"But you don't understand. I had fifteen thousand dollars in there. Part of it is operating money for the Journal. The rest is mine."

Orland sat staring at the floor. "Laura, can you set up the press today? I have stories on the table that are ready. Add those you have to it. I think I'll go home."

After presenting her stories, she'd hoped she could leave and rest. A terrible headache had come on, but she would make it.

"Everything will be fine here, sir. Go home and rest. When the posse returns, I'm sure they will have good news."

Orland strolled to the door and left.

She turned to the press to set the type for the first story. Her work in Boston never involved type setting or working a printing press. But Orland, upon hiring her, made clear she must learn all aspects of the business. The Journal mostly prints the day before distribution, but these stories were of the utmost importance and called for promptness.

Laura spent the next three hours printing. When she sat to rest at last, her mind turned to Big Jeremiah. *I must find an attorney for him.* There were two in Santa Fe, including Marcus Whiteman, who worked for the prosecution. The other was Weldon Bailey, but she knew little about him except that he often hit the bottle. Weldon was the best option unless she wanted to make a trip to find one from out of town.

She stacked the paper and made them ready for Benson Rupel to deliver to the subscribers. Benson knew nothing about delivering today's extra, though. *I'll go to the jail, see Big Jeremiah, and find Benson. And I wonder what Olivia has found.*

* * *

Big Jeremiah lay on the cot as Laura walked to his cell door. "How are you, Big Jeremiah?"

95

He leaped to his feet. "I suppose I'm fine. Still breathing."

"I'm on my way to see an attorney. Maybe he will visit you later."

"Can he get me out today?"

"I don't think that's happening. I'd say the sheriff will visit Judge Morley today. He will decide if there's enough evidence for a trial."

"What about why Teele didn't look for those Indian tracks?"

Laura realized Big Jeremiah was in a fix not of his making. But she wondered about the knife. "Jeremiah, did Teele have a knife?"

"Sure, most men who hunt carry knives for skinning. Why?"

"I'm only thinking out loud. But I want you to know that my friend from Boston, Olivia, a doctor, is examining the bodies."

"They dug them up, didn't they?"

"That's the only way to check them. She's measuring the width and depth of the wounds to determine if your knife could have done this."

"I didn't kill those folks, Laura."

"I believe you, but we need the judge to believe you. Or a jury if it goes to trial. Olivia is working to prove it."

"What if she can't?"

Laura could say little. She knew there was a possibility the knife used was the same size as Big Jeremiah's. "I'm going to leave now. But I'll try to visit later."

"Thanks for helping me."

"I have done nothing yet."

"At least you're trying."

She left the jail to find Benson Rupel and tell him the papers were ready for distribution, and then she walked toward Weldon Bailey's place of business.

The bell on the door rang as she stepped inside and took a seat, hoping the attorney had heard it. Soon another door opened, and a man in a tweed suit entered the room. He was spindly, middle-aged, wearing wire gold-rimmed glasses. From his vest pocket, a watch chain dangled.

He peered at her as she stood. "May I help you, ma'am?"

"My name is Laura Stone, and I'm looking for an attorney to represent a friend."

"Come sit in my office. Laura Stone. Are you from the Journal?"

"Yes, I work there."

"I've read some of your work. You are quite an accomplished writer."

"Thank you. I'd love to write more, but Mr. Flack tells me which stories to take on."

"Would you like some tea?"

In Boston, she had enjoyed hot tea with friends several times a week. The people in Santa Fe knew little of hot tea. "Yes, please. I haven't had hot tea since Boston, to be honest."

"You from Boston?"

"No, sir. I'm from here in Santa Fe. My father owned a ranch growing up. I went to college in Boston to be a journalist."

"You came back home."

"Well, it's a long story, but yes."

He poured hot water from a porcelain teapot and offered her sugar, a small container of loose tea leaves, and a strainer. "Well, who do you need an attorney for?"

"His name is Big Jeremiah, and he's at the sheriff's office."

"In jail. Would that be the fellow they brought in for the murders of the Wheelers?"

"Yes, but he didn't do it."

"You have evidence of this?"

"I don't, but I'm working on it."

"Oh? How is that?"

"I have a doctor friend from Boston performing autopsies on the bodies as we speak."

"Right now, this friend is doing autopsies? Now that's unusual for Santa Fe. When I was in school in St. Louis, we learned of the work of forensic scientists to use in court cases. What an interesting field. I hope the judge allows it since it's new to many here."

"He has to. Big Jeremiah has nothing on his side except for what my friend finds."

"That is a judge's decision, but we will see about finding more evidence."

"Thank you."

"May I ask, has the judge already declared that Big Jeremiah must stand trial?"

"I don't know. The sheriff was to contact the judge today, but now he's gone with the posse."

"Posse?"

Laura knew they didn't want everyone to know about the bank robbery. "I suppose I shouldn't have said anything. The sheriff and the posse are riding after the thief."

"I'll find out about the judge as soon as I can. And how do I get in touch with the doctor performing these autopsies?"

"She's staying at the hotel. Her name is Olivia Bunney."

"A woman doctor. Hmm. What an interesting trial for Santa Fe."

Laura didn't appreciate the last comment because it seemed to imply a lack of trust in women's abilities. Unfortunately, she had no other option for representation for Big Jeremiah.

"I'll leave this to you, Mr. Bailey. Will you see Big Jeremiah today?"

"Yes. I'll get to the jail soon and question him."

Chapter 17

$\mathcal{P}$astor West watched from the church as Laura walked to the old boarding house. *I wonder if that's where they are doing those autopsies.* He strolled to the place and walked inside, hearing voices as he drew closer.

"My measurements tell me Big Jeremiah didn't do this," Olivia explained. "Ever who did used a longer and slimmer knife."

"So that means they should let Big Jeremiah go," Laura said.

"I'm no judge, but this man couldn't have done it with the knife the sheriff showed me. Just doesn't add up."

Pastor West stepped in behind them. "Hey, ladies."

"Oh, you scared me," Olivia said.

"I'm sorry. That wasn't my intention."

"Hello, Pastor. So, when the judge hears this, what will he do?" Laura asked.

"I heard that Judge Morley is still out of town and won't be back for several days," Pastor West explained.

"Oh, no. That means Jeremiah will have to stay longer."

"Laura, I'm not trying to discourage you from helping Big Jeremiah, but I can tell you, the people of Santa Fe will want justice for these terrible murders. Judge Morley will know this. What you need is to find the person who did it."

"You mean Big Jeremiah may still take the fall for killing those folks unless we do something?" Olivia said. "If an autopsy like this doesn't help bring justice, then Santa Fe is not a town of law. In Boston, this evidence alone would cast enough doubt on anyone charged. No one should die for a crime unless there's absolute proof they did it."

"But this is the rugged west, where the law is not always the process followed," Pastor West said.

"Then why is there a judge? His job is to follow the law."

"There's something else," Laura said, "Big Jeremiah told me when I was in the sheriff's office earlier."

"Oh, really?" Pastor West asked.

"He said Teele carries a knife."

"Most men in these parts carry a knife and a gun."

"But Teele was there and *is* the person who accused Big Jeremiah of the murders. Jeremiah thought it was Indians because of the unshod pony tracks and told Teele, though he never looked. We saw the tracks too when we were at the Wheeler place."

"How does this help Big Jeremiah?" West asked.

"Well, it might," Olivia said. "Indian tracks offer something to cast doubt on him, and so does Teele's knife."

Laura stared at her. "We need the judge to send the sheriff for Teele so we can measure his knife. If Teele did it, he should pay the price, not Big Jeremiah."

"Yes, that would help clear things up."

"Olivia, have you documented what you've found here?" Laura asked.

"Yes, but I must make copies in my room."

"We should take this information to the sheriff."

"The sheriff is gone, remember?" Pastor West said.

"I know, and we need him here."

"Folks in Santa Fe may be more concerned about losing their money than the murders."

"But people died!" Laura said.

"I realize that, but I know these people."

"Then help me pray the posse returns soon with the thief."

"Well sure, Laura, I will. Did I see you were coming from Attorney Weldon Bailey's office?" Pastor West asked.

"Yes, why?"

"Then you should take this info to him. Let him argue for you. That's what attorneys do."

"He's right, Laura," said Olivia. "An attorney will know the correct procedures to have the charges reversed."

Laura flashed a bright smile. "Maybe Mr. Bailey can find a law forcing Teele to allow the measuring of his knife blade."

"I hope," Olivia said.

"So, Olivia, are you finished with the bodies?" Laura asked. "Yes."

Laura turned to Pastor West. "Would you send the undertaker for them? I want to make sure they get a proper burial. And I'd appreciate it if you would officiate the memorial."

"Sure I will."

* * *

Clayton Atwood sat at the sheriff's desk as Weldon Bailey explained the autopsy results.

"So, that doctor said it couldn't have been Big Jeremiah's knife?" Clayton asked. "But you know I can't release him."

"I know. You want to wait for the judge," Weldon Bailey said. "So, where is he, anyway?"

"I'm only here to make sure the prisoner doesn't escape. Judge Morley has a case in Albuquerque to take care of. They told me he'd be back in a couple of days."

"*Who* told you?"

"Councilman Gordon Andrews."

"Oh, my. Is Harley Dolton in town?"

"The mayor? Yes, I think so."

"Okay, with the sheriff out of pocket, I need you to bring in Walter Teele. There's a good chance he's the one you're looking for."

"Sorry. The sheriff hasn't trained me to go after people, Mr. Bailey. And from what I heard, no one has seen Teele commit a crime. Without evidence, I can't accuse or lock him up."

"You may have evidence if you bring him in and let the doctor measure his blade."

"You said it, Mr. Bailey, 'may have the evidence,' but to charge a man with a crime, we need more than maybes and possibilities."

"Well, what about the fresh Indian tracks around the Wheeler place? Everyone knows Indians have killed with knives. Doesn't that shed *some* doubt on Big Jeremiah's innocence?"

"Sure, it sounds wonderful for Big Jeremiah, but I still can't turn him loose without the sheriff or Judge Morley signing off on it."

Laura had sat to rest, listening and trying to stay out of it as her friends had suggested. But with all they had uncovered, Big Jeremiah was still in jail awaiting the judge. She stood and walked to the desk. "Gentlemen, may I say something?"

"Sure, Miss Stone," Clayton replied.

"I am confident Big Jeremiah did not commit these murders. His gentle spirit holds only the willpower to kill the animals he catches in his traps."

"Miss Stone—"

"Clayton, I'm asking that you release Big Jeremiah into my guardianship until he goes before the judge."

Clayton stood staring. "What? And what if he is the murderer?"

"He's not, and he'll not hurt me. I'm sure he'll promise to stay at the boarding house for a few days until this is over."

"I don't know."

Laura recalled hearing that Clayton, was an avid fisherman and hunter, and hoped the similarities might sway his opinion of Big Jeremiah. "Clayton, can you imagine what it must feel like for him? Never has he seen the inside of a jail before now. He's not visited towns much in his lifetime, either, only when there's a need. This man knows the woods, trapping and skinning animals, which he does for a living. So let him come to my place, which is still much like a jail for someone like him."

Clayton shook his head. "The sheriff is going to shoot me." Then turning around, he walked to the wall, removed the keys, and marched toward the jail as Weldon smiled at Laura.

"Laura, I'm wondering now if the education you received was all wrong," Weldon said.

"Why, sir?"

"Just sounded so much like a closing argument in a court case."

She laughed. "Just trying to help."

Big Jeremiah stepped from the hallway.

Weldon nodded. "Oh, it did, my dear."

"What's going on?" Big Jeremiah asked.

"You're going to my place," Laura said, "until the judge arrives from Albuquerque."

"So, it's over?"

"Not at all," Clayton replied. "This only means that Miss Stone has the care of you until the judge returns, at which point you will come to see Sheriff Ellison, and he will take you to Judge Morley. This also means that Miss Stone is accountable if you leave the town and would face the consequences. You cannot leave by law, so I urge you to stay close to where Miss Stone lives. Some folk around town are not happy about the deaths of the Wheelers."

Jeremiah nodded. "I'm going nowhere until you've settled it."

"When you go before the judge, Big Jeremiah, I'll be there with you," Weldon said.

"What for?"

"Well, the law expects an attorney to be present, and this young lady has gained my services for you." Weldon pointed to Laura.

"I see."

"Can I take him now?" Laura asked.

Clayton sat down again. "Not yet. I need you to sign a writ, and I'd like your attorney also to sign. Oh, the sheriff is going to shoot me."

After Laura signed the paper, she walked out with Big Jeremiah and turned toward Esta Dowd's boarding house.

Pastor West saw them and walked over. "Wow, I'm surprised they released Jeremiah."

"Oh, they haven't," Laura said. "I asked that Big Jeremiah be under my recognizance."

"Who's at the jail today?"

"Clayton Atwood is watching things until the sheriff returns."

"I wonder how that will go over with the sheriff?"

"I don't care, as long as Big Jeremiah doesn't have to stay in that jail."

"Amen to that," Big Jeremiah said.

"I'm glad Clayton went along with it."

"So am I," replied Big Jeremiah.

"Steven, walk with us to Esta Dowd's. I need to get him there."

"Sure. How is your friend Olivia doing?"

"Are you interested in her, Steven?"

"No, but I am the pastor in Santa Fe and was hoping to invite her to church."

"She's been already."

"Doesn't mean I can't turn on my pastoral charm and hope she continues."

"Is that the same allure you cast my way?"

"Oh, no. That deep charm I've never used before or since. You were and are still my dream."

They reached the boarding house.

"Laura, show me where to go," Big Jeremiah said, "then you two can talk out your affairs on the porch swing." He grinned.

After Laura took Big Jeremiah in, she returned to find Pastor West seated in the swing.

"This is quite a romantic swing, Laura. You should have told me about it."

She sat beside him. "Have you thought more about our situation, Steven?"

He placed his arm around her, smiling. "I'm leaning your way, but I might need more convincing."

She peered away with a slight grin. "I'm sorry, Steven. I'm just too tired."

"Did you have a bad day?"

"Terrible. Well, only physically. I'm thankful for what Olivia found and that Clayton heard me out. I think they know Big Jeremiah is innocent."

"Maybe so." He watched as she turned her head downward, sensing her fatigue. "Listen, I was about to ask you to supper at the hotel tonight. But seeing how tired you are, I can wait another day."

She turned to him. "I only need to close the Journal for the day. If I can rest a few hours, I would love to dine with you tonight."

"Wonderful. I'll come by around six o'clock then if that's alright."

"Certainly." She watched as the handsome pastor strolled away.

Chapter 18

The Queen Hotel housed the best restaurant in Santa Fe. Pastor Steven West drove the buggy near the door and reined the horse to a stop.

Stepping down, he made his way to the other side and reached for Laura's hand. "May I help you down, ma'am?"

"You may," she said, smiling. "Steven, are you sure you can afford this place?"

"Oh, yes. I eat here often."

She took his arm, and they entered the Hotel. The restaurant was sparse with customers, but they did not mind.

The waitress paused what she was doing and hurried to them. "A table for two?"

"Yes, please," Steven said.

They followed her to a corner table—a candle burned on the wall beside them. The dimness of the section presented a romantic touch.

"This is somewhat poetic, much like the descriptions in some novels I've read," Laura commented.

"Yes, it is," Steven said.

They placed their order and sat waiting.

"Laura, I have been doing some thinking."

"About us?"

"Yes. I know you enjoy writing. But of course, I'm traditional in my views of the woman's place. I believe God wants a woman to keep a close relationship with her home life. Still, I think for us, there's *some* compromise to discover."

"Oh, compromise," Laura said. "Whose compromise needs discovering? Mine or yours?"

"Um, let me finish, and I think you'll see. I wondered if your boss, Orland, would allow you to write your stories at home. You could take them to him, and he could print them in the newspaper whenever he wanted to. I thought you'd enjoy writing much more in the privacy of our home. Of course, you'll be there to help with other things." He paused, waiting for her response.

Laura sat gaping, searching for the right words. One thing was sure, she did not go through years of schooling in Boston to become a bound wife. "Steven, you don't need a wife. You need a maid." She stood up.

"Now, wait. Please sit down."

She sat again. "I didn't spend six years of my life in Boston, digging into school work, fighting to make good grades in the face of belligerent men, all so I could be someone's maid."

"I didn't mean it that way."

"Yes, you did. You believe God's perfect wife is a maid. Someone to clean your clothes, cook your meals, tidy up your house and who knows what else. I thought there'd be a negotiation, an arrangement with you. I heard only about me compromising what I love to do and what I trained to do."

"So that means you won't marry me?"

She drew a deep breath and allowed a slow escape through her nostrils. "Under these terms, *no*. I don't want to enter marriage, be unhappy, and get divorced. What a terrible mark it *would* be on you."

"Yes, it would."

They drank from the water glasses brought to the table. Laura peered around the room and saw Kenneth and Olivia at a dining table on the far side. "I didn't know Kenneth was back from the hunt."

"Oh?" Pastor West turned in his chair to get a glimpse. "I wonder if they saw us. The room is dark."

"Kenneth saw me, and I'm sure he mentioned us to Olivia."

"Yes. Maybe on the way out, we can sashay by their table."

"Sure."

The waitress brought a bowl of the daily special soup for each of them. She sat them down and returned to the kitchen.

Laura bowed as Pastor West said a brief prayer over their food. She peered at him as he finished. "Steven, I'm sorry that I'm not right for you. Someday a woman will come along who is everything you expect. You'll be glad then that you waited."

"After I ran into you that day at the mercantile, I determined that woman was you. I'm sorry for what *I've* put you through, Laura. I suppose how my family raised me influenced my ideas and, of course, the Bible. In Ephesians it says, *Wives, submit yourselves unto your own husbands, as unto the Lord. For the husband is the head of the wife, even as Christ is the head of the church: and he is the saviour of the body. Therefore as the church is subject unto Christ, so let the wives be to their own husbands in every thing.* I wrestle with it because I want to follow God's word."

"I understand, Steven. You're a man of God and should walk how the Bible instructs, but maybe your interpretation of *this* is skewed. I have no problem looking to you as the head over our house should we wed, but regulating every step I take seems more like a one-man rule or autocracy. I can't believe that is what God intended for the marriage between a man and a woman."

"There are various interpretations in the Bible. On this, I've chosen to follow a strong conservative approach I know. But I will offer fervent prayer, and maybe God will offer me another assessment."

Laura sat her fork down and half smiled at him. "Steven, that's an important step. But please don't alter *your* views because of mine. Make sure they align with your convictions."

"I will. If I spend enough time in prayer, *surely* God will give me an answer."

"And we'll always be friends, right?" Laura asked.

"Why do you ask that? Sure we will."

"Only that you might marry someone else someday, which could make friendship problematic."

"Laura, I'm certain I'll never feel about another woman as I do when I'm with you." He turned and peered across the room. "Are you finished with your meal?"

"I am."

"Let's visit Kenneth and Olivia and break up the romance." He grinned.

When they reached the table, Kenneth had hold of Olivia's hand. She jerked it away and sat back in her chair, blushing and smiling at them.

"Hello, Pastor and Laura," Kenneth said. "I didn't expect to see you here."

"Just getting a meal with a friend," Laura said.

Kenneth smiled. "Well, everybody has to eat."

"Olivia, how are you?" Laura asked.

"I'm fine. I finished the autopsy documentation, so Kenneth asked me if I had eaten."

"Good. They have fine food here, don't you think?"

"Yes, they do."

Laura turned to her brother. "So, did the posse catch up to Diedrick?"

"Yes, he rode into a canyon and thought he was safe to

110

make a camp. We followed his tracks and surrounded him. He's in jail."

"Oh, dear, that means the sheriff is back and will want to know where Big Jeremiah is."

"I was there when Clayton explained how you bullied him into letting Big Jeremiah go."

"I didn't bully him. I just impressed on him to release that man into my custody."

"The sheriff seemed fine with it. I heard Clayton saying that attorney Bailey wanted Teele brought in for questioning under some formality."

"So, the sheriff is going after Teele?" Laura asked.

"Yes, and he wants Olivia to measure and document Teele's knife."

"I doubt Teele will go along with this," Pastor West said. "He's a hard man with his own rules."

"So you believe Teele will buck the sheriff?" Kenneth asked.

"I'm saying he will."

Kenneth stood. "I think I should ride and help Sheriff Ellison."

"Then I'm coming along," Laura said. "I'll get my rifle."

"Well, I suppose I should help, too," Pastor West replied. "I'll get my gun and saddle my horse."

"And I'll leave the fun to you folks," Olivia said, "and go to my room."

"You're not afraid of a little gunfire, are you?" Kenneth asked.

"I'm from Boston, remember?"

Chapter 19

Walter Teele's farm lay five miles outside town in a hollow between two mountains. He had an ideal view of the road from his house. Laura, Kenneth, and Pastor West had met up with the sheriff a hundred yards before getting to Teele's place.

A shot rang out, ricocheting off the road.

"That's what I hoped wouldn't happen," said Sheriff Ellison.

"Find cover, everyone!" Kenneth cried out.

They rode behind a large boulder and dismounted.

"Kenneth, can you get around behind that house?" Sheriff Ellison asked. "I'm going to talk to him. Maybe I can convince him to come out without bloodshed."

"I'll go with you, Kenneth," Pastor West said. "If Teele doesn't come quietly, we can split up and maybe draw his fire."

Sheriff Ellison put a hand up to hold them back. "Wait a minute. I don't want any shooting if you can avoid it. We still don't know for sure that Teele murdered those Wheelers."

"Then why is he shooting at us?" Laura asked.

"I don't know, but if I saw this many ride out to my place, I'd be suspicious too."

Kenneth nodded. "Sheriff, Teele may not surrender without a fight."

"We'll do what we can," Pastor West said.

The two men ran back the way they rode until they found a place where the trees blocked them from the house.

When the sheriff thought they were far enough, he called out to Teele, "Walter, I need you to come with me and go over your story again!"

"I told you everything you need to know, Sheriff. Nothing to talk about," Teel shouted.

"Well, a few things aren't adding up. The judge will want to hear it from you."

"No, you got something up your sleeve. I saw four riders coming down that road. If all you needed was me to come in again, why all the riders and guns?"

He's not buying it. "We only met up along the way, Walter. Could you put your gun down and make this easier for me?" Sheriff Ellison said.

Teele then fired several rounds toward the sheriff, spooking the horses.

"Sheriff, he's not coming out," Laura said. "Why don't you let me speak with him?"

"What can you say differently?"

"Let me try."

"Go ahead, but it's your life. I can't protect you out in the open."

Laura stood and walked in front of Ellison. "Mr. Teele, it's Laura Stone. May I speak with you?"

Teel peeked out the screen door. "Don't see how it will do any good, little lady. I'm staying right here."

"Mr. Teele, there's an innocent man in the jail, the one you brought in."

"Now, how do you figure he's innocent? I saw Big Jeremiah kneeling over that Wheeler girl."

"You may not understand this, but recent evidence proves he didn't do it. They measured his knife and the wounds in the bodies and found they didn't match."

"What did you tell him that for?" Sheriff Ellison asked.

"Because nothing else has worked. I'm pleading to Teele's humanity."

The sheriff shook his head.

"If that's true, it means the sheriff has come to take me to jail because he thinks *I* did it," Teele said.

"What about the Indian tracks we found, Mr. Teele? Couldn't the Indians have done it? Why didn't you look at the Indian tracks like Big Jeremiah asked?"

"Miss Stone, I see what's going on here. You have this recent evidence that may prove Big Jeremiah didn't do it, but that town council plans to come through this looking good. They need someone to set these murders on. And since I went by the Wheeler place. Simple."

"But Mr. Teele, if the Indians did this, the sheriff needs to know. If we could measure your knife blade, it might eliminate you as a suspect."

"No! Ya'll just want to put me in jail." He raised his rifle and fired at her. Searing hot pain sliced her torso and she dropped to her knees.

"Laura!" Pastor West cried out when he saw her fall.

Teele turned and fired at Pastor West, who had hunkered down behind a wagon.

Knowing Laura had taken a bullet, Kenneth raised his Winchester and sent several rounds to the door frame, sending Teele searching for cover.

As Kenneth and Pastor West traded rounds with Teele, the

sheriff drew closer, taking cover behind the barn. "Teele! Walter Teele! I asked these men not to fire unless they had to. You started this and didn't have to. Now hold your fire and talk to me."

Teele aimed his rifle at the sheriff and sent a round, catching him in the leg. Sheriff Ellison stumbled to the ground.

"Pastor, can you hear me?" Kenneth cried out. "Fire at that door with all you have."

Pastor West unloaded his rifle at Teel's front door, sending chunks of wood into the air, then pulled his revolver and continued. As the bullets struck the doorway, Kenneth ran to the back of the house and pushed through the door.

Teele heard the crash and turned. "Barlow, you're not taking me in." He raised a shotgun and fired, missing Kenneth, sending a scatter load of shots into the kitchen cabinets.

Falling to the floor, Kenneth aimed and pulled the trigger, catching Teele in the chest. Teele collapsed to the surface, trying to reach his rifle.

"It's over, Teele," Kenneth uttered as he kicked away the shotgun.

Blood poured from Teele's chest and mouth. "Why did you...come here?"

"Just searching for the truth. Did you kill that family?"

Sheriff Ellison hobbled through the back door. "You get him?"

Kenneth didn't answer but kept his eyes on Teele. "So tell me."

"Grief and me...had an argu...ment. I killed him, but then...Ocie came outside. I couldn't have...witnesses. Luella came. I didn't...mean to kill her, but—"

"I gotta take you, Teele," Sheriff Ellison said, "For shooting at the Sheriff and a citizen of the city."

Kenneth peered at the man as he lay bleeding. "Sheriff, he's gone."

"Hmm, well. We'll have to carry him so the doctor can examine the body."

"Sure, where's Pastor West?"

"I think you know where he is."

"So, how *is* Laura?"

"Bullet caught her side and went straight through. I reckon she'll be down a while."

"Nah, you can't keep my sister down for long."

* * *

Pastor West ran to Laura. "Are you alright?"

She reached out and grabbed him around the neck. "The bullet went through. I tore off a piece of dress and wrapped it."

"We've got to get you home."

"Yes, but Pastor, find Olivia when we get there. Let her do the doctoring."

Pastor West ran for their horses and led them closer. "Let me help you on."

"I'm glad you were here, Steven."

"Oh, now it's Steven again. A few moments ago, it was Pastor."

Her weak body sent her thoughts drifting, and she pondered why she remained in Santa Fe when she could be in Boston, writing for almost any newspaper. But she supposed the times and circumstances had brought her home. At least now she could pen a story for the local paper about what had happened. She leaned toward Steven and lowered her voice to a whisper. "I'm thankful you are here. Can we leave it at that?"

"Sure we can. Now get on that horse."

She nodded. "Yes, sir."

Pastor West mounted his, and they rode to Santa Fe.

Chapter 20

O livia cleaned and wrapped Laura's wound with a piece of bed linen as a knock sounded on the door. "Wait just a moment! Laura, let's get this robe on you. I'm sure that is Pastor West coming to see how you are doing."

"I'll be fine now that you are here."

"Well, maybe you won't try something like this next time."

"The sheriff told me it was a bad idea, but I didn't listen. I was only trying to keep Teele from shooting because I knew how it would end."

"But Teele did shoot."

Laura nodded, offering a regretful expression as she tied the front of the robe. "You can let him in now."

Olivia pulled back the door. Standing, waiting, was Kenneth and Pastor West. "Come in, gentlemen. She's decent now."

Laura sat leaning on the divan, grimacing as they entered the room. Pastor West would no doubt do his job, but his most obvious motive for being there was not his interest in her well-being as much as her hand in marriage. "Thank you, Pastor West, for getting me back safe."

"Well, I care about you. You know that."

She turned to Kenneth. "While I was resting, Olivia measured Teele's knife and documented her findings."

"I know. I was at the sheriff's office with Pastor West. Sheriff Ellison has released Big Jeremiah."

"But the judge is not back."

"I suppose that doesn't matter now. There's insufficient evidence to hold the mountain man for the crime."

"The evidence points to Teele," Olivia said.

"Teele confessed to us before he died," Kenneth stated. "He said he argued with Grief Wheeler, which got out of hand. That's when Teele pulled a knife and stabbed old Grief. Ocie had come outside when they were fighting. He didn't want witnesses, so he killed her and the daughter. We supposed Big Jeremiah came by right after that. Walter must have gone inside the house to look around. Big Jeremiah was kneeling over Luella when he came out."

"I tried to get Teele to come to church many times," Pastor West said. "He wanted nothing to do with church. I believe if he had, none of this would have happened. Four people are dead because of some disagreement."

"That's so sad," Olivia said.

Pastor West turned to Laura, smiling. "I'm glad you're going to be okay. I'll leave you to heal. But if you don't mind, I will check on you until you're on your feet."

"I don't mind, Pastor. But don't anyone expect me to stay down long."

"You should follow the doctor's order, sister," Kenneth replied.

Laura shook her head, casting a demure smile at them. "I will try. Goodbye, Pastor, and thanks for stopping by."

Kenneth stood beside her. "I suppose I'll ride back to the ranch. Don't have anyone watching over the place now that the sheriff has arrested Diedrick."

"What are you going to do, Kenneth?" Laura asked.

"I'll do it myself until the right cowhand comes to town. Though I suppose I should pay more attention."

"Yes, I hope so."

"Olivia, now that you've examined the bodies, what are *your* plans?" Kenneth asked. "I'm friends with Doc Simms. Maybe I could speak with him about you joining his clinic."

"Thanks for offering, Kenneth. But I have other plans."

"Oh?"

"I bought that old boarding house where we performed the autopsies and plan to fix it how it should be. I plan to start a clinic of my own."

"Do you think that's a good idea? Doc Simms will not like that at all."

"Who cares what Doc Simms thinks? If I live here and become a citizen of Santa Fe, I have as much right as he does to be the doctor of this town."

"Oh, boy. I see a war coming."

"Not unless he starts it."

Kenneth turned to Laura. "Have you spoken with Olivia about her plan?"

"No, because it's none of my business. And I know a newspaper where she can advertise real cheap."

"You women make it hard on us men. We can't live with you and can't live without you."

Laura could see Kenneth was upsetting Olivia, so she reached for a shoe to toss at him.

"No, Laura, you'll open the wound," Olivia said, grabbing it away.

Kenneth seemed relieved until Olivia tossed the shoe at him, just missing. The women laughed as he ran from the room.

Mountain Confinement

Chapter 21

*P*astor West peered over the crowd before starting his sermon. "Well, what a delightful group this morning. Most are here, but has anybody heard from the Dunning family?"

Silence followed as the folks glanced around the room.

"I saw Orval yesterday at the general store," responded Gus Hewett. "He spoke like they would all be here."

"They never miss a Sunday unless something is wrong," acknowledged Morton Ackerman.

"I hope nothing is the matter with baby Clair," said Fay Brink.

"Now, let's not jump to conclusions, Fay," Pastor West added. "I'm confident everything is fine, and we will see them this week." But then he thought of an occasion in Orval's past when rye whiskey commanded him and hoped he had not stumbled into his former practices. "Let's get on with the service."

Laura sat hearing Pastor West's preaching, but her mind

wandered to the days of her arrival at Santa Fe. After a brief time, she discovered how mischievous folks here could be. Why did men turn to evil? Her father had died because of greedy men. The bank robbery attempt was another recent villainous deed. Then came the massacre of a family over a silly disagreement. She must make sure that someone asks about the Dunnings right after service.

As the church service ended, Olivia and Kenneth strode to Laura.

"Laura, will we see you at the restaurant?" Olivia inquired.

"I'm concerned about the Dunnings, so I thought I'd meet with Sheriff Ellison. Maybe I can convince him to ride and check on them."

"When you finish, come over."

"We'll keep a chair for you," Kenneth said.

"Sure."

After the people departed the church, Laura walked to the sheriff's office. Sheriff Ellison sat at his desk eating lunch when she went in. "Hello, Sheriff."

"Hi, Laura. It's good to see you are over the bullet wound."

"Yes, I'm doing fine. Go ahead and eat, but I have something important to ask you."

He nodded. "Okay, I believe I will."

"All the people customary for Sunday attended church today except one family. Do you know the Dunnings?"

He munched on a bite and gulped it down. "Uh, well, yeah. Everyone knows the Dunnings."

"They weren't at church today."

His eyebrows lifted as he shrugged his shoulders. "And?"

"They weren't there, and they always are."

Ellison swallowed a sip of his drink. "What are you trying to say, Laura?"

"Something must be wrong, and we're concerned."

"I'm sure people miss service all the time—when they

have a cow in a gulley, or the corn needs picking, or a mule is sick. Farming folk miss church all the time."

The Dunning family, who usually sat beside her during services, were absent for the first time since her arrival. Something was amiss. She just knew it. "Not the Dunnings. They are always there."

"Maybe since you've been coming, but I feel certain they've missed service before."

She paused, contemplating Sheriff Ellison's remark. "Maybe, but something seems wrong today." Relaxing her tone, she said, "Would you *please* ride out there and see if they are alright?"

"Can't."

"What do you *mean* you can't?"

"I can't. I have to ride to Pecos to escort a prisoner back here. Marshal Walsh foresees his arrival tomorrow and wishes to take him on the train to Albuquerque for trial."

Who could help if Sheriff Ellison could not? Kenneth was short-handed at the ranch, and she understood that Mayor Dolton had invited Pastor West to his home for lunch. "Thank you, Sheriff." She turned toward the door.

"They will be fine, Laura."

She twirled before him. "You don't know that, Sheriff."

"Your shoes must be painful to fill."

"What?"

"Well, it seems that anybody who happens along with a problem, you work up the urge to solve it."

Her eyes honed at him. Still, he was correct. She knew she tended to get involved in other people's lives. She was nosy—but this trait had helped her become a successful journalist, though it often led her into difficult situations. "I know that, Sheriff. I assume that's why journalism calls to me."

"Maybe so. If you must visit them, have Kenneth take you there. To reach their place, ride out on the north route and adhere to it until you see a little pond on the left. There's a turnoff lane beside it. They are the only place up the mountain."

She didn't respond and turned to leave.

Outside the sheriff's office, her mind reeled. Could Ellison have a valid point? What if she was worried about nothing, and they were working with a cow with complicated labor? Or Orval had to scout for a missing cow. But what if something *was* amiss, and they required help?

Desiring to change her wardrobe, she approached Esta Dowd's boarding house. After a brief walk, she was at the livery. Moving from the farm to Santa Fe, she housed Copper at the livery for convenience. She enjoyed riding him, and they had become close.

Copper spotted her and became excited. "Wow, boy. You are ready. I'm sorry it's been two weeks since our last ride. So many things have cropped up, though there's no reason to make excuses. I'll try to ride you more often."

She latched her rifle into the scabbard, thrust a package of bullets into the saddlebags, and mounted him.

A black fellow wandered in behind her and Copper. "Miss Laura. I would have saddled him for you."

"Hello, Ishmael. No bother. I'm used to the saddle."

"So, you going on a ride for a bit?"

"Yes, I'm riding down the north road to the Dunnings. If anybody inquires about me, that's what you tell them."

"Yes, ma'am. I will."

She reined Copper beyond Ishmael and gave a gentle kick. He dashed forward into an unbroken gallop before reaching the edge of town.

Chapter 22

*L*aura followed the directions Sheriff Ellison gave. When she had identified the turn, she gaped at the path, observing how vines and young saplings had flourished, overtaking the road. *Someone should help them clear this lane.*

Copper lunged forward when she urged him toward the trail. Soon she came to a clearing with a barn to her right near the dense timbers, and the cabin to her left, though not a soul could she see.

Dismounting as she reached the home, she tied Copper's reins to a sparse sapling at the corner of the residence. *This is strange.*

She peered at the broad field, the barn, and the garden section but saw no movement. *Where could they be?*

"Orval, Alice, where are you?"

Again, she called for them. "Orval, are you home?"

An unfamiliar sound then reverberated in the air.

What was that?

Speculating if the odd cry was a mule or a cow, she gazed

across the field and at the barn again but saw nothing that could have produced the noise.

Realizing Copper had become disturbed made her uneasy. *I'm not scared by much, but this is odd.*

As she turned to tap the door, she heard it again, stronger. Peeping over her shoulder to the barn, this time, she noticed movement. *Oh, no.*

A giant grizzly strode from behind the barn and spotted her. He raised on his hind feet and roared.

Laura's mind churned at what to do. She turned and beat hard on the door. Copper saw the grizzly and tugged against the sapling, tearing away from it. He raced down the lane and disappeared.

The door behind her opened, and Orval stood gawking. "Get in here, Laura."

She rushed through the entrance as Orval sealed the door behind her.

The grizzly beat on the cabin, growling loudly.

Orval held a shotgun in his hands, and he stared at the door. "What are you doing here, Laura?"

"You weren't at church, and I wondered if something was wrong."

"You figured right. That monster paraded in yesterday about the time I went to milk the cow. And like you, I just made it inside. Thankfully, the rest of the family were inside already."

"Where are they?"

He pointed the weapon at the loft. Laura spotted Tommy and Retha resting on the loft floor, their legs dangling over the edge. She nodded to them. Alice held little Clair, their two-month-old daughter. Laura recalled Orval had brought Alice into town on the buckboard to Doctor Simms. He had called on Olivia to assist when Orval feared losing Alice. She suggested a unique surgery to remove the baby and save them both.

"Is everybody alright?" Laura asked, peering at Alice and the children.

Alice tried to smile. "We are doing as well as we can."

"If only the town knew about this."

"What can they do?" Orval asked. "That grizzly is the largest I've come upon in these parts."

"There are men who hunt in Santa Fe. They can track it if need be."

"Well, even if they knew about it, they wouldn't have to track him. That bear believes he's discovered a new feeding ground. I expect he's already taken the mule."

"Oh, Orval. I'm sorry."

The grizzly had relaxed its ranting and returned to the barn. Laura sat in a chair, hoping to calm down, wishing Pastor West and Kenneth were there. The bear was just another obstacle in a series of challenges since moving to Santa Fe, including murders, cattle thieves, and attempted bank holdups. Now, a massive grizzly posed a threat to her and this family.

But Boston was not any better. There were three instances of robberies and homicides. Someone had killed a young man who attended her college.

Before her departure, she wrote and published a story exposing a scandal involving multiple city officials who were involved in concealing illegal moonshine sales, which helped fund their campaigns.

Trouble seemed to come no matter where she lived, and she must learn to rely on her faith in God through these difficult moments.

"Orval, do you have horses?" Laura asked.

"Two. They are for drawing the buckboard when we require supplies. I saw them in the pasture yesterday, but they ran away when they heard that beast. If they are alive, I presume they are on the backside of this place where there's water. I hope this thing doesn't become tired of the mule and head for them. They say bears can smell everything."

"You are correct. I roomed with a friend in Boston who studied zoology. I recall her telling me how they could smell us, even from a distance. You mentioned he might soon move for your horses. Wouldn't that be better than trying to come inside your cabin?"

"No, don't need him here, but I need those horses. We are ordinary folk. It took two years of hard farming to earn enough to compensate for those horses."

Laura lowered her head in disappointment. The appearance of the grizzly bear was the worst thing that could have happened to the Dunning family, other than the passing of a loved one. Like many others in the area, the Dunnings had worked tirelessly to clear land and cultivate their fields. Any progress they made was hard-won and significant. A hardship of this proportion would set them back years.

"Maybe the town will help if anything happens to them," Laura replied.

Orval turned to her, allowing a grunt. "I don't require their handouts! We've made it here by ourselves. We will make it just fine."

"But you need horses to gather supplies."

"I'll hear no further talk of handouts."

Laura had seen firsthand the painful precepts of pride in her father. He claimed that his own effort and intelligence for his success, asserting that nothing could happen without him. Over the years, he had overcome many obstacles, which only fueled his pride and made it all-consuming.

She had learned about the dangers of pride while reading about the early settlers who traveled west through the Rockies and suffered from freezing and starvation. While pride could be beneficial in moderation, it could lead to destruction if left unchecked. Laura prayed to the Lord to help Orval overcome his pride.

Orval scanned his place out the front window. "Laura,

watch for me. I can't see him out there."

"You're not going out, are you?"

"We must eat. To do that, we need firewood for the cookstove. I'm not worried about me, but Alice is nourishing Clair, and the children require food."

"Alright, but be prudent."

"I will, but I have to reach the side of the cabin to get it."

"You'll be out of our sight?"

"Orval, do you think you should?" Alice demanded.

"Yes, Alice. I will be alright. Laura is watching for me."

He gazed outside through the window again. "Alright, here goes." He tugged open the door and glanced around. When he did not see the bear, he walked out.

Laura observed from the door as he rounded the corner. *Oh, please hurry.*

Moments later, she saw Orval bringing an armload of split firewood. Then the bear turned toward the cabin as he approached the front of the home. "He's coming. Hurry."

Orval's eyes widened, and he stepped quicker until he reached the door and turned inside. "Seal it. Pull down the crossbars." He released the firewood beside the cookstove. "That blasted bear is not just stalking us. He's spying on us, hoping to catch us outside."

Laura sensed the bear had upped the ante. Perhaps it was his demeanor, but she could not shake the feeling that he was clever enough to have a strategy for securing his next meal. He was not just after any blood either. He wanted theirs.

Orval watched him rise on his hind legs and push on the cabin through the window. "I hope those timbers hold."

"God is watching and won't let death come to any."

Orval's eyes, as pale as daffodils, narrowed to slits. "So you're a prophet now?"

"No, but I know the Lord is good, and you should know, too."

Alice passed Clair to Tommy before descending the ladder. Orval scanned the room as he lit the kindling. "You know, we devote our lives to the church every Sunday, and still, God hasn't determined to reduce our endeavors. I had to dig a new well this summer. I never foresaw that coming. And as you may recall Alice's plight when she had Clair, we almost lost them both."

"We all have our trouble, Orval."

"Yeah. Do you have a grizzly in your yard?"

She kept her peace, realizing words were meaningless, hoping Pastor West could speak sense to him soon.

"Alice will fix up some supper," Orval said. "We will eat and then rest. I plan to sit in that chair and watch the door tonight. You can bed down in the loft with the family. Alice will prepare a place on the floor. I'm sorry, but it's cramped up there."

Laura strode to the stove. "May I assist?"

"We have little tonight, but sure," Alice said.

Laura noticed the anguish on her face and whispered, "God will save your family."

"I know he will, but you have to understand. We've gone through a lot."

Laura understood more than Alice knew. Her family's early years on the farm were challenging, with meals made of only cornbread and fresh milk. Yet, despite this, they were always content.

After finishing their supper, they found a spot to lie down for the night. Orval sat in a nearby chair, keeping watch on the door.

Chapter 23

Outside the cabin, they could hear the grizzly strutting, rumbling, and never relaxing. His presence kept all but the children from resting.

Laura raised from the blanket in the loft and went to the ladder. She lowered herself to the lower floor and found Orval where he had said he would be, holding the weapon in his hands.

"Orval, why don't you get some rest? I will watch."

"What kind of fellow would I be to let a woman take charge of a grizzly situation? No, I better have a watch."

"Orval, if matters turn, we will require you at your strongest. To do that, you must rest. I can shoot a gun fine and will watch so you can lie down."

Orval reflected on her suggestion. "Well, I am rather sleepy."

Finally, he passed her the weapon as he rose from the chair. "Only a couple of hours now."

Laura stood in front of the door, staring into the darkness.

Her mind took her to her home in Boston, with its elegant furnishings and stunning surroundings. The neighborhood was picturesque. The people in the community were elderly and kind-hearted. A woman named Ella had offered her cookies multiple times and invited her for dinner once. She assumed she did so because she missed her daughter, who had died during childbirth.

Boston had experienced break-ins and fires in her neighborhood, but had never encountered a grizzly bear. Even the zoo did not have grizzly bears on display, adding to the rarity of the situation. The critter's presence outside the cabin was alarming, causing her and the others a sense of fear and uneasiness.

She questioned why the bear would target a family farm when the woods offered plenty of food—had someone done something to cause him to turn on them?

Her eyelids batted as she resisted the urge to fall asleep. She must remain alert and watch.

As she sat fighting sleep, she was thankful for Kenneth. Would she have ever known about him if she had not returned to Santa Fe? The thought troubled her, and she could not help but question why her father had kept it a secret. Since his passing, it was a mystery she might never solve.

The grizzly roared again, and she pondered how long until he burst down the door and made his next meal within.

The morning sun seeped through the window, reminding her it was time to awaken Orval.

As she rose from the chair and turned to go after him, she noticed he had put one leg on the ladder. "I was about to wake you."

"I heard the griz. Alice is feeding Clair. She will make breakfast in a bit, but we have no fresh milk. The cow is in the barn where I left her unless the grizzly has broken through the backside."

An image of the creature tearing into the cow's flesh

133

landed in Laura's mind. What a dreadful picture of this family suffering. "Does Clair take the fresh milk?"

"Oh, not yet, but it won't be long."

"Maybe your cow is still inside and doing well, Orval."

"I figure when that bear has exhausted himself of mule meat, he will attempt to break into the barn if he can't get to us."

"Someone will show up soon."

"Who? Those in town could linger a week before deciding we might have trouble. I mean, who has heard of grizzlies settling in these parts?"

"I know what you mean. My father dealt with mountain lions."

"I remember. Horace wasn't the only one who had trouble with them, but he downed several. This grizzly is worse. I'm confident there are cattle dead around here because of him and not only on our place. If he moves on, I will need to get into town and round up some fellows to track him."

"How long do you figure he'll stay, Orval?" Alice asked as she descended the ladder.

"How's Clair?"

"She's sleeping again. Retha was holding her."

"I don't know how long that bear will stay. Too long already."

"Orval, we can't survive like this. We have children."

"Don't you think I know that?"

"You shouldn't have shot at him."

Laura knew something had happened. "What did you do, Orval?"

Orval combed his fingers through his hair.

"Oh, tell her, Orval," Alice said.

He gawked at Alice with his jaw clenched tight. "Uh, I was milking Rose when I heard a sound. So I slipped to the backdoor with my shotgun. I always bring it in case foxes come for our chickens while I'm outside. That grizzly had a grip on the mule. When I saw him thrust Henry to the ground, I knew it was over for him if I didn't do something. I raised the gun and blasted the grizzly. He let go of Henry and charged the door, so I rushed inside and fastened it."

Orval shook his head. "Watching old Henry that way, let me know if that bear made it inside, he'd kill Rose. I dashed out of the barn and raised my arms to divert him from wanting to tear into Henry more. The bear spotted me as I ran for the cabin. When I reached the door, Tommy stood there, mesmerized by the bear. I had to draw him inside."

"You caused him to target us," Alice declared.

"That wasn't my intention. How did I know that was how he'd behave?"

Laura rushed between them. "That doesn't matter now, Alice. What does matter is keeping everybody safe."

Alice started for the kitchen.

"I'm sorry, Alice. I've never heard of a grizzly acting this way before," Laura said.

Alice uttered nothing more.

"Ah, she gets this way, Laura. You should have been here when she was carrying little Clair. I wasn't even sure that it was Clair."

Laura grinned. She'd listened to Olivia tell of changes women went through having a baby. She called it hormones and learned of it in medical school. "I'm sure this is temporary, Orval. Once the bear is gone, everything will return to normal."

"Not everything. We've lost the mule, I know. But I still don't know about those horses and the cattle."

"We will figure all that out. Right now, we must pray that God sends someone to check on us. The church folks all noticed your family missing and were concerned. I passed this on to the sheriff, who figured you had cow troubles. He rode to pick up a prisoner for the marshal, but at least he knows."

"Psst, Ellison won't show up. That is the most passive sheriff ever."

"Well, Pastor West might."

"He might, but he has a church full to care for, and those elderly folk have him hopping. They keep him active running to meals—and trying to marry him off."

Laura smirked. This was true. The elderly women had taken an interest in finding a bride for Pastor West. They thought if they could prove to him what a woman's home-cooked meal was like, he would want a proper bride sooner than later.

"Laura, I wonder if your horse has gotten in with mine."

"Maybe. Either that or run to the ranch. I'm hoping the latter because Kenneth will see him and come."

"Yeah, Kenneth might come running for *you*."

But what if Kenneth showed up at the door as she had and became trapped the same way? "That may and may not be a great thing."

"Why?"

"Kenneth won't know there's a bear around. He'll do what I did."

"You're right. If we hear a horse trotting up, we must warn him."

"Why didn't you open the door earlier for me? I knocked several times."

"I'm sorry about that, Laura. After that bear came yesterday, I didn't sleep a wink. I had nodded off. Alice called out that someone was outside. That was the reason I let you keep watch for me. I fall asleep at night quickly."

"That's not good, Orval. You have a family to defend with a predator bear on the loose."

"I know, and there's little I can do about it."

Alice clanged the cast iron oven door shut. "Right now, you can come to eat while the food is hot."

Orval nodded. "That I can do. Come on, Laura, while it's calm outside."

Chapter 24

After breakfast, Orval sat in his chair. "Tommy and Retha, now that breakfast is over, I want you two to go back to the loft."

The children scampered up the ladder as their father had demanded.

"Alice, don't delay in that kitchen."

"I don't hear the bear. Are you sure he hasn't given up?" Alice asked.

"Oh, he hasn't given up."

Laura narrowed her eyes, studying Orval. "What are you thinking about?"

"I should get to the barn and milk the cow before she grows sick."

Alice shot from the chair, still nourishing Clair. "No, you're not, Orval. You just made it back here the last time."

"I should have milked Rose early this morning. If I leave her, she may catch a fever. We can't risk losing her."

"We can't risk losing *you*, Orval."

"Alice is right," Laura remarked. "You can't go about as usual with a bear stalking your place."

"I'll be alright. He may never know I'm there. I'll carry the shotgun. Rose and I will be quiet."

"Orval, are you crazy?" Alice said. "The grizzly can smell you."

"I'm hoping he's still feasting on Henry."

"You're hoping. That's not good enough."

"Will have to be." Orval rose, put on his hat, and grabbed hold of the milk pail and shotgun. "Watch for me, Laura. I may come running."

Laura shook her head. "This is senseless, Orval, and you know it."

"Look, I'm sure you had plenty of everything in Boston. But here, in these farming hills, we just get by. I propose to keep Rose alive for our future. I plan to toss some hay up against the rear wall. That won't cause much commotion but will help with the noise."

Alice rushed to him with tears in her eyes. "Orval, what you're about to do is dangerous. These children need you, and I do too. So you get back here soon."

"Everything's going to be alright."

Orval gaped through the front window, then opened the door, peering again across the space to the barn, and did not see the bear. "Here goes." He then opened the door and walked from the house.

As he took hold of the door, it screeched. Then hesitating a moment, watching for movement, he tried again, opening the door wide enough to slip through.

Rose saw him enter and started to bawl.

"No, Rose." He rushed to her and patted her forehead. "I'm here, but please be silent."

He grabbed the milking stool and pulled it towards the jersey cow. Without hesitation, he reached for a teat and began milking. Her bag was full, and he knew it was right to come.

Each squeeze of the teat shot milk to the bottom of the hollow bucket, echoing into the air. *Oh, no. That's too loud. The bear will hear it.*

Images of the bear tearing at the barn shot through his head. *I can't lose Rose. We will have to make it without milk.*

He reached and pulled the pail from beneath her and squeezed her teats, sending milk to the ground. "At least this will bring some comfort, oh girl."

When he had finished milking, he tapped Rose on the neck. "Please be quiet while you are here. I can't turn you out today. How about a taste of grain? Maybe this will bring contentment."

Roses' crunching the corn, though, was louder than he expected. *Too late.* He knew she would bellow if he pulled it away.

"Lord, help us. I should have already called on you. Well, I am now, Lord."

As Rose munched on the grain, Orval snatched a pitchfork and tossed hay against the rear wall. The hay would not stop the grizzly, but he hoped it would shield sounds from inside. Soon, he sensed it was time to leave.

Holding the shotgun, he pressed open the barn door and looked around. If the grizzly were close, he would spot him in the sunlight.

Not seeing the bear, he shut and fastened the door. He took three steps and paused. To his right, fifty feet away, the grizzly watched, waiting for the perfect instance to run after him.

Orval pondered going back inside, but he knew how hysterical Alice could be. *Time to run.*

He started for the cabin as fast as he could run. Halfway there, he yelled, "Open the door!"

Twelve steps from the cabin. Nine. Seven. The door opened, and he spotted Laura, eyes wide, watching the bear as he raced behind Orval.

Then short of warning, a burning pain ripped through Orval's back as the bear thrust him forward and to the ground, tossing the gun against the doorframe.

High-pitched screams from those watching sounded from within the cabin. Gripped with fear, Orval cried out, "Help me!"

He rolled on his torn back, facing his attacker raised on his hind feet as Orval scooted toward the cabin door.

A shotgun suddenly exploded above him, sending pressure to his eardrums, followed by a second.

* * *

"Help pull him inside," Laura demanded.

After they had dragged Orval inside, she sealed the door and placed the wooden latch in place. "Everybody stand away from it. Are there more rounds for this shotgun?"

Orval was in pain and not responding.

Alice stared down at him, writhing in discomfort on the floor.

"Alice, are there any more rounds for the shotgun?"

"Uh, yes, in the desk drawer."

Laura dashed to the desk, pulled open the drawer, and loaded the cartridges. As she turned to meet the others, she realized Orval needed tending. "Alice, let Tommy and Retha care for Clair. Can you find some bedsheets and divide them into strips? We have to stop the bleeding, or Orval will not make it."

"Oh, dear. What about the bear?"

"I don't know, but I know Orval doesn't have long unless we control this bleeding."

Alice handed Clair to Tommy. "Take Clair upstairs."

When she found the sheet, Alice hurried from the

bedroom. Outside, the grizzly roared louder than ever. "Do you think he will break down the door?" Alice asked.

"I don't know. If he does, I'll try to shoot him again. Help me take Orval to the bedroom."

"We *can't* move him."

Tommy rushed down the ladder to assist, and they dragged Orval to the bedroom on a rug.

Laura gaped at the man as he stretched beside the bed. Orval was no skinny fellow, but she knew they must lift him to apply the bandages. "I'll take his feet. Both of you grab an arm and help me lift him off the floor." She looked at Alice, remembering that only two months before, she had little Clair. "Alice, I know this will not be easy for you. But it's the only way we can save Orval."

"I'll do it."

"Alright then. Let's get him up."

They lifted with all the strength they had. The big man moaned as they lay him on the bed.

Catching her air, Laura looked down at him. "Now, we must roll him over."

As they rolled his body, they pulled him closer to the edge.

Laura stared at the deep gashes that poured blood. "Bring some clean water. I'll wash the wound and wrap it. Alice, do you have any healing balm?"

"Yes, I'll bring it with the water."

They had the wound dressed and covered in a moment and left Orval alone in the bedroom.

Laura reached for the shotgun and relaxed in the chair. "I don't hear the bear."

"I don't either," replied Alice.

Then came a roar.

"I guess he *hasn't* forgotten," Laura said. "Alice, move on up to the loft."

"But Orval may need me."

"I'm sure he will, but right now, his body requires rest so it can heal. I'll call for you if I hear him."

Alice peeped through the bedroom door, her eyes on Orval as he lay sleeping. "All that's taken place... I don't know if we should stay here. This land—"

"Is just like any other land. Troubles happen, Alice. Doesn't matter where you are. It will find you. That's why we must depend on God for help."

"Will he?" Alice asked as a rush of tears filled her eyes. "I see all that's happened, and he hasn't helped."

"I know it's been hard, but remember, it could have been worse. God has not promised our lives will be free from trouble. Job declares that, *Man born of a woman is of few days and full of trouble.*"

"Our days have been overflowing with troubles. I know that part's right."

"Another scripture says, The LORD is good, a stronghold in the day of trouble; and he knoweth them that trust in him. Alice, we must pray and trust the Lord."

Laura took Alice by the hand and prayed for them.

Chapter 25

*T*he bear had not retreated to his hiding place behind the barn, and Laura worried that it may have satisfied himself with the mule and now had an appetite for more. His growling intensified as he grew closer.

Everybody had moved to the loft, but what could *she* do if the bear smashed down the door? The wooden access could never prevent him if he wanted in. She knew Orval's double-barrel shotgun carried only two shells and feared the bear would never permit her an opportunity to reload.

Oh, Sheriff Ellison, where are you? Please, someone, come.

The grizzly continued to growl from the side of the cabin, and panic set in again. Laura's legs wobbled when she stood, but she must prepare to fire the gun if necessary. *Why has this beast focused his attention on the cabin?* She peeped over her shoulders into the bedroom, seeing Orval lying on the bed. *Blood!*

"Alice, I need you to come down, please."

"What? Why?"

"I expect the bear is smelling Orval's blood. I'm not positive that what I'll ask of you will help, but we must try something."

"What?" Alice asked as she settled to the lower floor.

"Light the lanterns and open everything smelly you have, licorice, spices, perfumes, any of it."

"How will that help?"

"I don't know that it will, but we must try. My hope is to prevent Orval's blood scent." Laura said as she reached and closed the door to the bedroom.

"Do you have any tincture? Whisky, maybe? Liniment?"

"Yes, for medicinal purposes."

"Good. Warm the kitchen stove, put on a water pot, and add some whiskey. When heated, throw a spoonful or two into the fire."

"But it will burn up."

"I know. I want it to create an aroma that spreads outside the cabin." Laura could see hope emerge on Alice's face.

Alice rushed to the kitchen and stoked the flame. Then pausing, she said, "Laura, I have an aromatic candle. My sister in New Orleans mailed it to me last year. I don't burn it because Donna has never sent me anything."

"I'm sure it's special to you, though so are your children. If you wish to use it, we will."

"Yes. It is on the desk."

"Alice, use another pot to melt the candle. The richer the aroma, the better our chance that grizzly will leave us alone."

Alice grinned and nodded as Laura took it to her. "Laura, I hope this works."

"What we are doing has to help. If his smell is as delicate as I've heard, this may frustrate him, so he withdraws."

Still, the grizzly roared, pushing again into the side of the cabin, jarring photos from the wall and stirring dust into the air.

"This is not working," Alice said.

"Momma!" Retha said. "He's going to break in."

Alice turned and gazed at her daughter. "Retha, pray the way we do at night. Ask God to protect us from this evil beast."

Tears rushed down Retha's face, and she said, "I will, Momma, and I'll pray for Daddy too."

Laura watched little Retha climb the ladder and then turned to Alice. "Alice, I can smell it."

"He's still growling."

"But he's not rushing the house anymore. Maybe it is working."

She strolled to the window to peep out. As she raised her face over the frame, an eye gazed back at her. She withdrew, but the grizzly spotted her.

He pushed his head through the pane, shattering glass across the room, pressing against the cabin and roaring loud as he worked to reach her.

Screams blared from the loft as the grizzly offered another loud snarl.

Fearful he might break down the cabin wall, Laura raised the shotgun and discharged it, striking him in the face. The grizzly departed, rubbing at his face and eyes, turning and sprinting to a reasonable distance, where he stopped. Then, contorting his body toward the cabin, he released a death-defying bellow as if saying their time was near.

Laura watched as the grizzly strode toward the barn, still rubbing his face and growling.

"Is he gone?" Alice inquired.

"Yes, for now, but I don't think he's concerned about getting to Orval now."

"What do you mean?"

"I defied him when I shot him in the face. The cabin detained him only long enough to fire on him, but I think that in his mind, he now considers me the enemy. You should have seen his eyes when I shot him, following me like I was an adversary."

"You are to him, but if he reaches you, he'll take us all."

"Let's pray someone comes before that happens. We know the grizzly has recently fed on your mule, but soon hunger will drive his appetite again."

"Why doesn't he leave and go back to the woods? There's plenty of food there."

"I don't know unless he sees Orval as a challenge."

"Laura, do you think it's safe for me to come down and cook something for us?"

"Yes. The grizzly is tending his wounds."

Alice handed off Clair to Tommy and descended the loft.

Laura could see the exhaustion in Alice's body. "Alice, you need rest. You're nursing and must rest, or Clair will suffer."

"How can I relax with all that's happening?"

"I'm sorry. This event can't be easy for you, but it will all be over soon."

Alice strolled to the kitchen and threw in a stick of firewood. "We must carry on for the children's sake."

Laura returned to the open window but could not see the grizzly.

She was mindful of her inadequacy against the massive and rebellious grizzly. No one could single-handedly defeat it, but she was determined to use all her might to protect this family from being devoured.

When this ordeal was behind her, she planned to write a narrative that would appeal to the men in the region to hunt down and kill or move these animals to a more suitable feeding ground.

But was she being too optimistic, presuming they could stop the mad bear?

I know Kenneth will come.

Chapter 26

S even cows had drifted from the main herd. Kenneth nudged the black horse until he galloped past them. Moments later, he had them turned and headed across the field where they would meet up with the others.

"Excellent work, Ace. How would I manage without you?"

One cow darted from the herd, but the black horse saw it and spoiled its plan.

Kenneth patted the horse's neck. "You're doing terrific, boy. After we bring these to the others, we'll rest awhile. I need some lunch."

He worked the small herd into the others and waited, ensuring they would remain. Then he urged Ace toward home. "We're riding in, boy, and I'll unsaddle you."

When they reached the barn, Kenneth led Ace inside, pulled off the saddle, and rubbed him down with a cloth.

"I didn't expect you'd sweat this much on a cool day. Guess I was mistaken."

Ace nickered.

"Oh, you *agree*, huh?"

A horse whinnied in the distance, drawing Kenneth's attention. *What horse is this, I wonder?*

Leaving Ace secured, he stepped outside and searched around the premises. Copper stood near the corral, staring back at him.

"Copper, why are you here? And where is Laura? Has she gone inside?" Then seeing the bridle reins dragging the ground, dreadful images came to mind. Why was Laura not with her horse? Had she fallen somewhere along the road? *Copper is not an easy horse to spook, so what happened?*

Where was he to search? There were questions and no answers. He hoped she might turn up unharmed along the road to town.

Copper stayed beside the fence as Kenneth walked to him and patted him on the side of the neck. "Hey, boy. What happened to your rider?"

He gazed over every inch of the horse and found no cuts or bruising. "So Copper, why is Laura not with you?"

He could only speculate that they rode across something that spooked the horse, and Laura could not mount again.

Another theory was Laura's inquisitiveness. She was too often daring with her journalism. Could it be that she charged into a story more dangerous than she imagined? Thinking of the bank robbery, she had requested to be there when they tried to counter it. Things could have turned much worse.

She had once told him of a time in Boston when she would not withdraw from a story, even knowing groups were fighting each other with guns over home-brewed whisky. She had observed the disputing as the bullets fell in near proximity. After hearing the story, Kenneth had termed it too dangerous for her, but Laura declared it was ground-breaking journalism, the kind that launched careers.

He tapped Copper on the neck again, knowing what he must do. "Boy, let's put you in the corral with Star. I have to ride to town and search for Laura. Don't you fret. I'll find her."

Star had heard Copper whinny. Kenneth watched as he raced across the field until he reached the other entrance to the corral and slowed to a walk.

"There you are, Star. Do you mind if I leave your old friend with you? Yeah, I thought so."

I wonder when Copper last ate.

After leading the horse into the corral and tossing hay for them, he strode to the barn where Ace stood waiting.

"Well, Ace. I wanted to rest this afternoon, but Copper says we're needed. Did you hear what he said? Something has happened to Laura, and we must find out. And don't you worry? I'll give you some extra feed when this is over, but let's bring you some water before we leave."

He drew a bucket from the well and emptied a portion into Ace's water pail. The black horse drank his fill and whinnied.

"We're going soon, but I need to offer these other two water first."

After watering all the horses, he grabbed his saddle and cinched it on Ace. "Hang on, buddy."

Kenneth bolted to the house and pulled open a drawer from the wooden cabinet and collected a carton of bullets, and ran back. He slid them into the saddlebags, mounted, and rode toward Santa Fe.

Chapter 27

K enneth checked the boarding house where Laura lived, but she was not there. The last time Esta Dowd had seen her was Sunday morning at church. His gut churned as he rode toward the parsonage.

Pastor West stepped out of the home. "Kenneth, what brings you today?"

Kenneth tied Ace to a tethering rail in front of the home. "Have you seen Laura since Sunday morning?"

"I haven't. Why?"

"I've not found her."

"I'm sure she's somewhere working on a story."

"Her horse, Copper, came to the ranch, saddled."

"To the ranch?" West said with a worried look on his face. "That means—"

"I don't know what it means. That's why I'm here."

"Let me help you. I'll take the right side of town and go door to door. You cover the other side."

"Sure. Let's meet at the sheriff's office when we finish."

They knocked on every door, questioning everybody they came to. Most knew Laura because of the stories she wrote for the newspaper.

Kenneth reached the Santa Fe Journal. "Mr. Flack, is Laura here today?"

He glared above his spectacles. "I have not seen that young lady, and I need her! You'd assume she would tell me if she's not coming to work. So if you see Laura, inform her that if she doesn't return soon, she may not have a job."

"Okay, thank you." Kenneth backed from the door and turned to the next business.

When he came to the end of the street, he spotted Pastor West across the court speaking to Verner Givens at the freight office. He hurried across, dodging buckboards and horses stirring about.

Pastor West saw him coming and walked to him. "Any word, Kenneth?"

"Nothing."

"There are several minor roads behind us. I suppose we should check them out."

"Let's not lose time with that. Someone would have already seen Laura if she had been anywhere around town."

"I expect that's true, but where *can* she be?"

"The last time I saw her, Olivia and I were headed to the hotel for lunch after church service. We hoped she might accompany us, but she never showed."

"Well, someone knows something," Pastor West said.

"Wait. I remember that Laura was uneasy about the Dunnings not being in attendance Sunday, and she was going to speak with the sheriff to see if he would check on them."

"Kenneth, I was concerned about them too because they seldom miss service, but Mayor Dolton had requested I come for lunch. I should have followed up on it."

"We don't know anything is wrong, only that Laura is missing."

"Right, but it's a good place to start."

"Did you go by the sheriff's office?" Kenneth asked.

"Not yet. You said to meet there last, so I skipped it."

"Then we should go together."

As they started for the sheriff's office, Ishmael Pepper from the livery ran up to them. "Mr. Barlow, I heard two men telling about Miss Stone at the livery."

"Go on."

"They say you asked questions and want to know if anybody had seen her."

"Yes, we can't find her."

"*I* seen her Sunday."

"We all saw her Sunday."

"After the church service, she walked to the stable and took out her horse."

"Did she say where she was heading?"

"She says, if anyone asks for her, that she be riding to the Dunnings."

"Ishmael, get my horse saddled," Pastor West said, turning to Kenneth. "I'll hurry to the house and get my guns."

***

Kenneth and Pastor West rode out of Santa Fe, checking the sides of the road, finding no tracks.

Soon they reached the road to the Dunnings' farm.

"This doesn't look right, Pastor," Kenneth said.

"No it doesn't. There are few hoof and wagon tracks to their place. They've not been to town in a while."

Kenneth didn't like the sick feeling that came upon him. He sensed something was terribly wrong and knew Laura was in trouble. "Pastor, when we reach their place, I want you to

153

hang back until we know what we're dealing with. There could be criminals, and Laura has run headlong into them."

"But it makes no sense about her horse."

"No, it doesn't."

As they neared the cabin, Kenneth raised a hand for them to halt. "I'll knock on the door. Keep your rifle ready. If anything happens to me, ride for help."

"I sure will."

Kenneth slowed his horse and made his way to the cabin. He peered around, searching for any trouble. Finding nothing, he stepped from the saddle, unlatching the tie-down from his gun holster.

He heard a voice and turned as he fastened Ace to the small tree.

"Kenneth, get out of here," Laura whispered.

Peering through the broken window, he saw her. "What are *you* doing here, Laura?"

Then he heard it—the roar from the barn.

"Get out of here, now."

Ace pulled against the reins, and Kenneth reached for them, calming him so he could mount again. Reining the horse around, he looked back. "Wow, you are a big one."

Gunfire sounded from behind him. Pastor West had spotted the grizzly and let off two rounds from his Winchester.

Kenneth turned back to the house, where Laura still watched. "I'll be back with help."

"Oh, thank God," she said as he rode away.

Kenneth looked over his shoulder and saw the grizzly standing on his back feet in front of the cabin. Then he reined up Ace to a stop. "That bear thinks we are after his prey."

"Do you think so?" Pastor West asked.

"Why else would he stop there? He's watched over this cabin for a few days and believes what's inside is his."

"I've never heard of a grizzly doing that."

"Me either, but I'm seeing it now," Kenneth said.

"What are we going to do? Our Winchesters won't touch that beast."

"We need bigger guns, some .50 caliber single-shot rifles. The kind the trappers and mountain men use."

"Yeah, but it's that single-shot part that terrifies me. I estimate it'll take several of those guns to bring that bear down."

"Pastor, I only know of a few in Santa Fe, but there might be more. The sheriff keeps two in his case for those long shots."

"Who else has one?"

"You will not believe it. Doc Simms has one. And we should check with the town gunsmith. Maybe there are more."

"Kenneth, we have to do this today. Those folks may not have much time. And if they are injured, they'll need a doctor."

"I never thought of asking her before that bear interrupted us."

"Well, we know *why* Laura was missing now."

"Yes. If only I could keep tabs on her."

They turned their horses toward town.

"Kenneth, pray with me that Laura will marry me. Yeah, I know she will always look for trouble."

Kenneth laughed. "At least you understand that."

Chapter 28

L aura sat, reassured something would happen now that Kenneth had visited the Dunnings' cabin. She gazed into the bedroom and noticed Orval had shifted positions. *He needs a physician—and soon.* There was so much blood, and she could not imagine he had more to spare.

She gazed upon the children, seeing the fear in their eyes. They would never be the same. The anguish this family had suffered would transform them forever. Each day they go out to milk the cow, gather the firewood, or pick from the garden, they would remember this dreadful moment in their lives.

They may never sleep without hearing the daunting roar of a grizzly in their dreams. And if another bear happens their way, they may not even notice until it is too late.

Laura knew she, too, must find the strength to look beyond this nightmare, or the misery from these days of forced cabin fever would rule.

She heard someone behind her and turned. "Alice, how are you?"

"I'm still breathing, but I must thank you for all you've done for us."

"Together, *we* did what we must, and it soon will be over."

"Do you believe that?"

"Yes, I do. I know Kenneth, and he will gather some men and return. They will devise some strategy to eliminate the bear once and for all."

"They *are* going to kill it, aren't *they*?"

"If not, your family will never leave the cabin."

"Oh, how I know."

Orval called from the bedroom. "Alice."

"How are you feeling, Orval?" Alice asked when they came to him.

"I hurt something awful."

Laura reached and touched him. "This may be over soon."

"What may be over?"

"The grizzly?"

His brows raised. "Yeah, him."

"Are you hungry, dear?" Alice asked.

"I'm starving."

"I have some soup from the jars. I'll heat it for you."

"I'll help him drink some water while you do that."

"Alright."

Laura pressed a pillow beneath Orval's head. "You should drink as much as you can. Our bodies can't survive long without water."

"Oh, yeah?"

He took a long sip as she held the cup to his mouth.

"Good. Now some more."

He stopped drinking and glanced up at her. "What did you mean by it might soon be over?"

"My brother Kenneth showed up a little while ago looking for me."

"Is he alright?"

"Yes. By now, Kenneth has gathered some men, and they will return."

"I hope he has some serious guns. That's no small grizzly."

"They will work something out."

"I hope you're right."

"Orval, when this is over, you will need help to get through this catastrophe. Not every day does a grizzly attack a farm and cause panic and fear."

"We will be fine once I mend."

"Orval, that grizzly has traumatized your children and wife."

"I don't know what that means, Laura."

"Yes, you do. People can live a lifetime and never experience what your family has faced the past few days."

"Maybe."

"Please keep that in mind because one day soon, you'll awaken to a screaming daughter having nightmares of grizzlies."

"Oh, that."

"Yes."

Alice returned with a bowl of soup. "Did he take some water?"

"Yes, but he will need more."

"I'll feed him and make him drink."

"Okay. I'm going into the other room to watch for the beast."

"He is a beast for sure."

As she turned to leave, Orval called out, "Laura, hold up."

She spun around, looking at him.

"Thank you for helping us. Had you not been here, I would be dead. I owe you plenty."

"You don't owe me anything. We are all to help our

158

brothers and sisters. I suppose it was my turn. This is a great lesson for us. People often find trouble, but we are so busy we overlook what they are going through. We should always watch our friends' lives for changes. If something seems awry, we should do whatever we can to help."

"You did that for us."

"I will write a story for the Journal to help inspire others to watch out for their neighbors. The Bible tells us in Philippians, *Let nothing be done through strife or vainglory, but in lowliness of mind let each esteem the other better than himself.* That's not simple to accomplish, but we must try."

"You sound like a preacher."

She chuckled. "I only try to follow what the preacher says."

"And so should we," Alice said.

"Alice, when Orval finishes eating his soup, I'll clean and dress his wound again. Do you think you can find another sheet?"

"I will."

"And when the bear is gone, we'll get Orval to Santa Fe so a doctor can look at it. Do you mind if my friend Olivia sees you, Orval?"

He stared, considering her statement. "I suppose. Ain't never had a woman doctor look me over, though."

"Olivia has intensive training in surgery and has plenty of medicines on hand. She dressed my gunshot wound, and I was up in no time. Remember, she did the surgery that saved Alice and Clair."

"Yes, I recall. Alright. Maybe we need a change. Old Doc Simms uses the same old method—some stinky liniment."

"Orval, we must change a lot of things," Alice said.

"You are right, Alice. One thing is for sure. We are going to have more faith. It could be we are alive because of Laura's faith. I need that kind of faith working this old farm."

159

"Yes, I do too."

They smiled at Laura before she stepped toward the other room. "I'll look in on the children."

Peering to the loft, she saw Retha with her legs hanging over the sides, but her face was that of fear.

That poor child. What an awful situation for her. The days ahead in Retha's life would be challenging, but somehow she knew this tough little girl would come through. Laura was like her growing up, though there were no grizzlies. Horace was brute enough—forcing her to ride a horse at a young age. He pressured her into herding when he found the cattle trapped in the gully. On another occasion, he had her drawing up buckets of dirt as he dug a new water well.

But did Retha understand what a harsh childhood was? Orval was a stern man with fixed ideas, no doubt from a harsh past. His daughter had experienced more in the first years of her life than anyone should ever endure.

Again, the grizzly's roar grew louder, and Laura could tell he was drawing closer. She raised from the chair and gazed out the window as he shuffled toward the house, growling, swaying his head as if to say, *I'm coming.*

She prayed the men showed up before the bear burst through the door.

Breaking open the shotgun, she saw the shells. The gun was ready, but was she? "Alice, do you have any more candles to burn?"

"None that are smelly. The bear is coming back, isn't he?"

"Oh, yes."

"Get me up, Alice," Orval said.

"No, Orval," shouted Laura. "You can't do this."

"I have to protect—" As he raised, pain exploded down his back and through his legs, and he settled back to the mattress. "Well, Alice, get to the loft with the children."

"I can't leave you."

"Yes, you can. Up there, you are safe."

Alice walked toward the door.

"Pull the door closed."

"I can't leave Laura to face him alone."

"Oh, Alice. There's only one gun, so there's nothing you can do."

Alice left, and with reluctance, complied with Orval's wishes.

The grizzly stood at the window, his roar deafening as Alice reached the top of the loft. Rising to his hind legs, he pushed against the cabin, hoping to press it over on them. Screams echoed from within as they felt the cabin's movement.

Laura raised the shotgun toward the window. She heard a crack as the grizzly thrust against the side of the structure and fired two rounds through the opening, striking the bear in the face.

The beast rumbled and slapped the window facing with a paw, tearing away an oak board inside the opening.

Laura reloaded as the bear moved away, though not far. Then he turned and heaved against the side. Having no success, he growled louder because he could not reach his prey.

Please, Kenneth, get here soon, or we are all dead.

Chapter 29

Kenneth and Pastor West arrived at Santa Fe and went to the sheriff's office. Sheriff Ellison sat in a rocker, watching them as they dismounted.

Kenneth dusted his hat against his leg. "Sheriff, we need help."

"What kind of help?"

"Men and guns."

Sheriff Ellison pressed up the front of his hat. "What do you mean?"

"Laura is at the Dunnings'," Pastor West explained. "They're cornered inside the cabin with a grizzly stalking them."

"A grizzly? We don't have grizzly in these parts."

"Not ordinarily, but one is here now."

"Do you fellows think we can kill it?"

Pastor West turned to Kenneth. "Yes, Kenneth thinks so with .50 caliber rifles."

"That might work. I have two, but they are single loads."

Kenneth leaned against the pole on the porch. "We heard Doc Simms had purchased an old .50 caliber. Hopefully, he still has it."

"Have you checked at the gunsmith?"

"I'll head there next. But we need men to help lure him away from the cabin."

"You mean like bait?"

"I guess so. Then someone can get inside and check if anybody's injured."

"You'll want to take Doc along for that."

"If he'll go."

"So, Kenneth, how do you want me to help?"

"If you can see that men gather someplace, the church, the street, would help lots."

"What about the saloon?"

"Not the saloon. We need every man sober so he doesn't get killed."

"Right. While you're speaking with Doc Simms, I'll walk around and spread the word. And Pastor, can you ride to a few ranches south and tell them what's happening? I'll have one of my deputies ride north. We should meet back here in about four hours."

"Sheriff, they may not have four hours."

Ellison sat thinking. "That presents a problem. Most men are old in the city. Those living on the ranches and farms are who you want because they have reason to kill the grizzly."

Pastor West raised from the rail. "Alright. I'll ride to Irvin Speers and Arche Barto's place. They both have cattle to lose, they hunt, and are used to guns and should help."

"My deputy can ride after Shep Forrest. He should want to help. Maybe with them and a few others from town, we can take that bear down. Kenneth, are you positive you need those .50 caliber rifles?"

"That's a magnificent bear, Sheriff. I'm betting Orval already tried his hand with a shotgun."

"Yeah, and that means he's madder than a hornet, and perhaps why he's stalking the cabin."

"Huh?"

"I saw something like it once before in Colorado. Some grizzlies zero in on prey like a target. They set their mind to the quarry and don't let go until they have it."

"That's what I assumed," Kenneth replied. "When I got to the cabin, he ran out from the barn and started toward me like he was defending them."

Sheriff Ellison raised and spat out a match stick from his mouth. "Have you fellows considered how serious this is? There's a good chance someone will get hurt or killed."

"We can't leave those folks to fend for themselves, Sheriff," Pastor West said. They may have someone injured already.

"I know, but others may get killed trying something you don't know will work."

"Yes, it may be risky, but we have to try," Kenneth replied. "There are three children and two women inside besides Orval."

"I'm not saying I blame you or you shouldn't because you're right. You have no choice. I only want you to realize the danger."

"I'm riding south," Pastor West declared as he stepped from the porch.

"I'll have my deputy go north. Let's meet back here in an hour. Kenneth, accompany me," Sheriff Ellison said.

* * *

Men from town stood outside the sheriff's office, waiting and wondering what to do. Sheriff Ellison sat in his rocker, waiting for Pastor West's return.

164

Several men had heard about the bear and walked away, refusing to get involved.

"Sheriff, how much longer?" demanded Gus Hewett. "I'm building a porch."

"As soon as Pastor West returns, Gus. The lives of the Dunnings and Miss Stone is way more serious than your porch."

Kenneth stood leaning against a post beneath the overhang, remembering all too well the fierceness of the bear. Should he have stayed and helped? He could have shooed Ace away, gone inside, and done something. But then, as he reasoned, he knew Laura would have requested him to ride and bring help.

The sound of hooves brought relief as Pastor West, and the other two men rode near and dismounted.

They walked through the crowd as Sheriff Ellison arose. "Men, thank you for showing up. I'm not happy we have to reach so far out for good folks like yourself. But I've requested you because a family of our own is in trouble. Everyone here knows the Dunnings. You've seen them around town or in church. They are a fine family with three children, one an infant."

"What's happening, Sheriff?" Barney Cutts demanded.

Ellison stared at them. "They are trapped inside their cabin, with a grizzly at the door."

As his comment settled in, several began chatting among themselves. Being old, more bailed, others walked away cowardly, but it was for the best. They need only those who would improve their chances, not work against them.

"What are we to do, Sheriff?" Morton Ackerman asked.

"The first part of the plan is to entice the grizzly from the cabin so Doc can go inside and find out if they're hurt."

"And how do you entice a grizzly?" questioned Barney Cutts.

"We ride near him and gain his attention. Then turn your

horse and let him follow."

A rumble came over the crowd as they expressed disapproval until Kenneth raised a gun and fired a round into the air. "We have people inside that cabin right now. The grizzly is stalking them and will murder them if given a chance. He has already tried to shake the door loose and get inside. Laura Stone is inside with the Dunnings. Now, no one is suggesting you engage in a fight against a grizzly. But once we fire on him, he will turn to us.

Several heads nodded, and Kenneth thought he had persuaded at least a few. "We must do this directly because we don't feel they have much time."

"Count me in," Gus Hewett replied.

"I'll go too," answered Clayton Atwood. "We got to get Miss Laura out of there."

Kenneth looked at those who agreed to go. The sheriff was right—someone might get injured or killed. These were not marksmen or even gunmen. They were laborers, store owners, businessmen, and cowboys, though eager to assist where required.

He looked up as another man pushed through the crowd toward him, holding a .50 caliber Sharps rifle.

"Kenneth, I've come to help," stated Big Jeremiah. "Don't much like wrestling with grizzly, but I heard you say Miss Laura was in that cabin."

"That's right. We accept your help. You can give some insight on the grizzly so none of us get hurt."

"Or killed."

"Right."

"I'll do what I can. Tell me what you know."

Kenneth took Big Jeremiah into the sheriff's office, accompanied by Ellison and Pastor West.

Kenneth pointed out how they would use folks to draw him out. Jeremiah shook his head. "Won't work."

"What do you mean?"

"If that grizzly has marked the cabin as prey, no one is getting inside easy."

"But we will draw him away," Pastor West explained.

"He won't go but so far."

"There has to be a means to get him to leave the cabin," Kenneth said.

"Meat. Do you have any fresh meat?"

"I'll check with the men," said Pastor West.

"You believe that's the best way?" Kenneth asked.

"That's the only thing that will capture his concern."

Pastor West came back inside and shut the door. "Clayton Atwood says he has a fresh deer at home."

"I'll wager he's bled it already," Big Jeremiah said. "That would have served us better, but might still work."

"I expect we should head that way," Sheriff Ellison suggested. "I'll order the men to their horses."

In ten minutes, the men had their gear prepared and started for the Dunnings' place.

Chapter 30

he men halted a hundred yards from the Dunnings' cabin, awaiting orders from Sheriff Ellison or Kenneth. The grizzly was not around as they peered ahead.

"I don't see him," said Gus Hewett, gazing through a spyglass.

"He's there," Kenneth replied.

"But he might have left already."

"No, Gus, he's there. He's penned them down for days."

"I'll take your word for it."

"Doc, we need to get you inside," Kenneth said. "We'll see if he'll take the bait long enough for you to get inside."

"I hope you don't plan for me to be the bait because I'd rather *not* be his meal."

As they were talking, the grizzly walked from the barn to within feet of the ranch house, raised on his hind legs, and gave a powerful roar.

"Oh, my. He's a big one," Clayton Atwood said.

"And I suppose you want us to ride straight through to the other side of the place without getting killed," said Arche Barto.

"Yes, but not yet. Let him growl a while and go back to the barn. You men with the .50 caliber guns can follow me. I'll find a way around to the other side. When the bear follows you, Clayton, we will shoot and take him out."

"That should work," Sheriff Ellison said. "Clayton, you can cut up that meat now. If it bleeds, that's fine. Put some on the back of the horses."

Kenneth spotted the bear through the spyglass as Clayton cut the deer meat. He spotted markings on its face. *From a scatter load.* "Looks like they may have shot him."

"Let me see," Sheriff Ellison said and took the spyglass. "At least they've been fighting back."

"But it also confirms a shotgun won't kill him," Kenneth said. "We may have to give all we have to put him down."

"With Big Jeremiah, we have four, though they are only one shot apiece."

"Then we have to keep reloading until we take him down. Listen up, everyone. Those with the .50 caliber rifles, let's not fire all our rounds at once. Someone should reload as others shoot."

"Kenneth, when is the best time to move?" Sheriff Ellison asked.

"We'll wait until that bear gets back to the other side of the barn. We stand a better chance of getting him to follow us from there."

"Alright then, fellows. We know what to watch for. The men carrying the meat will ride through that opening between the barn and the cabin one at a time." Sheriff Ellison pointed ahead. "Make some noise, and don't ride too fast unless he gets after you."

Gus Hewett chuckled. "That might be hard to do. My horse ain't going to enjoy having a grizzly on his tail."

"We *hope* he gets on your tail and follows you away from the cabin. We sure don't want to shoot those big guns toward it."

The men understood and nodded.

"Kenneth and I will take the shooters to the other side and prepare. Wait until you see our signal."

"What if we can't see you from here?" asked Clayton Atwood.

Kenneth turned his horse toward them. "Clayton, take this." He handed Clayton the spyglass.

"Good. I'll use it."

Sheriff Ellison rode in beside him. "I sure hope we can pull this off. If not, we'll have a monster on our hands."

"But monsters make good rugs."

"You better hope so."

* * *

Laura peered out the window. The bear was moving back to wherever he hid out. On the other end, there were riders, but it seemed like they had no plan and only sat watching.

"What are they doing, Laura?" Alice asked.

"They are sitting there."

"Oh, my. They don't know how to kill the bear."

"Ladies, they will try something," Orval said. "Give them time. My bet is they will split up. Some will draw him out, and others will shoot him. I only hope they bring big enough weapons. What most folks carry won't touch him."

Alice walked toward the bedroom and peered inside. "Maybe they plan to draw him away from the cabin."

"I hope they do more than that because this is no ordinary grizzly, and you can't treat him like one."

Laura saw one man peering through a spyglass, but nothing happened. *Where's Kenneth?*

She hoped Kenneth had not chickened out because of the bear, though he wasn't the type to walk away from a fight. "Something is happening."

"What?" asked Alice.

"Riders are coming through."

"Riders?"

∗ ∗ ∗

The first rider trotted through, yelling. They heard the bear roar, but he didn't come out. The second rider trotted his horse through, calling out as he went by. Still, the grizzly only roared.

Doc Simms tied off his mount behind a thicket and ran toward the cabin.

"Doc, what are you doing?" asked Irvin Speers.

"I'm going inside."

When he reached the cabin, he knocked, watching behind him and waited. "Open up inside. It's Doc Simms."

The door opened, and Laura stood staring. "You are going to get mauled."

"I'm here to see if anyone needs doctoring."

"Come on in. Orval's in the bedroom. Doc, what are they doing riding through?"

"They are trying to distract and lure the bear away, but I can't tell it's working."

Doc peered out the window. "Here comes the last rider."

When Clayton reached the cabin, he slowed a bit. The grizzly roared and then ran out after him. Clayton's horse reared, almost throwing him off. He darted toward the shooters, the bear close behind. Holding tight, Clayton peered over his shoulder, the bear seeming to gain ground.

A blast sounded from Clayton's left, and the grizzly stopped and raised on his hind legs toward the shooters.

171

Another gun sounded, hitting the bear again.

"After you fire, load those guns!" Kenneth shouted. "Shoot him again."

Bullets pounded the grizzly. He turned toward Clayton, spooking the horse. Clayton tried holding him steady, but the horse reared, tossing him to the ground, then ran away, exposing the young man to the bear.

The grizzly burst toward Clayton as he attempted to get up and was on top of him in a hurry, pouncing. He swiped at Clayton with a paw, slicing into his body.

Three bullets hit the bear in succession, turning him to face the shooters. He stumbled, grunting, reaching for those who fired on him. Blood poured from the wounds on his sides and he groaned before his body gave up, falling to the ground.

Kenneth rode to Clayton as he lay on the ground in pain. "Clayton needs help, men. Someone see if you can find Doc Simms."

Irvin Speers raised a hand. "I'll get him from the cabin." He rode toward the cabin as Pastor West followed behind.

The cabin door opened wide, and Laura came out.

"Laura, are you alright?" asked Pastor West.

"I'm fine. Doc Simms is tending to Orval."

"Is he going to make it?"

"Yes, he will be fine."

Irvin exited the cabin, Doc Simms behind him, and they started up the hill toward Clayton.

Laura ran to Pastor West and hugged him.

"Laura, I'm sorry for all this trouble. I should have checked on the Dunnings."

"You couldn't do that with your other obligations."

"I have obligations to all the members of the church."

She reached to his face and turned him to her. "Listen to me. You are only one man. No one expects you to be in two places at one time."

"But I feel terrible that I didn't and to find you trapped by a—"

"A maniac bear?"

"Yes."

"Steven, why didn't you bring Olivia?"

He gazed at her, wondering how to answer. "I suppose we didn't think of her at that moment, Laura."

"What will it take for this town to give her a chance? Olivia is a fine doctor, but if the people of Santa Fe don't use her, she will leave."

"But if she does, we still have Doc Simms."

"Doc Simms is old, and his medical training is old, too. Olivia is fresh out of school with new ways to doctor people, and she's knowledgeable of the latest medicines."

"You're right. I apologize for not thinking of her. Olivia is a wonderful addition to our town, but I don't know what it will take for the people to trust her services. Maybe it's something I should speak to the city council about."

"That might be a good start."

Laura turned when Kenneth rode up.

"Are you alright, Laura?"

"Yes, I'm fine. But Orval tried to milk his cow, and the grizzly caught him outside the cabin. It raked his back, but he'll be alright."

Doc Simms walked over after treating the young deputy. "We lost Clayton. He lost too much blood. There's nothing I could do."

"I feel terrible now, asking folks to help."

"Kenneth, this isn't your fault. The fault belongs to that grizzly lying on the ground."

"Doc's right," Laura uttered. "If people had not come to help, we may have lost everyone. The grizzly had set his eyes on us and had already broken the glass window." She turned and pointed.

"Maybe."

"He tried once to push through. I shot him twice, or he would have torn down the cabin wall to get inside. The three children stayed in the loft, but I don't believe it would have kept them safe if he got inside."

Doc Simms slapped Kenneth's knee. "You did everything possible. Go home and be thankful nothing more happened." He nodded and walked toward his horse.

Pastor West stood holding his horse's reins. "Kenneth, we should set up a shrine commemorating today as a special memorial. People sacrificed to save others, and we will never forget what they've done. And for Clayton, we must keep him in front of us forever because of his sacrifice."

"I like that, Pastor," Laura said.

"I do, too," Kenneth replied.

Soon, all the men had gathered around the cabin. Sheriff Ellison looked them over. "You all did very well. The Dunnings will be fine now. We lost a man and will remember him for what he did."

"Sheriff, may I say a word?" questioned Pastor West.

"Oh, sure."

"What Clayton did today doesn't compare to what Jesus did on the cross. But he gave his life so others could live—and we should never forget. This is the love that Jesus wants for his people. And while our hearts remember Clayton, don't forget that God has shown favor and blessed us this day." Pastor West mounted up. "Let's go home."

Former Acquaintance

Chapter 31

℘he woman stood looking at the dark hotel room. The spindly man who volunteered to take her luggage to her room smiled, bearing his missing teeth as she handed him an unexpected tip. He turned and left the room, and she closed the door behind him.

I suppose this will do, but I'm ready to see him.

She wrapped a shawl around her shoulders, stepped through the door, and walked down the stairs.

The lady at the counter turned when she saw the woman walking her way. "Are you finding everything suitable, ma'am?"

"I wouldn't say suitable, but I suppose it will suffice. Could you point me to the church?"

The clerk gaped. "Are you in need of the pastor, ma'am?"

She grinned. "Oh, I am in need of him. Yes, I am."

"The church is at the end of the street." The clerk pointed toward the door and to the left.

As the woman stepped through the doorway to leave, a man with a star on his vest happened by. "Are you new in our town, ma'am?"

"I don't see that it's any of your business, sir."

Sheriff Ellison crossed his arms. "For your information, I know everyone in my town. And when new folks arrive, I make it a point to know who *they* are and where they are from. Folks elected me to do just that. So, again, are you new in our town?"

"Yes, I arrived on the train just a while ago. My name is Adeline Favor."

"And what business do you have in Santa Fe?"

Adeline hesitated. Giving out her intentions was not her practice. "I don't care for others knowing my business, but for you, Sheriff, I'll oblige. I am here to see an old friend, Steven West."

"The Pastor? *You* are an old friend of Pastor West?"

"Is that so difficult to picture?"

"Uh, no, I guess not. You'll find the pastor at the end of the street. Would you care for an escort?"

"If I need an escort, I will ask." She turned and strolled away.

Sheriff Ellison watched as Adeline Favor drew her dress above her shoes and crossed to the other side of the street. "Oh, Pastor West, if only you knew the insolence coming your way."

Adeline peered at the wagon at the mercantile store as she approached. A farmer and an elderly man in a white apron stood talking, studying her as she passed.

Both hicks, for sure.

Once beyond the mercantile, Adeline spotted the little white church at the end of town—a frequent country design— the place Christians took to on Sunday. *I can't believe Steven is a pastor.*

She marched up the steps and opened the heavy wooden door. Peering around the spacious chamber, she realized it was vacant.

"Steven, are you here?" Her inquiry harmonizing with the occasional creaking of the building.

As she advanced towards the pulpit, memories flooded Adeline's mind. She remembered the day she stood in another church, rehearsing for her wedding with Welford Harp, New York's most eligible bachelor. But it crushed her dreams when she caught him having lunch with the stunning Countess Eloise Bourgogne. Her courtship with Welford had come to an end.

Welford, of course, made excuses, saying he hoped to add

Eloise's father to the New York banking system. His explanation sounded legitimate, but she had witnessed him reaching across the table for the Countess' hand and staring into her eyes, using the same persuasion he had worked to win Adeline's heart.

A sound from the back caught her attention. Assuming there was an office beyond the door, she pushed it open.

Steven stood staring down at the Bible, quoting it out loud. *"For the word of God is quick, and powerful, and sharper than any twoedged sword, piercing..."* He raised his head to look at her.

The auburn-haired woman wearing an Eastern hat and matching dress smiled, her white teeth beaming, her eyes full of life. "Hello, Steven."

* * *

Pastor West was at a loss for words. He couldn't believe the woman he once loved had come to Santa Fe.

After the cattle drive, he traveled to New York and met this beautiful and spirited woman. They soon fell in love and talked about marriage. But he soon realized her attraction to him was his Southern behaviors and nothing more. "Adeline, what are you doing here?"

"I came to see you, Steven."

He seemed confused.

"What's wrong? Can I not come to visit my friend?"

"How did you know I was in Santa Fe?"

"News travels. I saw a man who journeyed here by train looking to add a bank."

"We already have a bank."

"So he discovered. I shared a meal with him, and he spoke of the people in your town. As we talked, he mentioned a pastor wearing a black hat and coat whose name was West. So, of course, I became interested and asked more questions. I soon realized it was *you* he spoke about. Though I never believed you would become a preacher."

"Life has its surprises, Adeline."

"So it seems. I've never forgotten the great times we shared, Steven."

He knew she was right, except for the other man in her life. "Yes, we had some good times, but you lived another life that did not include me."

"Oh, Steven, you misunderstood me. Don't you remember how I was assisting the bank fetching new clients?"

He had never heard this. Why had she not mentioned it before? "Well, that was then, Adeline. We both have our lives."

"But I'm here now. Can't we try again?"

"I don't know that this is a good idea."

"Oh, you mean you have someone you are close to?"

Laura came to mind at the question. Asking for her hand in marriage had not turned out as planned. But the truth was, there was no one close except for God. He and Laura were friends, nothing more. "I have close friends, but not a relationship."

She smiled. "There you are. We can be more than friends now that I'm staying."

"What happened to St. Louis? And weren't you planning to travel? I seem to recall your dreams being the other problem we encountered. You had said when your traveling was over that you hoped to land in St. Louis and live out your life there."

"Well, as you said, life has its surprises."

He sensed something had changed, making him question whether the current plea was genuine or another of her many games. "I don't know what to say. You told me about your dreams of visiting places and were unbending towards those ideas. Are you saying none of that was real?"

"Oh, I traveled to *many* beautiful cities, New Orleans, Denver, San Francisco. I even went on a voyage to France and stayed there for almost a year."

"So what happened?"

"I told you my father owned a manufacturing business and a newspaper, right?"

"Yes."

"Father overestimated his worth and could not pay his debts. So when he passed, I discovered there was negligible available for traveling. Father had always enabled my care and travel expense, so to realize he left me so little was a shock."

He sensed sadness. "I'm sorry, Adeline. Things must have been horrible for you."

"But the worst part was losing Father. I loved him so much."

"What would you like to do?"

She pursed her lips, drawing in a deep sigh. "Just to have dinner with me. That is a start. I'm staying at the hotel."

What could a dinner hurt? "Alright, Adeline. I'll come by tomorrow evening. I have appointments today."

"That's wonderful. Thank you, Steven. I know we will enjoy our time together."

* * *

Laura peered from her desk through the window of the Santa Fe Journal noticing a beautiful woman walking away from the church, having auburn hair and dressed in clothes much above the status of the community. "Mr. Flack, have you heard of any newcomers in town?"

Orland stepped closer and peered outside. "Are you talking about that woman?" He pointed.

"Yes, I haven't seen her before."

"No, neither have I. Maybe you should check her out. Might be a story there, but not today. We have too much work to do."

"The hotel should know something."

"I'm sure they will at another time."

"I'll go by there when we finish here."

As Laura watched a moment, she determined the woman's dress looked Eastern, similar to those from New York. *Oh yes, there has to be a story.*

Maybe her account was like her own, she thought. Laura had moved from Santa Fe to Boston and returned after hearing of her father's death. She must find out what brought a woman of her position to a Western town comprised of hot air, cactus, and unforgiving soil. *I'll find out before she leaves.*

Chapter 32

$\mathscr{P}$astor West sat in the front pew, exhausted from running errands and speaking with some families from the congregation. He closed his eyes to pray, but his mind kept wandering to Adeline's arrival.

Five years ago, he had thought their relationship was perfect. Despite her father's demanding nature, Steven satisfied expectations by sharing a passion for hunting.

He and Adeline had enjoyed a special time together. They spent their days watching plays at the theater and sitting in the park, talking. Her father had reservations about his occupation, but Adeline did not mind Steven's past as a cowboy.

During this time, he felt the Lord's calling on his life, but his love for Adeline made him hesitant to commit until her sudden change of lifestyle.

Should he have discussed his passion for God with her? Would it have made any difference for their future?

Adeline's arrival in Santa Fe was an inconvenience. What was he to believe? Was she ready to settle down? Could she see herself in a role as the wife of a minister?

When he remembered their first kiss, so passionate and sincere, his life now seemed so empty. He could stand a woman's touch and thought he had found it with Laura, but she turned him down.

"Lord, I give this matter to you. Keep my heart safe. Please reveal if there's a path for Adeline and me."

He left the church and walked to his home, changed clothes, and prepared for their dinner together.

✳ ✳ ✳

Adeline opened the door when she heard the knock. "Steven, right on time."

"Are you hungry?"

"Yes, I am. Let me grab my shawl."

They walked downstairs to the Queen Restaurant. The patrons examined them on their way to a table with curious eyes.

The waitress soon came. "May I bring something for you to drink?"

"I will take some red wine?" Adeline said.

"We don't serve wine, ma'am. You may find that at the saloon."

"Well, then I'll take tea, hot."

"We only have cold, sweet tea and water."

Adeline drew in a breath and pursed her lips, peering at Steven. "Okay, bring me cold, sweet tea."

The waitress smiled at him. "And you, sir?"

"Hello, Gloria," Pastor West said. "I'll take sweet tea as well."

Gloria left to get their drinks.

"She's flirting with you."

"Oh, just being friendly, Adeline. Gloria visits the church

and may be curious that I'm sitting with you."

"I'll bet many women from church flirt with you."

"Oh, I pay no attention."

"A woman can tell, you know."

Gloria brought their drinks and set them down. "Do you know what you want, Pastor West? And what about you, ma'am?"

"What are today's specials?" asked Pastor West.

"Only one. We have beef vegetable stew with cornbread."

"Okay, give me that. What about you, Adeline?"

"If that is good, I'll take it."

Steven turned to her. "I've had it before, and it's good."

"Alright then, I guess that's it."

The waitress turned and walked away.

"She's quite homey," Adeline said.

"This *is* a country town, and I'm sure you'll find the rest of the townsfolk are much the same."

Adeline gazed into his eyes. "Are you happy living here, Steven?"

"I am. Santa Fe is a fine place to be with some good folks. I suppose we have our problems, as most towns do."

"Do you think *we* could ever be an object again?"

He looked at her, wondering why she asked, recalling how their past had floundered. "I don't know. I'm a church pastor now with a calling on my life. Can you deal with that?"

She thought about the comment. "Sure. How difficult can it be? I'll always know I can trust you, you being a pastor." She chuckled.

"Adeline, the one I'm closest to is the Lord. So there can be no jealousy of my relationship with God."

"I understand, I think."

"Does that change your outlook?"

"No, but when I learned you were a pastor, I figured you'd

already be married. Now that I know you are not, I can think of no expectations."

This might work, he reasoned. "So, are you finished with traveling? Because I cannot travel as a pastor. The congregation needs me."

"How do they need you?"

"A pastor's job is to encourage and bring them a spiritual message from God's word. There are also times when they will need me to pray for them. Sometimes, I must offer a peaceful word when a loved one passes."

"Sounds special."

"Special? No. Essential may best explain my role," Pastor West said, unsure that Adeline grasped it. "Maybe we should take things slow until we understand the other better."

"Okay, but what's slow?" She leaned closer to him and placed her hand across his arm. "I remember how close we once were."

Steven looked upon her lovely countenance, her skin so smooth and alluring, yearning to press his lips against hers. He then turned his head, scanning the area behind them to ensure no one from the church was watching, and then leaned in and kissed her passionately.

Catching himself, he withdrew. *That's not slow.*

"That's how I prefer to kiss."

His face reddened, embarrassed. "I'm sorry, I didn't mean to—"

"No, it's alright. I always enjoyed your kisses," she admitted, grinning and tapping his arm.

"I should be cautious."

"Steven, are you ashamed of me?"

"Not at all. It's just that people expect good morals from their pastor."

"But it's only a kiss."

"And that's all it might take to start rumors."

She lifted her chin and narrowed her gaze. "They shouldn't be so conventional! People have to live a little."

"Not pastors. If you stay, you'll find this town is very traditional."

"Steven, I *am* staying and have no plans to travel again."

He turned his head, spotting Gloria bringing their meals. "Um, our food is coming."

"Wonderful. I'm hungry."

Gloria smiled as she presented them with the stew. "Here you go, and some cornbread." She sat the bowls and the plate of cornbread before them. "So, is there anything else I can bring you, Pastor West?"

"I think everything is perfect, Gloria."

"Alright, if you need anything, just call out." Gloria stepped toward the kitchen.

"Well, shall I pray?" Steven asked.

"Oh, yes, by all means."

He bowed his head, and Adeline followed suit as he prayed over the food.

West picked up the soup spoon and caught her staring. "What is it?"

"Oh, it just hit me that I had never heard you pray."

"Then you should come to church Sunday. I also preach."

"I will."

Chapter 33

*E*sta Dowd stood speaking to a man wearing a bowler hat and a suit as Laura passed by. "Miss Stone, may I introduce you to Benson Driskell? Mr. Driskell will be staying with us for a while."

The man reached for Laura's hand, smiling. "Call me Benson."

"Okay, and I think you heard my name," Laura replied, trying to retrieve her hand. "I'm sorry, but I must leave."

"I was hoping you'd have supper with us," Esta expressed.

"Sorry. I have to meet Kenneth. He's buying my supper at the Queen."

"So, you already have a man friend," Benson said.

Laura thought it best to keep things about her life private. "Sure."

"Oh, he's your brother, Laura," Esta said.

Benson's grin renewed. "Well, then. Maybe we can have lunch sometime."

"I'll think about it, Mr. Driskell." Laura spun and walked away.

"Please, Miss Stone, it's Benson," he called out.

"Yes, I know," Laura replied as she exited the boarding house.

Kenneth arrived as Laura reached the hotel. "Hello, sis. You looked like you've been running a race."

"Not running, avoiding."

"Avoiding what?"

"Oh, it's nothing. Esta has a new boarder, Benson Driskell. And he asked me to dinner."

"And you're avoiding that?"

"I don't know the man and have never asked Esta to match-make me to anyone. She opened the door for Driskell to impose on me."

"Maybe you don't know this, but lots of men in these parts don't have a woman. Some are talking about bringing in mail-order brides."

"You're not serious?"

"Very serious."

"That's dangerous."

"Maybe and maybe not."

Laura pointed to the door. "Let's go in and talk. Besides, I'm hungry, and you promised to buy."

"I suppose I did."

Laura sat across from Kenneth, and soon the waitress approached their table. "What will you drink this evening?"

Laura thought a moment. "I'll take the sweet tea, Gloria."

"Yes, for me too," Kenneth answered. "And I want a thick steak cooked with a bit of pink in the center and some potatoes."

"What about *mashed* potatoes?"

"That's perfect."

"And for you, Miss Stone?"

"Do you have soup today?"

"We have vegetable stew."

"That's great."

"I'll bring it out to you soon."

Gloria walked away and moments later returned with their drinks. "Here you go."

As she departed, Laura turned to Kenneth. "What's so crucial you must ride into town to meet with me?"

"Did I call it a meeting?"

"Well, you wanted to talk."

"Yeah, I did."

Laura thought Kenneth looked nervous. "What's going on?"

"Well, I'll just tell you. The ranch is not making much money. I had to bring a few cows in and load them out to get the funds to survive. But when I sold them, the market was down more than expected, and I made about half what I usually do."

"Okay?"

"Well, as you know, the herd has grown, so I could use some help. But there's no money to hire. After the sheriff arrested Diedrick Simms, that was the last of hiring hands because of the funds."

"Why didn't you say something before now?"

"You stay busy writing for the Journal, Laura, and I didn't want to bother you."

"Kenneth, Horace was my father, too. We are both connected to the ranch."

"But you brought me in. You didn't have to do it, and I feel terrible that I've let you down."

"I *involved* you because I wanted to and needed your help. Besides, we both knew this would be uphill for a while."

Kenneth gazed away and then turned again to her. "Well, I need help and don't know what to do."

"For starters, I can move to the ranch to help you."

"What about the Journal?"

"Orland should not mind me writing from the ranch. But I'll need to ride into town several times a week, give him the stories, and pick up my new assignments."

"Are you sure Orland will go along with that plan?"

"If he doesn't, he'll have to write everything himself, and he's gotten used to me giving him a break. He knows the Journal has sold more papers since I started working for him."

"Maybe it will work, Laura, because I need your help."

"There's something else, Kenneth. I sent my novel to a publisher friend I know in Boston. He just mailed me back a contract. He'll put my book on the market as soon as I return it."

"That's wonderful news, but what does this mean for you?"

"Right now, I don't know. Once he markets my book, then he can judge the sales."

"So tell me, what's the book about?"

"It's about a small town in Texas."

"Texas? Have you ever lived in Texas?"

"No, but it's fictional. I used character ideas from Santa Fe and changed people's names to avoid hurting feelings. Keep that to yourself. Folks can be weird about such things."

"Oh, sure."

"You're in it, Kenneth."

"Me?"

"I didn't use your name, of course, or your current occupation. I'm hoping the folks from Santa Fe will not realize the difference."

Gloria strolled up with their food and set it down. "Kenneth, cut through that steak and tell me if it's okay."

He picked up a fork and knife and made a slice. "This looks good. Thanks."

As Gloria set down Laura's stew and walked away, Kenneth peered around the room. "Laura, who's that with

Pastor West?"

"Where is he?"

"Sitting at the corner table in the dark."

Laura turned in her seat to look. Pastor West sat with his back to them and the woman opposite him. "I've never seen her before today."

"Maybe she's an old acquaintance."

"She's very friendly," Laura alleged.

Kenneth grinned. "You know that Pastor West likes you a lot, right? I don't know why you two haven't gotten married. Didn't he ask you once?"

Her mind darted back to the day West and she sat in the same restaurant when she told him she could not marry him. Steven's ideas and hers were not one and the same. "We talked about it, but sadly, we think about marriage differently."

"I'm sorry to hear that."

"Eat your steak, Kenneth, and stop worrying about me."

"I'm not worried, but I can tell when you look over there that she and Pastor West concern you."

"No, I'm not."

He took a bite and swallowed. "Yes, you are, and they call that jealousy."

"Jealousy?" She said it louder than she wanted to. "I'm not jealous. Steven can have any woman he wants. Besides, we don't even know who she is."

"So it's Steven now."

Her mouth took a hard slant but said not a word.

Kenneth swallowed a sip of tea and set down his glass. "We know she's friendly."

Laura turned her gaze again to Pastor West and the visitor. Kenneth was right. They seemed close, maybe closer than the two had been earlier. *An old girlfriend, maybe? A close friend, for sure. Someone in Santa Fe knows about her.* "I bet they know something at the hotel."

"So, you're going to go snooping around asking questions now?"

"I'm a journalist. That's what I do."

"Laura, every person who comes to Santa Fe is not a story."

"This one is."

"Why?"

"First, because she's spending time with our pastor and people will want to know about her. And have you seen how she dresses? Her clothes did not come from any shop in Santa Fe. They are from the East."

He shook his head. "Well, if you must snoop, ask Sheriff Ellison first."

"Oh, you think he'll know?"

"Maybe. If so, he'll come more to giving up the information."

Laura scooped her spoon into the bowl and took a bite of soup. "Are you still seeing Olivia?"

"When we have time. You know Olivia almost has her clinic ready for opening."

"I thought she needed another month?"

"She still had remodeling to finish and told me she was waiting for some paperwork to arrive. Maybe the carpenters have wrapped it up."

"I suppose I should visit her. I planned to write a story to give her some exposure."

"Laura, most everyone in town knew this day was coming. She'll do fine."

"But she's a woman doctor and will need all the introduction she can get, though I'm sure Orland will fight me on it."

"Do you need me to speak with your boss?"

"Not at all. You'll cause me to lose my job. But of course, that's what you want since I'd always be available."

192

He grinned. "Yeah, I need help at the ranch, but I don't want you to lose your job."

"You'll get my help soon enough, but you'll have to give me time to discuss the details with Orland and Esta Dowd."

"Sure."

She turned again, watching Pastor West putting a shawl around the woman's shoulders. "I need to find out who that woman is." She spun back to face Kenneth.

"Yep, that's jealousy," he said.

"No, it's not."

"Uh-huh."

Chapter 34

$\mathcal{T}$he carpenters had completed the remodeling project at the clinic and were gone. Olivia peered at the surgical instruments, preparing them to use. Now it was up to her.

She had spoken to several women around town who promised they would come to see her. But she wondered why their husbands fought against the opportunity to use an updated and well-trained physician. Dr. Simms had dominated the field of medicine in Santa Fe for all these years, but that had to change, even if she was a woman.

The door opened, and Laura stepped inside. "Now it looks like a clinic."

"One with no patients."

"To be expected at first, but they will come."

"I hope so because I've spent most of my savings on this place."

"Have you treated anyone yet?"

"I treated Orval Dunning and his wife, but that was because you urged them to see me."

"There will be more. I'm doing an article on you that

should bring in some clients."

"Laura, you don't have to do that. Won't that make me appear desperate?"

"You've seen how the advertisement worked in Boston. This is no different."

Against her will, moisture flooded Olivia's eyes. "But Dr. Simms is...is al...ready telling lies about me. He's ruining me before I get started."

Laura hurried to her friend, wrapping her arms around her. "You must not allow that doctor or his lies to upset you. There is room for two physicians in Santa Fe. He will have to move over at some point."

"He has all the men hating me," Olivia replied.

"Don't worry about him. Stand firm and go on with your plan. Don't let that man dissuade you. When women come to see you and have excellent results, that will cause their husbands to change their minds."

"You are always so optimistic, Laura. Please pray that I see things the way you do."

"I will. Olivia, I must help Kenneth, but I'll stop by later."

"Help Kenneth?"

"I'm going to move to the ranch for a while to help."

"Today?"

"Today, I'm riding there only to help. Then after I speak with Orland, I'll move back. I'm hoping Orland will let me write from the ranch."

"I won't see you as much, will I?"

"I'll still have to ride to town and leave my stories on occasion, and I'll visit unless you are too busy."

"Too busy with—"

"Don't fret, Olivia. Things will turn around for you."

"I sure hope so."

"I'll see you tomorrow for an interview and get a story out."

Olivia watched as Laura left and walked toward the livery stable. *I hope she's right.*

Bored out of her mind from waiting, Olivia grabbed a broom to sweep the floor again, her mind whirling. How could she survive in this country town if not as a physician? Was all that time in medical school wasted? Since she was very young, she wanted to be a doctor.

But her life was miserable in Boston. The male physicians were obstinate and heartless, eager that their female counterparts failed. She remembered two of her friends turned to the nursing field, believing it offered a better future. Maybe they were right. Or should she trust Laura's optimistic ways? Would this town someday opt for her assistance? Even if only women came to her, she must view it as a victory.

A knock sounded on the door.

Olivia opened it to see Dr. Simms standing there, his brown eyes beneath thick brows, staring, bearing a dismal expression. "Well, I didn't think I'd catch you."

"You did. So how can I help you?"

"I want you to stop this nonsense. I am the doctor in Santa Fe."

"Doctor Simms, I did not go to medical school for six years to work in a bank or restaurant. I am a doctor."

"Well, go somewhere else."

"It's too late for that. I've invested too much in this clinic to leave now."

"You should never have come here. My patients are mine. Do you hear me?"

Olivia felt her face reddening. "We'll see about that! I'm not leaving Santa Fe. There is plenty of room for two doctors and maybe more."

"Uh, no, there's not. I am the only doctor Santa Fe needs, and if you try to treat any of my patients, I'll—"

"You'll what? You don't own this town, Doctor."

"I'll...I'll."

"That's what I thought."

"Lady, you best get out of town because trouble is coming." Simms turned and walked away.

"You don't scare me, old man!"

Olivia slammed the door, pleased and smiling, absorbing the doctor's threat. Simms exhibited the same attitude as the male physicians at school. Rather than acknowledging her achievements as an intern, they remained mulish and egotistical.

Could that be the answer? Dr. Simms' attitude corroborated prejudice against the opposite gender. Perhaps he didn't want to be shown up by a woman.

Laura was right. Things would start slow but gain momentum over time. The women of this town were her targets. She must win them over by treating illnesses and their female medical issues. Only then would their husbands turn to her for treatment.

And one well-known fact was in her favor. Women would rather not expose themselves to a male doctor. She could earn their trust by restoring their health and offering the comfort that only a woman doctor could.

She sat thinking about her new goal, realizing there was hope.

Chapter 35

*C*opper neighed as Laura reined him closer to the barn. He pulled against her as Star trotted to the fence. "Easy, boy. You can't play with Star today because we've got to find Kenneth." She kicked a spur to his side and forced him away.

She had ridden for ten minutes when she came to a hill. Near the top, she spotted a group of cows and rode toward them.

Kenneth turned when he saw her. "I didn't think I'd see you this soon, but I'm glad you came."

"You needed help, so here I am. I still haven't spoken with Orland or Esta, though. Maybe tomorrow. What do you need me to do?"

"The grass around here has gotten mighty thin, so I want to split these yearlings and take them where there's grass. Take half these and move them to the eastern field with those momma cows."

"So that's all you're doing these days, moving cattle around?"

"Yeah, pretty much. We're running out of grass. And

winter is just around the corner."

Laura remembered a conversation she had with Horace once. "But why do you have to do this? Father said there was plenty of grass on this place."

"Maybe there used to be, but weeds have pushed out much of it, and the herd has grown."

"Then it's time we restore it, don't you think?"

"Laura, that's another expense. Plus, I don't have the time to plow or sow. We'd have to hire the work done."

"Do it, Kenneth, and I'll pay for it. My guess is Father never sowed winter grass here all these years."

"I've not seen any. But I'll look into getting Harmon Long or one of his sons to harrow the ground and prepare it for seed. Then we'll have to keep the cattle off it because we don't have fences to separate them."

"We can do it. Maybe next year, we can start adding new fences."

"Alright then. Grab those yearlings, and I'll push the others to the south field."

Laura gathered her herd and rode away with the yearlings as Kenneth moved his group in the other direction.

A half-hour later, Laura spotted the east field and the cattle through the trees. When she had the herd in place, she paused, looking them over. *Our cattle are in excellent shape. Kenneth has done a fine job.* Then, spotting something on the ground several yards away, she rode to it. "Oh, no."

She dismounted and examined it. Kenneth said her father had mentioned mountain lions and that he killed three once. She remembered finding the dead calf remains not long ago. Now another lay dead in the field. *More mountain lions...*

She mounted Copper and rode toward the southern field, where Kenneth took the others.

Laura knew working with the cattle would be challenging, especially with her job writing stories for the Journal. But writing was her life. Owning the ranch was unexpected and only came at the loss of her father. She had considered selling her part of the ranch to Kenneth, but seeing him under this financial burden pushed the idea from her mind.

Kenneth watched the herd from his horse as Laura rode upon him. "Another nice-looking bunch, Kenneth."

"Yes, they look fine, but will lose weight unless we keep them on good grass."

Laura sighed. "Well, you have another problem."

"Problem? What problem?"

"Mountain lions."

"Not again. I thought I had rid the property of those cats."

"You have at least one cat."

"You keep saying you. But it's *we* that have at least one."

"Right. And that dead calf is an indicator they are here."

"But only one, right?"

"That's all I found."

Kenneth blew a strong blast of air from his lungs as he removed his hat and wiped his forehead. "Our stock can't grow when something comes along and takes our offspring."

"No, it can't."

"I'll start riding the fields in the evenings when I'm not moving the herd around. These cats seem to stir before dark, maybe preferring not going to bed hungry."

Laura nodded. "I wish I were here to help you, but until I move, I'll have to ride back to town each time."

"You could spend the night at the ranch. I'll give you the bed, sis. I'm used to sleeping on the ground."

"Oh no. I have a bed to bring for the spare room."

"Was there never a second bed?"

"Yes, but gold wasn't the only thing thieves discovered after Father died."

"I'm sorry, Laura. Must have been a difficult time for you."

"Some of it, but I learned I had a brother. I believe Father would never have told me."

"I hope you don't struggle with Horace not telling you."

She peered at the ground. "I try not to dwell on it. Some days are easier than others."

"I'm sorry and wish I could help."

"I'll be fine."

"Maybe you should ride back to Santa Fe before dark."

"Yes, probably."

"But before you leave, tell me what you found out about our unknown visitor in town?"

"Not yet. I hoped to investigate, but Orland kept me busy. And then, as I left work, I visited Olivia."

"Oh, good."

"Kenneth, she's under a bit of emotional stress with so few patients coming to visit. And now Dr. Simms is telling lies about her to keep people away. I tried to encourage her, though I'm not sure if I did her good. I told her I was writing a story about her clinic opening."

"What did she say to that?"

"She wondered if it might make her seem desperate."

"How could it? You're only giving the folks the truth."

"I know, but Olivia may not find any optimism until she treats those in need."

"Maybe you should hurry that story along."

"I'll work on it tomorrow, and I hope Orland will allow it."

"When you have things settled about your job, I'll bring the buckboard in for your things."

"We may have to make two trips."

"How much stuff do you have?"

"I'm sorry, Kenneth. What I've purchased is too beautiful to throw away. I just can't part with any of it." She grinned.

"Oh, sis." He shook his head.

"I suppose I better start back."

"Before you leave, will you grab the papers with the finances and look them over?"

"Sure. I'll do that tonight. Bye."

Chapter 36

The next afternoon, Pastor West borrowed a buggy from a friend. He snapped the driving reins onto the horse's bridle, recalling when he had paid for a buggy ride for him and Adeline. New York was unlike any place he had been, its countless attractions and noise.

Upon her request, he took Adeline to a play at the theater that night. The people gathered for the event were extraordinary: a crowd of bankers, owners of manufacturing companies, shipping merchants, and fine restauranteurs. He remembered feeling out of place in their presence.

Adeline stood on the porch waiting when he arrived.

"You are right on time, Steven."

Pastor West had learned that Adeline was a person of delay, which always annoyed him. "I prefer promptness."

Moments from the past came to Adeline. "I remember," she whispered, bristling as he pounced from the buggy and walked to the other side.

"Give me your hand," he said, reaching for her.

She zeroed in on him with a squint. "You were always the

stickler for time, and I remember how my tardiness got under your skin."

He helped her into the buggy. "Well, some things never change, do they?"

"Yes, it would seem that is true." But what are a few moments when a woman is dressing, she thought? After all, they had more to do than a man.

He hurried around and got in. "Let's not speak of the past, please. I've learned to be prompt as a pastor. Folks want the church service to begin when we advertise, and I suppose that practice has settled into my ways over the years."

"I don't know about out that, Steven. You've always been this way."

"Can we drop it, please?"

"Sure."

"I have our food in the back and some water."

"So, you no longer drink?"

"No, Adeline, I don't."

"Hmm."

He slapped the reins against the horse, and it darted forward.

A few miles from town, West pointed to a pond as they drew near the location he had in mind. "Well, I hope this place is satisfactory for our picnic."

"Oh, Steven, it's lovely." She reached for his arm. "But how many women have you brought here?"

There was the jealousy he remembered, though he wondered if Adeline even realized it. "None."

"None? That's hard to imagine. So, you saved this picturesque setting only for me?"

"Well, I wouldn't say that. I knew it was here from some rides I've taken. Just never had the opportunity to visit for a picnic until now."

"Is that what I am to you, an opportunity, a chance

meeting, a bit of favorable time?"

"Oh, Adeline, stop picking out my words so you can start an argument. I didn't even know you were coming to Santa Fe. Certainly, you are not some twist of fate. Just please understand that I've given my life to serving God. But I won't allow you to make this into something it is not."

Her mouth skewed sideways. "Steven, I'm not. I'm delighted you are not married or entertaining female friends at this lovely picnic spot." She swallowed hard. "I'm sorry. I have no right to be jealous of you."

"Are you jealous?"

"That's silly, isn't it? You've done nothing to deserve it. But I'll be honest. I was always jealous when women fawned over you."

"Over me? I wouldn't know it."

She touched his face and caressed it lightly, recalling a time when they were eating in the park. A beautiful young woman had come to them, asking questions Adeline no longer remembered. The young woman's eyes hardly left Steven. Then even as she stepped away, she continued to gaze back at him. "I saw it in New York. Women always know these things about men."

"Maybe women should leave well enough and not allow this evil spirit to control them. For envy and strife are carnal and can only hinder relationships."

"That's not so easy for some women."

A soft smile shadowed his handsome face. "Jealousy is not of God. So I'll pray for you, Adeline, and I know God will help you control it."

"Thank you, Steven. I knew you were good for me."

He turned to face her, his brows arched high and kissed her, and then stared into her eyes.

Her heart lurched, feigning a heavy sigh as he leaned to kiss her again. She reveled in his warmth as he encircled her with his arms.

After a moment, Pastor West pulled away. "Um, maybe you are good for me, too."

She blinked wide, her eyes following his. "You know, I've never stopped loving you. Yes, I've made some mistakes. But if you will, help me find forgiveness with you and God. Then maybe we can pick up where we once were."

He smiled. "I can help you." And he kissed her again.

* * *

Laura saw the buggy leaving town as she mounted Copper. *Where is Pastor West taking her?*

After following behind them at a distance, she saw they had stopped and turned near Mac Frazier's pond.

She came to the lane leading in and reined Copper to a halt. She could see from the road that they were lying on a blanket.

Spying on people was not her way, though journalism often called for it. To watch this woman strolling around town in her Eastern attire sent up red flags. Unlike those down-to-earth, hard-working women of Santa Fe, she did not measure up to a pastor's lifestyle. No, this was all wrong. So what did she want with Pastor West?

Laura tied Copper out of sight and settled to watch them. Lying on the blanket, the woman peered at West, smiling, often laughing. She could not tell if Steven enjoyed the conversation, but indeed, there was something Pastor West loved about her since going to the trouble of retrieving a buggy and a horse for their outing. Did he not realize how his association with her made him look? She was no saloon girl, but folks in Santa Fe may not view her otherwise.

Adeline lunged forward to kiss him, but he turned his head away. Determined, she grabbed his head and pulled him to her, kissing him.

Laura shook her head and grabbed her mouth, impeding

any foolhardy outcry. *Shush, Laura. The woman is pushy, but does Steven even like it?*

She wished she had gone to the sheriff's office and asked about the visitor. *I will find out tomorrow.*

She watched for a short while as Pastor West and the woman ate their food from a basket.

I must leave to help Kenneth. She hurried to Copper, mounted, and rode toward the ranch.

Chapter 37

Outside the Journal, men around town had formed a protest group carrying signs that read, "NO FEMALE DOCTORS."

Laura stood peering at them through the window, shaking her head, saddened that a woman had little liberty to explore a career for the well-being of people's lives in this town. "I don't understand the complaint. Olivia is a fine, well-trained doctor. Instead of fretting, these men should be happy she is here in Santa Fe."

Orland stepped up beside her to look. "This is not Boston, Laura. Maybe one day things will change."

"Someone has to lead the way. But I'm sorry that someone is Olivia. She doesn't deserve this chauvinistic treatment. No woman does."

"I don't know what we can do about it. Do you have any suggestions?"

Laura recalled that in Boston, not long after she had arrived, the town's women rebelled against the men because they could not vote. Of course, they did not win the argument in the end, but she learned that because of their undertaking, the men of Boston leaned toward a change in the future. "What if the women here protested? What if I could convince some of them to refuse Dr. Simms?"

"That might start a war." Orland smiled. "But what a story we'd have."

"Orland, this is more important than a story. Women should be free to take on the same jobs as men."

"I wouldn't go that far. Can you see a woman as sheriff in Santa Fe?"

"Yes, I can, Orland, if she is qualified."

"Now you're making too much of this craziness. I won't allow you to write an unconstrained account in the journal. We must not cause discordance."

"We already are causing discord. Today's main article was about a woman doctor, which is why those men are protesting."

"But you don't mention a woman sheriff or any other civic employment."

"Is not a doctor who can save people's lives as important as a sheriff, mayor, or city council member?"

Orland thought about it. "Well, maybe. But how do you convince *them*?" He pointed through the window at the horde.

"Leave that to me." She laid down her pencil and started toward the door.

"Where are you going?"

"I want to speak with Esta Dowd. If I can convince her to see Olivia, that would be a start."

"I hope you are right."

Laura exited the newspaper office and could hear the men shouting louder.

"We don't need a women doctor in Santa Fe," came a lone outcry.

Another said, "No woman doctor will ever be allowed to

209

touch my family."

Laura kept walking as they bellowed their criticisms so all could hear. Partway to the boarding house, she walked headlong into Pastor West.

He smiled, pausing in front of her. "Laura, I've been meaning to speak with you."

She turned to view the protest group in the streets. "Um, I'm busy right now." She stepped to leave.

"Wait a minute. I need to say this."

"Say what?"

"An acquaintance of mine from New York has arrived. I'm sure you've not seen her."

"Yes, I know of her and have seen her."

"You have?"

"You were at the hotel restaurant when I was several days back."

"I'm sorry I missed you."

"You seemed quite distracted."

He lingered, considering his next words. "Well, I hoped to speak with you about Adeline."

"Adeline? That's her name? I'm happy for you. But right now, there's something urgent I must attend to." She turned to view the protesters.

Pastor West rotated to observe them as well. "Concerning those folks?"

"Yes."

"What is going on with that?"

"They are protesting because of the article I wrote about the new doctor in town."

"Olivia? They are protesting about her?"

"Yes. These men don't want a woman doctor."

"I didn't think—"

"Olivia needs our help, Pastor. Could you please mention

her to the women from the church?"

"I don't know. Their husbands might not like me taking sides."

"You're not taking sides if you tell them we have a new doctor if they are interested."

He shrugged his shoulders. "I'll do what I can and hope Olivia stays with us."

Laura cast a wary look at him. "Pastor, I'll see you later." She took two steps and halted. "Wait, Pastor. Do you think I might have an interview with you and your friend, Adeline?"

"Why?"

"I'm sure the church folks will want to know who this woman from out of town is visiting their pastor."

Looking at her, he furrowed his brows. "Um, do you think it seems immoral for me to be with Adeline?"

"That's not for me to judge, but I believe an article in the journal might benefit."

"I'll speak with Adeline and let you know."

Laura turned and walked away.

* * *

Esta was busy in the kitchen cleaning dishes when Laura arrived. Laura sat at the table near the boarding house owner. "Esta, I need to speak with you."

Esta wiped her hands on a towel and tossed it over her shoulder. "Are you here to apologize?"

She recalled Esta introducing her to Benson Driskell a few days before, and Esta's invitation to dine with the tenants. "I'm sorry I couldn't stay to eat with you. I already had plans."

"But you could have come to any meal when Benson was here, and now he's gone."

"Esta, I'm not interested in Benson if that was your intention."

"Well, you missed out on a wonderful opportunity. I heard him speak of his employment with the banking system. Benson is well-known and has a stable hold on his career. A man like that would have freed you to write your books."

Laura rose and walked to Esta. "I am free to write, and I have been."

"Well, I still think you missed your chance at a good marriage."

"Maybe so, Esta. But I came to speak with you about our new doctor."

"You mean the one you wrote about in the Journal?"

"Yes, Olivia."

"What about her?"

"I hoped I might talk you into seeing her. She needs to get her business off and running."

Esta crossed her arms. "I think there's more to this story."

Laura sat down again and motioned for Esta to join her. "There is. The men of this town are protesting against a woman physician."

"Why?"

"I believe it's because she's a woman."

"You know, I was going to see Doc Simms about this twinge in my hip. I will see Doctor Bunney instead."

"Good. May I have an interview with you after your visit?"

"Why not?"

"Thank you. I hope you'll point other women to her who want to see change."

"My friends from the bridge card group might see her. It's only right that a woman sees a woman doctor for her more delicate needs rather than old Doc Simms."

Laura grinned. "You are so right, Esta. Let's get the word out that the men in this town are trying to stop Olivia from doctoring folks."

"You bet I will."

Chapter 38

Kenneth loaded the last of Laura's things onto the buckboard. "So, that's all of it?"

Laura wrapped a blanket around a lamp to secure it for the trip back to the ranch. "Yes, that's it. Kenneth, I have to work today and tomorrow at the Journal, and then I'll be available to help."

"How are you handling Pastor West having a new friend?"

"Whatever he wants. Life goes on, and people must as well."

"If you say so."

"I'm interviewing them today for an article in the Journal."

"Now you're getting personal."

"No. Depends on the questions."

He peered at her. "You're doing this to find out more about her?"

"That's not true. This is an interview for an article."

"Maybe, but *you're* prying for personal reasons and you'll take things farther than you should."

"Why do you assume I love Pastor West?"

213

"Laura, because it shows. You say you've moved on, but your actions tell a different story. In the restaurant, you couldn't stop gawking at them, and now you have this interview. Lord knows the depths you've gone to understand his interested in her."

She peered at the ground, a blank expression on her face.

"What have you done?"

"Oh, I might have ridden upon them a few days ago on the way to the ranch. It was an accident. They pulled out in a buggy ahead of me."

"Did they see you?"

"I'm sure they didn't because I was a long way behind them. They turned in at the pond there on the left."

"Mac Frazier's pond."

"Yes. I stopped Copper and got off to look."

"So you spied on them?"

"I wasn't spying, Kenneth. I'm a journalist and have a curious nature."

"You justify spying by your job? Laura, you crossed the line."

"I know and feel terrible about it, though I could only hear a little of what they were saying."

"Did they kiss?"

She turned her head away from him. "Yes."

"That should tell you what you need to know. That pastor has feelings for her."

"I know you are right."

"So is this interview more of the same—prying, spying?"

"No, it is not. Orland and I spoke about it because she is new to the town and interested in one of our prominent men. The people have a right to know about their pastor's interest in an unknown woman he may marry."

"Marry?"

"Well, I don't know that he will, but who knows where this

is leading?"

"Laura, promise me one thing: that you will not try to influence their relationship."

"I promise."

"I'm worried about you, sister. You should spend some time praying about this first."

"I'll be fine! Don't you have things to do?"

He stepped onto the buckboard, sat shaking his head, and then slapped the reins to the horses and pulled away.

* * *

It was almost two o'clock. Laura walked from the Journal office toward the church. They had agreed to have the interview at Pastor West's home. She held in her hands some paper, a pencil, and her reticule as she knocked.

The door opened, and Pastor West stood smiling. "I've been expecting you, Laura. Come in."

He led her to the living area, a modest room lacking a woman's touch. She peered at a small table centered in the room where a colorful flower ornament sat atop.

"Adeline thought I needed to decorate and brought that arrangement as a gift."

"Yes, it's beautiful. Where is Adeline?"

"She's not here, but I'm sure she is on the way. May we sit?"

She sensed a moment of déjà vu as she sat on the divan. Not of any visits to Pastor West's home, but of their time together. Those moments had been extraordinary, and though she failed to admit it then, she felt comfortable and safe with him. "Um, is Adeline always late?"

He grinned. "I suppose that is one of her flaws. But of course, arriving late where she comes from is optimal for exposure."

"I saw much of that in Boston, the upper class competing

for publicity. I thought it was childish."

"You're right. I do not view it as maturity either, but in the Eastern culture, it seems ingrained."

"So, you know about the East?"

"Yes. I lived in New York for a while. That's where I met Adeline."

"Then I'm glad we are having this interview. The folks in Santa Fe may learn a lot about their pastor, as will I."

"Laura, I hope we don't get too personal."

"I will only use what you share."

A sound came from the door.

"That must be her." He hastened to the front of the house.

"Steven, I'm sorry I'm late," Adeline said, standing at the open door.

"No, no, come in, Adeline. Laura is here and waiting."

"I am so sorry."

He led her to the divan.

Laura rose and reached for her hand. "Thank you for giving the interview."

"Certainly. Steven and I are happy to oblige."

The women turned and sat beside each other.

Laura peered at her notes. "I wrote a few questions, and I may think of others as we go along."

Adeline nodded at Pastor West.

"Laura, before you ask your questions, we have an announcement," Pastor West said.

"An announcement?"

"Yes, Adeline and I are getting married."

Those words sent waves of heat through Laura. "Um, Steven. I mean Pastor West. That is...a surprise."

"Yes, it was for us as well. But you should know that Adeline and I were very close when I lived in New York and had planned to marry. I won't go into why we didn't, but I hope you understand how we could establish again our relationship."

Laura peered at him, still shocked by the comment. "Sure, I can see that."

Adeline watched Laura as she took in the announcement. "You care a lot for Steven, don't you?"

"Why would you say that?"

"Adeline, please," Pastor West said.

"She does. Is there something between you two that I don't know about?"

Pastor West's face turned beet red. "There was, months back, but no longer."

"Months back, interesting. Steven seems to attract many sorts of women. I'll admit that when I look at you, I didn't see this coming."

"Adeline, stop this," Pastor West demanded.

"That's alright, Pastor," Laura replied and turned to Adeline. "You should know that I broke things off."

Adeline set her full lips in a moue of distaste. "Well, there's that. When the interview ends, I expect you to keep away from him."

Laura swallowed as lines of despondency etched into her brow. "You have nothing to worry about. May I get on with the interview?"

Pastor West nodded. "Please do."

"My first question was where you are from. I suppose that is New York, Adeline?"

"No, I'm from Virginia City. I moved to New York in my youthful years. A friend, Natalie Carmichael, invited me to join her, hoping to find work at a bank. For a month, we struggled. But soon we found jobs, and things improved."

"How's that?"

"Men from the bank would ask us to go with them to dinner and the theater. I met the influential people of the city during our time at the theater and became friends with them."

"How long after that did you meet Pastor West?"

"He was not a pastor then. I suppose a few years later."

"Pastor, what was your reason for being in New York?"

"I was curious growing up. I was roughshod, always finding trouble. Joining the cattle drives served me well. You see, it was on the cattle drives I started reading the Bible each night around the fire. One night while praying, I thought I heard God speaking, which startled me. Looking back on those days, I realize my New York adventure was me running from God."

"And how did you meet Adeline?"

"By chance, I suppose. We were in a shop looking at various things when we bumped into each other, literally."

Adeline smiled. "I offered my name, and he was polite, took my hand, and told me he was sorry. He was handsome, and I worked my way into his heart."

Pastor West grinned and shook his head. "You weren't difficult to be close to, if I recall."

"So, how long did you see each other before deciding to marry?" Laura asked.

"I don't recall the exact time frame, but I would say a month." He looked at Adeline. "Does that sound right?"

"Yes."

Laura turned to Adeline. "Did you ever set a wedding date?"

"No, but we were about to when...."

"When what?"

"I'd rather not say."

"Laura, this part is personal," Pastor West said. "You should leave it alone."

"Yes, I will. But tell me, have you set a wedding date since you found each other again?"

Pastor West smiled. "Yes. We'll marry three weeks from

this Saturday at the church."

Laura wrote the date on her paper. "So, Adeline, may I ask you one more question?"

"Sure."

"How do you feel knowing you'll soon be a pastor's wife?"

"Wonderful. I know it will be challenging, but I'm up to the task."

Laura rose from the divan. "I will finish the story today, and it will print tomorrow."

"That's great, Laura," Pastor West said as he walked toward the door.

Laura stepped through the doorway, gazed back at him, and turned toward the Journal.

Chapter 39

Twenty-three women lined up outside Olivia's clinic door, awaiting an examination. A group of men, mostly husbands, stood across the street, calling out names, badgering the women.

Olivia thought they were just like the men in Boston who tormented women, who seethed with envy that a female had the same qualifications and capabilities as a man. The pressure was overwhelming, almost causing her a breakdown until an elderly man, Dr. Harold White, explained their resentment. He said, "I heard some talking. They realize your intelligence and worry that you will surpass them in promotions." But even if he was right, it did not dismiss the torture they brought.

The women watched as Laura pushed her way through to find Olivia.

One lady barged in front of Laura. "Get in line, lady, like the rest."

"I'm not here as a patient, only as a journalist."

"I don't care."

Olivia spotted Laura in the doorway. "Ladies, please let Laura through. I asked her here." She led Laura to the next room. "I'm glad you're here."

"Do you need me to help?"

"I could use help, but I know you are busy at the Journal."

"I can stay for a while, but I need to tell Orland."

"Do that after I take in a patient. Call in one person at a time in the order they have arrived. I also need to set up the women with new appointments. There is a paper pad with the names of those in the wait area. When someone comes, have them sign the sheet of paper."

"Got it. Are you ready for one?"

Olivia nodded. "Yes."

Laura called out the first woman's name, and Olivia invited her into the examination room.

The taunting from the men in the street drifted through the open doorway. Several women returned comments.

An angry woman hollered, "Billy Joe, if you don't leave the street, I'll not make you supper tonight."

"You can't speak to me that way," replied Billy Joe.

"I am speaking to you that way. You leave, or things at home will turn awful for you."

Kenneth pushed through the door and saw Laura sitting before the women. "What is happening out there?"

"Seems the women are rebelling against Dr. Simms."

"I heard the town's men calling out awful things."

"But the women may have the upper hand. One woman said she wouldn't fix supper for hers."

"Now, this could turn ugly."

"I wonder if the sheriff is watching?"

"Sheriff Ellison won't get involved in domestic skirmishes unless someone gets hurt."

"Well, someone *may* get hurt if this continues. He should come shut it down."

Kenneth pivoted his head to her. "But you want him to shut down the men, even though the women are just as much to blame."

"Not hardly. The women are declaring their right to choose, and the husbands are mad about it. They should just get over it."

"You're wrong, Laura."

"So you think all these women should go home?"

"Maybe."

"Don't you realize this is what Olivia needs?"

"Yes, but it's gotten out of hand, Laura."

"There would be no problem if the men would move toward the other end of town."

"Forget I said anything. I came to ask how your interview went?"

A patient stepped from the examination room and walked toward the door.

"Hang on a minute, Kenneth. Katie Barns, it's your turn to see Dr. Bunney."

Katie Barns entered the examining room.

Laura stood. "It went well. The article is in the paper today."

* * *

"And speak of the devil," Kenneth said. "Here he comes."

Pastor West stepped through the doorway. "Lots of commotion in town these days. Is there anything I can do to help?"

"Yes, Pastor," Laura replied. "You can call Olivia's patients in order when she needs one. Write their names down when they come in. I have to get back to the Journal."

"Sure, I'll take care of it. I'm sure so many showing up delighted Olivia.

222

"Yes, she is, but the threat outside has us worried."

"I'll keep an eye out. If it gets out of hand, I'll fetch Sheriff Ellison."

"Thanks." They left the clinic.

West gazed through the windows and noticed that Adeline had strolled up near the men. Weldon Bailey, the attorney, had separated himself from the others to speak to her. Adeline chuckled. He laughed and said something more, seemingly amused that the lovely woman gave him attention. Weldon reached and took her hand as they continued in conversation.

What a fool he had been, West thought, to think she had reformed. Anger rose within as he watched Adeline and Weldon carry on out in the open, where all the men could witness them. The undertaking was equal to what she had committed in New York. *Adeline has not changed.*

Laura's article about them had hit today's Journal, revealing his forthcoming marriage to the woman from New York. And now Adeline was making a fool of him. Was this her plan all along?

He returned to his seat and waited to call the next patient. He set his mind to a time in New York when he witnessed Adeline's flirting gestures as she and another man stood waiting for a buggy. After boarding, he saw them kiss from a distance, and it was the day before he broke off the relationship.

But by this time, God was tugging at his heart to become a minister for the gospel, so Adeline's involvement no longer affected him. Until now, he hadn't allowed their relationship to disrupt God's plan. But he watched as Adeline's attitude toward him transformed the day he admitted it to her.

He stood and walked again to the window. Adeline was gone, along with Weldon Bailey. At least he learned an important lesson before they became husband and wife.

* * *

223

Kenneth and Laura went to have lunch together while he was in town. They sat at a back table waiting on food when Weldon Bailey walked in, and he was not alone.

"Who is that with the attorney?" Kenneth asked.

"That's Adeline Favor, Pastor's fiancé. Oh, my goodness. The Journal released the article in today's paper about their forthcoming marriage."

"I thought that was her, but I'd only seen her once. So Laura, what's going on?"

"During our interview, I sensed a strangeness from the woman. I think she was jealous of me. Maybe she's trying to make Pastor West jealous."

"No. What she is doing to him now can only be fueled by anger.

"And puts his character under attack. Adeline should never expect him to marry her after this disgrace."

"Laura, she may have never intended to marry him, only to ruin his reputation and make him look foolish."

"That may be. Do you think the people in the church will forgive him?"

Kenneth peered around the room. "I don't know, and some are here today watching Weldon and her now. Everyone in town has heard about Pastor West and the woman from New York."

"If they hadn't, they'll know when they read the story. Oh, Pastor, if only—"

"If only what?"

The waitress brought their food and set it on the table. "Is there anything else I can get for you?"

Kenneth looked up at her. "No, Gloria. Everything looks wonderful. Thank you." Gloria left for another table. "So, if only what?"

"You know he had asked me to marry him."

"Yes, but you never told me what happened."

"We didn't marry because he wanted me to stay home, to be his maid."

"Oh, it couldn't be that bad."

"Kenneth, he didn't want me to write. We discussed it, and he thought he was compromising and spoke mostly about me cooking and cleaning. I told him I didn't attend those years of school in Boston to become a maid. I don't mind sharing the household chores, but I'm a journalist and want to write."

"I didn't realize—"

"Well, you do now. Pastor West has some old fashion beliefs about a woman's duties to her husband, which is why I'm surprised by his infatuation with Adeline."

"She *is* beautiful, Laura."

"But he's a pastor and needs a woman who can fulfill those roles besides the ones at home."

"Sounds like you've thought a lot about it."

"At one time, yes. Right now, Pastor West will need our support and friends who will stick by him through this ordeal."

"I'll stand beside him. That New York woman has hoodwinked him, and I'll be there for him. Now, tell me about your book. Have you heard anything about it?"

"Yes, I have. My publisher, J.D. Goslin, sent a telegraph last week saying they would release it in a month. I will have him send me some when I know for sure."

"That's great. What is the name of your book?"

"I titled it West Texas Trail since the story is based in San Antonio, Texas."

"I can't wait to read it."

"I hope others like it."

"They will."

They finished their meal and left the hotel.

"Kenneth, before I head to the Journal, I'm going to check on Olivia."

"Don't you think you should leave that alone for a while? You already gave that job to Pastor West. His seeing you again might spark memories of the interview and his marriage."

She smiled, pondering what he said. "You may be right, wise brother. The pastor needs time to think, but I can pray for him."

"Yes, you can, wise sister." He mounted Ace. "Will I see you early enough today to help gather those steers for the market? I've got to bring them to town before the train leaves."

"Sure, I'll come as soon as I can. And then next week, I plan to work from the ranch and help you more."

"I look forward to it." He turned and rode away as Laura walked toward the Journal, observing that the rowdy men outside Olivia's clinic had dispersed. "Good."

Chapter 40

*K*enneth rounded up the last yearlings he wanted to sell, herding them in with the others. "That ought to do it. We'll push them to the ranch house, then drink some coffee before pushing off."

Laura rode in beside him. "I didn't think it would be so cold this morning."

"Yep, mornings of late have been a bit nippy. But I bet you're used to laying up." He smiled.

She narrowed her eyes and furrowed her brow. "I don't lay up! I've always been an early riser!"

"Wow! Don't bite my head off!"

"Then you best tell no one I'm lazy getting out of bed."

He chuckled, more amused than offended. "I'm sorry, but we still know little about each other."

"Maybe my moving here will help solve that. Just don't expect me to do all the cooking and cleaning." She gave a slight grin.

"I won't. I'll do my share. As a matter of fact, I'm a decent cook."

"With what, steak?"

"Yes, I have some beef quarters hanging in the smokehouse now."

"Well, we are going to plant a garden next spring."

Kenneth peered at her with curiosity. "Where are you going to find the time? You have plenty of work to do on the ranch and write for the Journal."

"I'm also writing a book."

"I thought you already wrote a book."

"And published it. I'm writing a memoir."

"A memo...what?"

"Memoir, a book that tells about my life. I thought I might write about those times when I was a child helping my father with the ranch. But I also will include my years in Boston."

"I might read it."

"Which part?"

"All of it."

* * *

After leaving the ranch with the herd, a steer darted away. Kenneth rode after him into a creek area. "You come on here, buddy."

The steer went to the water and drank.

"Mister, I think your cow there is thirsty," came a husky voice behind Kenneth. "We'll take him and any others." The man cocked his weapon and pointed it at Kenneth.

"Now, mister, I didn't come here asking for trouble. This is just an old steer getting off track."

"Rope, don't you think he's trying to make trouble?" said another voice Kenneth didn't recognize.

"Yep, Brad, this man's causing a lot of trouble. So let's take him out so the law doesn't have to."

A lever on a rifle cocked not far away. "You stop right

there, or I'll shoot you both. Throw down those weapons and put up your hands."

Kenneth knew right away it was Laura's voice. "Better do what she says, boys. She's mighty good with a rifle."

"A little woman like her can't be that good, Brad," Rope alleged.

"I don't know," replied Brad. "I think she's got one of them advantages on us."

"No, I don't think so." Rope spun and pulled his weapon from the leather. But Laura was too quick and put a bullet in the side of his neck. His gun went off into the dirt as he fell to the ground, grabbing for the wound. "Brad, help me."

Brad had reached for his weapon, but Kenneth had turned Ace and aimed his gun at him. "Laura, are you alright?"

"I'm fine. But do you mind if I look at this man? He's bleeding pretty bad."

"Yeah, check him out."

Kenneth urged Brad away from his partner. Laura kneeled beside him and saw the blood pouring from his neck.

Brad peered into her eyes, grinning. "I'm sorry. You'll...have to...live with this, y...you know."

"I'll try to help you, mister."

"Oh, it's...too late." The breathing ended, and he closed his eyes.

Laura peered down at him—a young man, maybe twenty years old, dead now because of her.

"Laura, can we get him on a horse?" Kenneth asked.

"Won't help. He's dead."

"Well, he shouldn't have pulled his weapon on you. You had no choice."

"I know it. I'm just sad about it."

"Come watch this one, and I'll put him on his horse. We'll take these to the sheriff."

After Kenneth had the dead man on his horse, they

gathered the herd and headed toward Santa Fe.

* * *

Sheriff Ellison stepped from the saloon to finish making his morning rounds when he heard an odd sound. He turned and spotted cattle coming into the main part of town. "I've said it over and over. Do not bring cattle straight through town."

He walked to the middle of the street and waited. "What is this?"

As they drew closer, Ellison realized Kenneth had a rope in his hand leading two horses. Behind him, Laura herded the cows down the street. Kenneth reined Ace to a stop.

"Who you got there?" Sheriff Ellison asked.

"I don't know much. These two tried to steal our cattle." He pointed to the dead man. "This one drew, and Laura nailed him."

Ellison took off his hat and leaned down to glimpse the face of the dead man hanging from his saddle. "I believe I have a poster on this one. You'll maybe get a reward."

"Not me, Laura."

"Does she need help with the cattle?"

"Yes. If you can take these men, I'll help her."

"Head on," Sheriff Ellison said. "I got 'em. But I'll need a statement when you finish there."

"Sure." Kenneth handed off the rope and rode away.

* * *

When Kenneth arrived, Laura sat on Copper outside the corral, staring into the distance.

"Are you alright, Laura?"

"I killed that man, Kenneth."

"He had it coming. You cannot blame yourself for what

happened."

"But he was so young."

"And it could have been me who killed him."

"Does it bother you to kill someone?"

"Sure it does. But when men decide to rob others, they make a choice. So don't take this on, Laura. Nothing about what happened back there was your fault."

She breathed out a long breath and stared into the corral. "I know, and I'll be okay."

"Are you sure?"

"Of course."

A man walked into the corral and soon herded the cattle through to a scale.

"They should bring a fair price, Kenneth. I heard the price for beef is up."

"I know. Much better than the last time. I was desperate then."

"Sure, you were."

"Laura, I need to sign off on these with the stockman. Time is close for them to load up."

"Go ahead. I'll wait for you."

Kenneth rode away, and then she watched him rein up Ace at the stock buyer's building and dismount. As she leaned in the saddle, she spotted a woman in an elegant dress walking beside a man carrying two suitcases as they entered the ticket area. "Adeline."

I suppose this was bound to happen. That made two women poor Pastor West lost in recent months. And Adeline's leaving would be difficult for him.

Kenneth rode up beside her. "What are you looking at?"

"The ticket station."

He pinched his brow, wondering if she was alright. "I know killing a man can be hard on folks, but you've got to let it go."

"Forget about that. I'll figure things out."

"Then what are you doing staring at the ticket office?"

Laura turned in the saddle to Kenneth. "I saw Adeline go in."

"Adeline?"

"I am surprised. I thought she had old Weldon wrapped around her finger the way they carried on in the restaurant. But I guess Adeline didn't want Weldon. She must have learned he was no sugar daddy."

"A what?"

"I heard the term for the first time in Boston. They said it was when a woman goes after a man of means and wealth but doesn't love him. Many women in Boston come from backgrounds often unsuitable for the upper class. But the single, wealthy men are so desperate for someone they fall for them."

"Ah, I get it—a man who can sweeten the pie. So, that's what she first saw in Pastor West?"

"I don't know. Pastor West doesn't fit that mold, so I don't understand what happened. I guess it's possible that she loved him."

"No, she couldn't love him and do what she did."

"People do strange things for love, Kenneth."

"That they do."

"What about you and Olivia?"

"We are doing fine, but we need to figure out how to have a life together. There's her clinic, and we still have the ranch to run, which takes up much of my time."

"Kenneth, don't let the things of life interfere with your happiness. I did that, and it's not fun," Laura said, turning to look at the ticket station. "There she goes."

"Adeline *is* leaving, which might benefit the town. I have to wonder if she'll someday return."

"We may never know."

"You're right."

Laura peered down the main street at the buildings. There were two rows of stores on opposite sides of the street. Townsfolk moved about walking, looking, and buying. "Kenneth, Santa Fe is growing. Just look."

But Kenneth had his eyes on Adeline as she boarded the train. The conductor took hold of her bags and carried them on board. "Yeah. But sometimes purging is *good* for growth, don't you think?"

They laughed.

"Kenneth, let's get something to eat. I'm buying."

"I can't. I still have a mountain lion to kill at the ranch."

"You'll have time later."

"Well, okay, since you're buying."

MICHAEL J SPANHANKS

Restricted Passage

Chapter 41

*K*enneth peered at the ground as he rode the black gelding, following the tracks along a muddy trail. With three calves dead already, he knew he must put down the mountain lion. Taking out animals trying to feed themselves was unpleasant, but the cattle ranch was a business, and that's how it had to be.

He surveyed the trail as it turned into the woods, observing the tree branches where big cats often sit and search for prey.

Where did he go?

He recalled some large rocks laid behind the patch of woods. Mountain lions loved it high because they had the best view, which made him wonder why this one had come to these low hills when the Sangre de Cristo Mountains lay only a few hours away. Was it possible that feeding there had dried up?

He heard a roar as he came to the edge of the wood line. *Alright, where are you?*

He reached and pulled out his Winchester rifle and

cocked it, laying it across the saddle horn.

The sun filtered through the pine and pin oak trees near the small mountains, casting its shadow against them. Before he reached the tree line, he heard the cat's warning roar echo through the rocks. He reined the black horse to a stop, peered to the high points, and saw it. The cat thought he was safe, positioned high.

Kenneth dismounted and led the horse to the trees, aware the mountain lion kept his eyes on him. After tying the horse, he stationed himself beneath a medium size pine, hoping to use it for bracing. Then he searched for the large cat but could not find it. *That's not good.*

He thought about waiting, but images of the cat pouncing on him came across his mind. *I need to leave.*

He turned to reach for the reins when a branch snapped behind him, causing him to spin around. The mountain lion had him in his sights.

No time for a rifle. He tossed it and reached for his sidearm. And as the cat pushed off the ground, he pulled back the hammer and fired two rounds.

* * *

Laura had called out to the cattle, hurrying them to a safer place, awaiting Kenneth's return, when she heard the shots ring out in the distance. She thought it sounded like they came from the hills.

Copper took the kick as Laura punched his sides with her heels. She knew Kenneth had gone searching for the mounting lion earlier. But knowing the cats were dangerous and hearing the shots cast a fear within. And having only recently learned of her brother months before, she could not lose him to a mountain lion.

Something moved ahead in the trees. Kenneth raised from the ground with his skinning knife in hand. He turned to

236

her as she rode up close.

"You scared me, brother."

"Nothing to worry about, sis. An old mountain lion is not much."

"So, where was he when you shot?"

He grimaced and said, "Right about where he is, I reckon."

"That thing could have killed you."

"But it didn't."

"I told you that you needed another person along."

"Laura, he's dead, so you're fretting over nothing."

She dropped from her saddle. "Only a few months ago, I found out I had a brother—"

"Half-brother."

"My only brother! And my only brother went chasing a mountain lion, whom we all know are dangerous."

"He's dead, Laura. The thing you're concerned about is laying right there and not moving."

She stared at the furry creature, mouth exposing its sharp teeth for killing, long piercing claws for grabbing prey and pulling them down to their end. "They just scare me."

Kenneth reached for her, pulled her close, and wrapped his arms around her. "They scare me too, sis. But we have cattle that call for our protection. They can't hold off creatures like this, so we must do it for them."

"I know, even so, they scare me."

"Well, hopefully, this is the only one. We'll know if the killing stops."

She pulled away. "So why are you skinning out the cat?"

"I thought I might make a rug out of him."

"Oh, Kenneth. Don't put it in the living room, please."

He laughed. "Okay. I'll put him in the bedroom where I sleep. But he has to cure first."

"While you finish here, I'll push that herd onto the north

pasture."

"I thought you'd have that done."

"I would have if I hadn't heard the shots. Once I get the herd settled, I'm riding to town. Steven wants to have dinner tonight."

"You two are having lots of dinners together these days. One might think you're planning something."

"I'm sure he would."

"So you still don't think Pastor West is what you want?"

"Sure he is. Steven just needs to loosen the ball and chain."

"Well, keep at him. Before long, you'll have him trained right."

"Huh, now that wasn't nice."

"Laura, I see how you're tweaking him. Little by little, you're showing him what you want."

"I'm not forcing Steven to do anything."

"But that's what you expect before you tie the knot."

She mounted Copper and smiled. "A woman knows how things should be." She turned and rode away as he watched, shaking his head.

* * *

Laura peered around the town, watching the stage as it pulled to a stop. She reined up Copper near the livery stable. Ishmael spotted them from inside and ran out.

"Thank you, Ishmael. Could you give him extra oats tonight? Copper worked very hard today."

"Sure, ma'am. If Copper worked, he deserves it."

She headed toward the newspaper office. Orland Flack stood watching from the doorway, smoking his pipe. Laura loved the pipe's sweet aroma when he lit it.

"Laura, how's the cattle business?"

"It would be better if mountain lions didn't take our little ones."

"Mountain lions? Goodness. They are dangerous. You should speak to the sheriff about it. He might call in hunters for you."

"No need. Kenneth already took it down."

"That brother of yours is the real deal when it comes to cowboying."

"Yes, he is. I hope the last of those cats, but I remember my father had trouble with them, too. I remember how he stayed up watching over the cattle until he had killed the mountain lions."

"Is that right? Maybe there's a story there."

"Hmm, maybe. I've got two here for you today."

"That's it?"

"I'm sorry, Orland, cattle need watering. And we've had to move them around because of the cat."

"Well, remember that I said you could keep working if you handed in three to four stories a week."

"And I have, for the most part. I have to go now, but I'll work on keeping up."

"You do that."

She stepped through the door, turning toward the hotel. As she walked inside, an older couple stood at the counter while Lidie Atwater set them up in a room for the night. Lidie saw Laura and waved.

In the dining area, she noticed several unfamiliar faces. Santa Fe was a through-town and a stopover for folks heading west, so seeing new folks coming through was not unusual.

Hearing the couple talking as they started up the stairs, she returned to the counter and walked closer. "Hello, Lidie. How are you today?"

Lidie looked at her with sad eyes. "Okay, I suppose."

"What's wrong, Lidie?"

"I think I have a woman's issue, and it's painful."

"See Olivia."

"She is gone to deliver a baby. Someone said she might be out of town for several days."

"Then you must get to her office as soon as she returns."

"I will."

"Is it possible for a bath?"

"Sure. I'll have the boys bring in some hot water. I suppose you want my extra room to change."

"Yes, if it's available. I am eating dinner with Pastor West in a few hours."

"How romantic. That Pastor is a stunner."

"Yes, he is."

Lidie turned to the wall behind her and reached for a key. "Here you go. You can head up, and I'll let you know when the water is ready."

"Thank you."

Chapter 42

$\mathcal{P}$aul Albrecht and Isaac Brandenberger sat on their horses, peering at the road before them.

"I'd say dere's a town nearby from da looks of the wagon trails," said Paul.

Isaac sighed. "We need supplies, but I not looking forward to another town. So much trouble before."

"We'll be fine, Isaac. The Lord has brought us this far."

"And it's not been easy. It seems like we traveling all my life since we leave Germany. I'm tired, Paul."

"I am too, Brandenberger. But one day, we will have a nice farm—plenty of land in America."

"Well, let's turn south, Paul. Maybe not far."

Paul raised an arm high and motioned for the four wagons to follow Isaac. He watched as they passed by, his second in line.

Eli, his eldest son, had a smile on his face as he walked beside the wagon. "There's a town ahead, Father?"

Paul nodded.

Eli whooped. "We're going to town, folks!"

The others offered joyful comments, voices more energetic as each wagon caught on to what was happening. Twice only since leaving St. Louis had they stopped for supplies. When the goods ran low, they survived hunting in the nearby woods.

Isaac saw smoke ahead several miles away and halted the small wagon train. Paul rushed to the front as his friend stared down the old road. "What is it, Isaac?"

"Smoke, not far."

Paul pondered their situation. "Maybe they travel like us. Take out the rifle."

Isaac spun his head. "The Lord would have us follow His word, Paul."

"Only lay it out in the opening. Maybe dere is no problem."

Isaac slowly slid the shotgun from the leather pouch and laid it on the saddle before him as they rode toward the smoke. When they drew close, a tall man wearing brown pants held by suspenders and a light shirt stood watching. A dark hat sat on his head as he carried an armload of wood. He dropped the firewood on the ground near a blaze and stood smiling. "Hello, friend. Where you from?"

Paul nodded. "New York City."

"New York City? My goodness. That's a long way." He peered beyond them and spotted the wagons. "You moved the whole bunch, didn't you?"

"Yes."

"So, are you heading west?"

"We are."

"Oh, my name is Findley, Morgan Findley."

"My name is Paul Albrecht, and my good friend is Isaac Brandenberger."

"Well, come on down and rest a spell. My family would love to visit with you. You see, we're from North Carolina.

Heading to Oregon, where my brother and his family have moved. They left for the West three years ago. He wrote that they have land now and are working it for the first time this next spring."

Paul turned to Isaac. "Did you hear that, Isaac? Dey have land. We must speak with this man."

"Yes, I'll tell the others we stay the night."

* * *

After visiting for a long while and eating supper, the families headed to their separate wagons.

"These people are not Christian, Paul," said Ruth Albrecht as she pulled herself beneath the covers. "We should not have children around them."

"Why do you fret so much, Ruth? We need information."

"Paul, I only want to see dat we raise da children to love de Lord."

"And we do. They know dat."

Ruth lay quietly resting and then thought of something more. "Will we have a church in Oregon, Paul?"

"Yes, we will. If dere's no church, we will build one."

"We must. Our children must follow the Lord all the days of dere lives."

The darkness hindered Paul's smile from his wife. "Let us first get to Oregon."

"I rest now."

The night grew on as everyone slept until a cry came across the camp.

"Paul, what is that?" Ruth asked.

Paul listened for a moment, then raised. "That's not our people."

"Go see if they need help."

He rose, put on his overalls, and stepped from the wagon

as Ruth rolled from the bed.

After a moment, Paul stuck his head back inside. "I believe it's a child. I will ask if dey need us."

He ran toward the Findley's wagon and met Isaac returning.

"Paul, Mr. Findley's son, very ill. Stomach pain and diarrhea."

"Must leave early, Isaac. Tell our people to stay away."

"Stay away? We should help."

"No, we should leave," Paul said. "They find de doctor in town."

"I don't tink the Lord will like dat."

"It's wisdom. We have long trip to Oregon," Paul said. "We can't afford to lose our children to sickness."

"Alright, but I think you're wrong," Isaac replied.

As daylight approached, Paul watched as Morgan Findley stepped from his wagon and headed toward them. "Mr. Albrecht, we're going on to Santa Fe to find a doctor. There's enough light to see now, so we should get on."

"I'm sorry for your son," Paul said. "Maybe doctor know how to help him."

"I hope so. A few coals are in the fire. Help yourself and stoke it for breakfast."

"We'll do that. We will stop at Santa Fe to see how he's doing."

"Thank you." Morgan walked away and climbed into his wagon, and popped the reins against the horses.

Isaac walked beside Paul with a cup of coffee. "We stay for a while?"

"Long enough to eat. But I have bad feeling about dis."

"About breakfast?"

"Nah, nah, about sick boy. The children play with the young man before bedtime last night."

Isaac stared into the distance. "God will protect us, Paul."

"God has been good, but sometimes we do tings that test him. Are we not to defer from testing our God?"

"Yah, but are we testing him, Paul?"

Paul stared at his friend, turned on his heels, and walked away.

* * *

Morgan Findley pushed the team until he saw the city come into view. As he entered Santa Fe, he spotted a man in a dark hat and waved at him. "Mister, can you help us?" he said as he stopped the team.

The man walked closer. "Maybe." He reached up to shake hands. "I'm Pastor West. What can I do for you?"

"Is there a doctor in this town?"

"Yes. There are two. You rode past a good one—the gray house. Stand in your wagon, and you can see it."

Morgan stood, peering behind him. "Yes, I can see it."

"Turn on the next street and go around. The road will take you right there."

"Thanks, Pastor."

"You better get some water in those horses."

"Sure."

Morgan Findley slapped the reins to the team to move them forward, and Pastor West watched them pull away.

When Morgan reached the gray house, he jumped from the wagon and ran to the door, knocking hard.

The door opened wide, and a woman stood before him. "I am looking for the doctor. Is he in?"

Olivia grinned. "Yes, she is. I'm Dr. Bunney."

Morgan's eyes grew large, and he became nervous. "I'm sorry, ma'am, but I heard another doctor is in town."

"At least tell me what's going on."

Morgan peeled his eyes to the wagon. "My son is sick,

ma'am. His stomach is hurting awful, and he's fevered."

"I should be able to help you. I studied in Boston, sir, and I'm capable."

"I guess it won't hurt for you to look at him. I'll bring him in."

Morgan held his oldest son and carried him to the door.

"Follow me," Olivia said.

She showed him to the examination room, and Morgan put his son on the table.

"My name is Dr. Olivia Bunney. What's yours?"

"Um, Morgan Findley."

Olivia turned to the patient. "I've not heard that name."

"We're from the Carolinas. We were making our way to Oregon when this happened."

"Oregon? That's quite an adventure."

"Will he be alright, ma'am?"

"I don't know yet. What's *his* name?"

"Tobe Findley."

"Tobe, are you hurting now?"

Tobe moaned. "Yes, please help."

"Mr. Findley, why don't you gather your family and bring them inside the waiting area? I'll look your son over. Examining your son won't take long."

He paused, watching her, then turned and exited the room.

Olivia took Tobe's temperature and asked him several questions.

The backdoor sprang open, and Laura walked in, smiling. "I caught you home. I heard you delivered a baby."

"Laura, forgive me. Unfortunately, I can't talk now, and you must leave."

"Leave? Why?"

"There's a strong possibility I have a contagion here."

"Which one?"

"Let's just hope it's only typhoid, cholera, or mountain fever which have similar symptoms and are the least contagious. But until we know, stay away from here and ride back to your ranch."

"And if it isn't any of these?"

"Then we have an epidemic on our hands."

"Oh, no. You're sure I can't help?"

"Not really. I'm treating this young man, but they must leave town immediately. And if you tell anyone, they will bring trouble for them."

"And what about you?"

"Don't worry about me. I have a job to do."

"I will pray for these folks and you, Olivia."

"Their last name is Findley."

"If you need me, leave a visible sign in your mailbox with a note."

"Alright, now get on."

"I'll see you then."

Chapter 43

 he wagons progressed down the trail beside the farms and ranches. Paul led them to the main road when someone called out. "Who was dat?" he asked.

"I don't know," replied Ruth. "Maybe you should stop."

Ruth halted the team, and Paul rode beside the wagons, soon noticing Amos Miller waving his hand.

Amos cried, "Come, Paul."

"What is it?" Paul asked as he approached them.

"Rachel, my second daughter, is sick, like the Findley boy."

"Oh, dear Lord." Paul pondered how quickly the sickness had found Amos' daughter. "Spreading fast."

"May we camp?"

"I'll find a place ahead. Santa Fe is close, so maybe I ride to see a doctor, and they come here."

Ruth urged the lead team on as the others followed.

When Paul sensed they were near town, he found a place in an opening near a creek, guided the teams into a circle, and dismounted.

"Gather men," Paul said, waving them at him.

Abner Bawell was the first to come. "What we do?"

"Wait for others."

When Isaac and Amos had reached him, Paul turned to them. "Amos has a daughter sick as the Findley child. We cannot go into town."

"But we need supplies," Isaac expressed.

"I will take two horses and go for supplies. Before I leave de town, I will stop to see de doctor. Maybe dey comes here."

"We will pray," Abner said.

"Yes, good idea."

* * *

When Paul rode up, Gordon Andrews was outside the mercantile putting tool handles in a wooden barrel. He turned when he saw the middle-aged gentleman in overalls with a black hat and beard. "May I help you, sir?"

"I'm here for supplies."

"Do you live nearby?"

"Oh, no. Our wagons wait outside of town."

"You are travelers heading westward then."

"Yah."

"Come on in. I can fix you up."

Paul stood inside the door, searching over the sizeable facility. He saw a blue dress and thought it might fit his wife. *Maybe another time.*

Gordon turned to him from behind the counter. "So, what will it be today?"

"Legumes, flour, ground corn."

"By legumes, you mean beans, rights?"

"Yah."

"And ground corn, I suppose, is meal flour?"

"As you say. A large bag of each and a bag of coffee."

"Any bacon? Have some fresh today?"

"Yah, give me three kilograms and some bacon grease."

"Sorry, mister, I don't know kilograms. I'll tell you what, I'll show you when I'm ready to cut it."

Paul nodded. "Good."

Laura entered the mercantile. "Good morning, Mr. Andrews."

"Oh, good morning Laura. I'll be right with you after I help this gentleman."

She turned to see Paul standing watching her. "I don't believe I know you, sir."

"Wagon train moving through," Gordon said as he stepped through a doorway and headed to the rear of the store.

"Oh, going westward." She smiled at Paul.

"Yah, name is Paul Albrecht. We travel from New York— a long way here."

"Laura Stone is my name. You have a long way to go, Mr. Albrecht. So why are you traveling south?"

"Ah, yes. See friends in Arkansas before moving on."

"I see. So, where is your final destination?"

"Oregon."

"I hear Oregon is beautiful."

Gordon came through the door with a large bag of flour.

"Mr. Andrews, I only need some coffee beans," Laura said.

"Then get what you need, and I'll put them on a writ for you."

As Laura dipped coffee beans into a bag, Paul went outside to help Gordon tie the flour to his horse. "I got one pound of coffee beans, Mr. Andrews," she said, leaving.

"I'll put it down for you, but hold up. I need to speak with you."

"Alright, I'll wait a moment."

Gordon stepped inside, returned with a bag of cornmeal, and heaved it onto the horse as Paul tied it down with a rope.

"Mr. Andrews, is there a doctor in town?" Paul asked.

"Are you sick?"

"Nah. One of our children."

"Well, Doc Simms is right down the road here." He pointed to a light blue house only a short distance away. "If he's home, he'll take a look."

"I was hoping the doctor might follow me to the camp. We don't know the sickness and try to be cautious."

"I see. Well, talk to the doc. I'm sure he can help."

Gordon headed inside as Paul tied the supplies when Laura caught his sleeve. "Why didn't you tell him about Olivia?"

"Because Doc Simms has been here a long time, and he's a good doctor."

"I think Olivia can treat this better."

"Why would you think that?" Gordon paused, waiting for an answer. "Doc Simms has seen it all, Miss Stone."

"But he may not be up on all the latest treatments."

Gordon saw Paul heading toward the door. "If you know something about this, maybe you should tell the doc."

Gordon walked behind the counter. "Let's see. We need to get your bacon and fat."

As Laura watched them working, she decided Olivia should know—the sickness at the camp may be the same as the young boy she treated.

"Gordon, I have to go." She turned and walked toward the door.

Gordon raised and saw her leaving. "But I still need to speak with you."

"Later."

Gordon shook his head. "Are your women as stubborn, Mr. Albrecht?"

"Yah, sometimes."

***

Laura reached Olivia's clinic and saw the sign on the door. She dismounted and walked closer to read it. CLEANING. COME BACK IN TWO DAYS.

How can two days help?

She knocked on the door. "Olivia, I need to speak with you."

"I told you to stay away," Olivia said.

"I have some vital information about your sick patient."

Footsteps sounded on the hardwood floor. "I'm not opening the door."

"You don't have to. But tell me, is the boy still here?"

"No. I sent the family out of town. Mr. Findley said they would camp nearby because I promised in a few days to check on him."

"I'm not so sure that's a good idea."

"Why not?"

"I saw a foreigner at the mercantile buying supplies. He's with a wagon train heading west. He asked for a doctor for one of their children, a girl. Gordon sent him to Dr. Simms."

Olivia yanked the door open wide. "He didn't."

"I'm afraid he did. Do you think Simms can treat whatever this is?"

"Stand back from the door. Yeah, he'll treat it alright, with quinine."

"Isn't that poison?"

"Yes, and will do more harm than good."

"Surely he knows better."

"He's from the old school, Laura. They taught them to treat diseases with these useless remedies. If it's typhoid, you only need to give them something for the pain and hydrate them with clean water. We know it originates from unsanitary water and living conditions."

"What will you do?"

"I'll speak with him. Maybe I can catch him before he leaves out." Olivia stood thinking, staring at her friend. "No, I can't."

"Why?" Laura asked.

"I could have been exposed, so I need to stay away from people long enough to help identify this."

"That's why you have the sign posted."

"The sickness may not affect me, but I wanted to keep patients away until I've had time to boil my instruments and thoroughly clean the room. I have to be sure before they return."

"I'll tell him."

"He may not listen."

"I'll make him listen."

"Tell him everything I told you. But wait." Olivia turned away, leaving the door open. When she returned, she had a book in her hand. "Give him this. Show him the marked section on page three hundred and twenty. The booklet explains the latest treatments, reactions, and outcomes using the old medicines."

Laura turned to leave. "Okay, I'll give it to him."

"Please, be careful. I don't want to see you sick."

Laura nodded and started for Copper as Olivia closed the door.

Chapter 44

L aura watched the townsfolk rambling in the streets, window shopping and gossiping. *I hope this sickness doesn't come to our people.*

She rode Copper toward Doc Simms' place when another horse whinnied.

Kenneth shook his head as he slowed Ace beside her. "Laura, I thought you were coming to the ranch today?"

"I'm sorry. I was about to leave, but something has come up."

"Something always comes up when we have work. Mr. Flack, I presume, wants another story."

"He always wants stories." She hated telling Kenneth that Olivia had come in contact with a sickness. "I have something to tell you."

"Okay."

"A man brought a boy into town sick. Olivia thinks it might be Diphtheria, Typhoid, or something with the same symptoms."

"She saw this boy in her clinic?"

"I'm sure she didn't know what it was at first."

"How did you know?"

"You know me. I burst in, though Olivia stopped me right away and made me leave."

"So, is it contagious?"

"She hopes it is diphtheria or typhoid. Typhoid transmits through food and water and is easier to control."

"How do you know this?"

"I read a lot about these when I was in Boston. We carried a story about Britain when they had typhoid in many places."

"I don't like hearing this."

"Kenneth, there's more. Come with me to Doc Simms' office."

"Oh no. You think you have it."

"Not me. Come along, and I'll explain."

Gordon Andrews stood outside the general store smoking a pipe and waved at them. He watched as they rode toward Simms' office.

The doctor turned toward the examination room with a patient as they walked inside. "Hello, Kenneth and Laura. I'll be right with you."

They waited until Doc Simms had finished with the patient.

"How can I help you?" Simms asked.

"Did you speak with a man earlier about a sick child?" Laura asked.

"From the wagon train, yes."

"I would have thought you'd be already gone to see them."

"I couldn't run off from my other patients, but I'm heading that way now. Would you both like to come along?"

Kenneth's eyes sharpened. "Is it safe?"

"I don't know. The man told me of the symptoms, but I'll need to examine that child."

"Doctor, you should know that Olivia treated another child this morning from the same camp," Laura explained. "She believes it's diphtheria or typhoid."

Simms stared at her through narrowing eyes and gritted his teeth. "I'm the doctor in this town! My diagnosis alone will determine whether we have a disease of such nature in Santa Fe, not this…pretender!"

"Olivia is no pretender. She went to school the same as you. There is plenty of room for more than *one* doctor in Santa Fe. And by the way, she told me the treatments are not the same as in the days of your training."

"She did, did she?"

"Here is a textbook Olivia sent you to assist with the treatment."

"Get that book out of my sight! You can saddle up and follow along, but do not bring that abominable writ." He stormed to the back of the clinic.

"What a gripey old man," Laura said.

"That doesn't matter, but I suppose we should get our horses and wait for him," Kenneth commented.

"Yeah, maybe we can help."

"I'll ask Pastor West to ride along. I think he'll want to pray with them."

"Good idea, Kenneth. I'll wait for you outside."

✳ ✳ ✳

They spotted the smoke from the campfires before they reached the wagons. Simms drove his one-horse buggy down a bumpy trail as Kenneth and Laura followed on horses. Simms recognized one man and went straightway to him. "Mr. Albrecht, I'm sorry for the delay. I have patients to see. Where is this young person?"

"The last wagon. We made them park far away."

"I'll look at her, then let you know."

"Yah." Paul nodded.

They reached the wagon. A man about fifty years old, in blue denim overalls and wearing a straw hat, stood waiting. As Doc Simms stepped from the buggy, a young boy around seven years old ran to him and touched his leg. "Hello, young'un. What's your name?"

"Vernon. Are you going to fix my sister?"

"I hope so."

A man drew closer, with veins of anguish etched on his face. "Thank you for coming, Doctor. I'm Amos Miller. We don't know what to do."

"Is she feverish?"

"Yah, much."

"I can surely give you something for that."

"What about other symptoms? Mr. Albrecht thought there was stomach pain."

"Yah, and head pain too. But now she not waking."

Maybe Ms. Bunney was right. "Sir, that's her body trying to heal itself. You must get her awake to take fluids. You will have to push her. Some broth would be beneficial and especially clean water. Boil the water and let it cool."

"Boil the water?"

"Yes, boiling takes away impurities."

"Okay, yah."

"Let's see the girl."

He led Doc Simms to the back of the wagon, where they climbed inside. Simms kneeled beside the pallet of blankets and found the girl lying and breathing, though unresponsive when he touched her arm.

"Yes, she has a high fever—a sign of infection. I want to offer her opiates, but if I do, she may not take the fluids. I know they would help with the pain. We need her awake. Can you help me with her?"

"Yah."

They raised Rachel in the bed and she opened her eyes.

"Rachel, I'm Doc Simms. I'm here to help you, young lady. You must work with your parents when they give you medicine and broth. That will help you recover."

Rachel blinked her eyes a moment, then closed them.

"Okay, lay her back down, Mr. Miller. Boil the water and make her some broth. Also, make sure your family drinks only the boiled water, which may be how this started."

"In the water?"

"Maybe, though we don't know with certainty. If the water is safe and this sickness keeps happening, there's another problem."

"I see."

"Um, Mr. Miller, there was another child brought into town. Is he here now?"

"Findley. Their boy was sick, so they went to town to find a doctor. We don't know what happened to dem."

"Did your children play with the Findley boy?"

"Yah."

"Do you know if they drank their water?"

"I don't know. Maybe."

Simms noticed the frustration on Mr. Miller's face.

"Don't blame them," Simms said. "I'm sure they didn't know about the sickness when you saw them."

Doc Simms leaned to the back of the wagon and motioned for Kenneth.

"What is it, Doc?"

"This is most likely typhoid. So, listen, I need someone to ride down the road and find a man named Findley and his family."

"Laura and I will do it. Pastor West is praying with these folks."

"Kenneth, the Findleys should be in a covered wagon, the same as these. Maybe they camped nearby. Let me know when you find them. I will be here with the Millers. I'm waiting for Rachel to take some clean water and broth. Then I may give her a little quinine or opiates."

"Sure."

Laura heard the word quinine and remembered what Olivia had told her. She decided at least part of the treatment seemed correct and thought it was best to let it go.

"We won't take long, Doc," Kenneth said as they mounted up.

Chapter 45

S everal townsfolk had gathered outside Doc Simms' office. A man with a burly beard and brown hat continued to knock on the door, but no one answered.

Sheriff Ellison was making his rounds when he noticed the crowd. *What is this?* He strolled closer to find out the problem. "What's the difficulty, people?"

"Sheriff, a man came into town sick with cholera or some other disease," said Morton Ackerman. "We want to know what the doctor plans to do about it."

"Is the man in town at this moment?"

"Gordon said he rode out."

Gordon overheard and hurried across the street. "I did not say he was sick. You made that up, Morton. The man said they had a sick child in their camp. So he kept them outside of town. He did not say what it was, though. "

"Wait a minute," said Burney Cutts. "Maybe there's something else going on."

Everyone turned to Burney. "I saw a man in a covered wagon come through and stop at the new doctor's place at the end of town. I thought little about it because folks heading west sometimes come through Santa Fe. But later, I was outside the barbershop and noticed him leaving. So I stopped him to ask if they needed help. He said that Doc Bunney told him their child was sick and that maybe I should stay back."

"Okay, so that's two stories about sick children," Sheriff Ellison said. "But as far as you know, none of our townsfolk is sick with cholera or any other contagious disease?"

"But Sheriff, we don't want it here," Burney said.

"No, we don't. But right now, you folks should get back to your business. I'm sure the doc is on a call. When he returns, I'll get to the bottom and tell you if there's a problem. Now go home."

Sheriff Ellison had seen diseases before in the war. Dysentery took out several regimes of good fighting men. On another occasion, there was typhoid fever. He recalled the muscle and headache pain, the stomach cramps, and the diarrhea many had suffered.

He turned toward the end of town, still watching folks as they searched for answers. He reached the large gray house at the end of the street. A sign near the white picket fence said DOCTOR OLIVIA BUNNEY in bold letters. Something was hanging on the door, a handwritten sign. He stepped closer and knocked.

A voice from inside said, "Come back later. Can't you see the sign?"

"Uh, Doc Bunney, Sheriff Ellison here."

"I can't open the door."

"Would that be because of the sick child you treated?"

"How did you know?"

"One of the townsfolk stopped him leaving town."

Olivia swung open the door. "I've been waiting it out to see what it is. I wouldn't want it spreading to folks."

"If it is typhoid, you know it came from bad water, right? I saw it in the war."

Olivia stood staring at him.

"You will not catch it from him. But of course, being a doctor, I thought you'd realize that."

"Sheriff. Yes, I know that. I suppose because I'm new here and still trying to get my business going, I figured it was best to close."

"You're making sure no one can blame you if it spreads."

Olivia smiled. "Is that so wrong? We don't know for sure that it is typhoid."

"Not at all. So do you think this is typhoid?"

"Ninety percent."

"Can't be a hundred?"

"Maybe if I followed through with the care."

"I see. I also thought you'd like to know that there may have been another young child sick with the same outside of town."

"Oh?"

"A man came to the mercantile earlier for supplies. Gordon Andrews said he asked about a doctor. He pointed the man to Doc Simms."

"Where is Doc Simms now?"

"No one knows for sure. The townsfolk believe Doc's treating his regular folks somewhere outside of town, but maybe he took his buggy to the camp where that sick girl is."

"A girl?"

"Yes, I think it's a girl that's sick."

Sheriff Ellison raised his hat at the front with a finger as Olivia watched him. "You think I should ride and help him?"

"I know it would be in your best interest. Then the townspeople might come to know you care about them. Might help your business."

"I suppose you're right."

"And you won't be treating typhoid in town. So how could the town blame you if one of them here caught it?"

"You know, Sheriff, I've heard some things about you, and I'm not sure they are all true."

"I figure most of it is. But beyond what people say about me, I love this town and watch out for its people, even you, Doctor."

Olivia grinned. "I'll get my bag and start that way."

"Oh, and just so you know, I saw Laura, Pastor West, and Kenneth riding along with Doc Simms in his buggy."

"You knew all along where Doc Simms went."

"I had a pretty good idea when I heard folks talking about sick children."

"But you didn't meet the man earlier, the one who told Mr. Andrews about the girl?"

"I only know how involved Miss Stone sometimes gets and that it would be nothing for her to be right there where they are camping."

"And that worries me. Laura doesn't know how to protect herself against these diseases."

"But Doc Simms surely knows."

"Maybe not. Times have changed, and better treatments have emerged since Doc Simms trained."

"Simms was a military doctor, Olivia. I'm sure he treated typhoid in the war."

"And how many died, Sheriff?"

"Well, that's another thing. So if you don't mind, I think I'll ride along in case Simms and don't see eye to eye on this."

"Might be a good idea," Olivia said with a firm stare.

"You do have a horse?"

"Yes, Kenneth bought one for me. Ask Mr. Pepper at the livery to saddle her, if you will. I'll get my things."

"I'll tell my deputy."

Chapter 46

*L*aura and Kenneth found the Findleys several miles away. Morgan Findley sat on a log near the campfire, cooking food in a skillet as they arrived.

"Your name is Findley, right?" Kenneth asked.

"That's it."

"We understand you have a sick child."

Sadness showed on Findley's face as he bowed his head.

"Are you alright, Mr. Findley?" Laura asked.

Findley pointed to a place beneath a tree with a grave beneath and a handmade cross. "My middle son, Tobe, died yesterday—buried him this morning."

"I'm so sorry, sir," Kenneth said.

"That ain't the worst of it. My daughters Rose, and Lena, my youngest son Luke, and my wife Eileen is now sick with a fever."

Laura moved to dismount.

"Don't," Kenneth said. "You can't help them, and you could become infected."

"We need to help."

264

"Doc Simms is better prepared to help."

"I don't want anyone else to catch this," Morgan Findley said. "What about the others in the wagons?"

"One girl is sick," Laura replied.

"Oh, dear Lord. If I had known, I would never have asked them to stop and share our camp."

"No one is blaming you, Mr. Findley," Kenneth said. "There is a doctor in their camp now. He asked us to return and tell him if we found you. Maybe he can help. Our pastor is at the camp praying for the sick, too. We will let them all know where you are, and I expect you'll see the doctor in a short while."

"No, tell him not to come."

"Mr. Findley, Doc Simms will do his best to treat your family."

"Or Dr. Bunney," Laura said. "I'll try to get the other doctor to come out."

Kenneth reined his horse around, and they rode away.

"Why did you bring Olivia into this?"

"Because she's a doctor, Kenneth, and a good one."

"I don't want her around this."

"Kenneth, I told you that typhoid is not in the air. Olivia said it happens because of bad food or water. Doc Simms cannot take care of both camps."

"If you're sure, then ride to get her. I'll take this information to Doc Simms."

Before they made it to the first camp, they spotted two riders coming on the west road.

Laura pulled against Copper's reins. "That's Olivia."

Kenneth halted his horse. "Share with them what's happening, Laura. I'll ride on to the other camp and tell Simms."

"Where's he going?" Ellison asked when Laura reached them.

"To the first camp. Olivia, there's another camp behind me that needs you. They lost their boy yesterday but have several others sick. Sheriff, I don't know about you, but maybe you should ride and ask Doc Simms if he needs supplies. There was one sick in that camp when we left them earlier, but who knows how many more this will find?"

"I'm concerned those in town will hear."

"Why are you concerned about it?"

"Townsfolk can sometimes become paranoid when it comes to disease. I don't need them stirred up and taking matters into their own hands."

"Let's pray that doesn't happen."

"I'll find the other camp." Ellison rode away.

"Follow me, Olivia."

When Laura and Olivia rode into the camp, they spotted Findley climbing from the wagon. He ran to them when he saw them.

"How are they?" Laura asked.

"Fever is bad, Miss."

"Call me Laura. This is Olivia Bunney. She's a doctor."

"Yes, we've met."

"How is your boy?"

"We lost him, Doctor."

"Oh, no. I'm sorry. Maybe we can head off this thing."

"Come with me. They are in the wagon except for Oren and me. We haven't taken sick yet."

"Maybe you won't if we can change your food and water."

Findley stopped walking. "Food and water?"

"Yes, typhoid shows up with unsuitable food or water. I gave you something for the pain and told you to boil the water. Boiling the water removes bacteria. You'll see the same results if you keep drinking from the same water."

"I'm sorry. I never heard this, and I suppose you, being a woman, I figured you were wrong."

"Mr. Findley, Olivia studied in Boston for years," Laura said. "She knows more than most country doctors."

"I'm sorry. I know you're right. I suppose then it's my fault Tobe died."

"No, it's the fault of typhoid," Olivia said. "But you best learn to prepare your food and water, or you may never make it to Oregon."

"Yes, we will."

"Mr. Findley, let's see your family now."

They reached the wagon, and Mr. Findley fumbled for Olivia's hand. "Let me help you up, ma'am."

"Yes, please."

He held her hand until Olivia gripped the wagon and climbed inside. Findley walked to the rear and climbed up so he could peek inside.

Olivia kneeled to the floor beside Findley's wife, Eileen, and felt her forehead. "Her fever is too high. We must get it down."

She moved to the children, touching their foreheads and stopping at the last one. "This child may be the worst."

"That's my youngest, Luke."

"I'll administer some medicine for the fever for each one."

"Will that heal them, Doctor?"

"No, it will only help with the pain." She reached inside her satchel and pulled out a paper sack. "We need to heat some water to make tea."

"What is that you have?"

"Red cedar leaves. The idea came from the Indians. We discovered this treatment during a research trial that was part of my training, but I've never used it. Cedar leaf tea is helpful for many things, but we saw a reduction in fever during our trials."

"I'll heat some water."

The sound of horse hooves filtered into their ears. Laura

looked at Olivia from the front of the wagon. "That must be Kenneth." But turning, she saw a man in a buggy. He stopped when he saw Morgan Findley. "Oh, no."

"What is it?" Olivia asked.

"I believe his name is Shep Forrest, a rancher."

"And what's the problem?"

"Sheriff Ellison wanted to keep this from the townspeople, fearing they may start something."

"Start something, like what?"

"Anything, but I'm afraid it might be too late. The look on Shep Forrest's face tells me Findley told him."

"What can you do about it?"

"Can't take it back, but I can ride and tell the sheriff so he can watch out if they want to try something."

"The camps are so far out of town, and there's no way these folks can cause them harm. And besides, they would have to drink the same water or eat the same food."

"But people do strange things in this town. So I better find the sheriff."

Laura reached the turn toward the other camp and saw the dust left by Shep Forrest's buggy. *Too late.*

The sheriff stood beside his horse, speaking with Kenneth and Pastor West as she rode hard into the camp.

"Did someone else die?" Ellison asked.

Pastor West ran to her. "Laura, are you okay?"

"I'm fine, but we may have a problem."

"Seems that's all we have," Ellison said.

"What you feared may come our way."

"Explain yourself."

"Olivia was treating patients when Shep Forrest came by in a buggy."

Ellison shook his head. "Oh no. Shep's the worst gossiper."

"I don't know what Mr. Findley told him, but I saw the

look on his face, and it wasn't happy."

"The entire town will know before the hour. I better ride back and see if I can head this off."

"I'll ride with you, Sheriff," Pastor West said.

They mounted and left the camp.

Chapter 47

When Sheriff Ellison and Pastor West reached Santa Fe, people were in the street gathered together as Shep Forrest spoke to them from the porch at the mercantile.

"Oh, this can't be good," said Pastor West.

Sheriff Ellison pushed his horse until he reached the crowd.

Someone cried, "We got to run them out, or we'll all be sick with it!"

"Listen to me, folks!" Ellison roared as he dismounted. "No one is getting near those camps. You hear me."

"Now you listen, Sheriff," uttered attorney Weldon Baily. "You don't own us and have no right, according to the law, to stop the people from protesting."

"Yeah, that's right," touted Burney Cutts. "We've not hurt anyone."

"Maybe not," Sheriff Ellison replied. "Just remember, those camps are off-limits."

"You can't stop us from going there," said Gus Hewett. "That land is government owned. We have as much right to visit as those pioneers."

Ellison pushed his way through the crowd to the porch and stepped atop. "Now, hear me. I just rode from the camps and have spoken to one of the doctors. She says typhoid comes from food and water and won't spread unless you drink bad water or eat contaminated food."

The words typhoid sent fear into their hearts, and the men roared back at the sheriff.

Ellison raised a hand. "Hold it down, men. This is not as bad as you think."

Gordon Andrews stepped away from the mercantile doorway. "Yeah, we hear you, Sheriff, but reporting what that new female doctor says is worthless. We need to hear that from Doc Simms. We know little about this Doctor Bunney."

"She's good enough," said Eleanora Queen, the owner of the Queen Hotel and Restaurant in Santa Fe.

The people laughed at the comment.

"What are you laughing at? You'd rather trust a man best suited to be a horse doctor than a proper physician who has the latest techniques and medicines at her disposal. So go ahead with your old ways. But I'll trust Doctor Bunney."

"We don't need no woman doctor in this town," someone called out.

"Yeah, it just ain't right," said another.

Pastor West spoke up. "Hey folks, I'm no doctor, but you all know me. I would never lie to you. Even Doc Simms has the camps boiling water to purify it."

"That doesn't mean it won't spread to our town. I saw it in the war," said Irvin Speers.

"That's right," some shouted.

Several men turned toward their horses.

"Now wait a minute, you men," Sheriff Ellison said. "It may not be lawful, but if necessary, I'll jail every last one of you who goes near those camps. Don't you get it? The camps are where you *can* catch this, but you are safe in town. Are you hearing me?"

Some folks nodded and began filtering to their homes.

Sheriff Ellison's brother, Deputy Elijah, ran across the street. "How will you keep 'em from riding out there? They got a mind of their own."

"I have three deputies, Elijah, but that's not all we must watch for. The camps may come for supplies, and that can't happen either. I want you to set up a watch at the end of town. Find a place to perch, and keep your eyes peeled. If anyone rides out who doesn't live that way, call 'em back. If they don't stop, come get me. And if you see those pioneers heading in for supplies, you stop them."

"Sheriff, folks in this town may shoot if I try to stop 'em."

"So, you better be on your toes because I'm heading back to the camps."

Pastor West stepped up beside him. "I'll get my sidearm. We may need them."

A scream sounded from near the end of the street.

"Jimmy Baker's boy has a fever!" someone shouted. "Where's the doc?"

"That's it, folks. We have to do something!" shouted Weldon Bailey.

The men in the streets headed for their horses.

Sheriff Ellison turned to Pastor West. "Forget the gun, Pastor. Ride and prepare those camps for what's coming."

* * *

Sitting in his buggy, Doc Simms saw Pastor West riding in fast. West spotted Kenneth and reined his horse toward him.

When Simms realized something was wrong, he climbed down and walked their way as Pastor West gave the update.

"The town roused over Jimmy Baker's son having a fever, believing his is the same as these folks," Pastor West said.

"Several men from town are on their way here. Sheriff Ellison worries they will try something crazy."

"Surely, they won't," Kenneth said.

"They seemed very riled to me, and I think some were drinking."

Pastor West turned to Doc Simms. "Doc, is this thing contagious? Could Baker's son have gotten it from these folks?"

"I don't see how, but until I examine him, I can't know for sure."

"Does it spread through the air?"

"What I saw in the army was from bad food, though bad water can cause it too. Unless the Bakers have been around these folks, I'm doubtful it's the same problem."

"Needless to say, we have trouble on our hands. There's no telling what these rowdy men have in mind."

"Pastor, here they come," Kenneth said.

Seven riders and one buckboard drew near and slowed. Barney Cutts sat on the buckboard, holding a rifle. Riding horses were Cooper Tillman and Reeves Fincher, Verner Givens, attorney Weldon Bailey, Morton Ackerman, Gus Hewett, and ranchers Shep Forrest and Irvin Speers.

"What's going on, Weldon?" Kenneth asked.

"We're here to run these folks away from our town."

"I can't let you do it."

"Kenneth, I've always been your friend, but you need to step out of our way right now."

"Can't do it."

"Why don't you allow these folks to heal?" Pastor West asked. "They will move on soon enough."

"We've already got one sick in town," said Gus Hewett. "They need to go before things get worse."

"Alright, alright, listen to me," said Doc Simms. "You don't know what you're talking about. The Baker boy could not have gotten sick from these folks."

"We heard that one of them went to the mercantile. How do you know he didn't spread it to us?" asked Shep Forrest.

"Because it doesn't work that way. Typhoid is not an airborne disease. It comes from bad food or water."

Morton Ackerman pushed forward toward Doc Simms. "We best not take a chance, men. Light up your torches and burn 'em out."

"Yeah," cried Shep Forrest as he lit a match and put it to a torch.

Kenneth jerked his sidearm and shot the fire from the torch, and the band aimed their sharp looks his way.

Irvin Speers cocked his Winchester, pointing it at Kenneth. "Get out of our way, Barlow. We can't have folks coming through Santa Fe leaving behind their diseases."

A horse trotted up behind them.

"Put down the guns, people!" Sheriff Ellison said, pulling his weapon. "It's time you men head back to town. This assembly is over."

The sheriff's voice surprised Irvin Speers. "Now, Sheriff, you best leave this all to us and return to your duty in town."

"This is my duty, Irvin."

Irvin sat unmoving for a brief moment. His gun stayed on Kenneth.

"Put it down, Irvin," Weldon Bailey uttered. "Let's get on to town."

Irvin eased his weapon downward and released the hammer. "Sheriff, if more of our people come down with a fever, we'll return and finish the job." He shoved the rifle into its scabbard, turned his horse, and followed the others away from the camp.

The sound of more horses caught Kenneth and Pastor West's attention when Laura and Olivia rode in.

"Was that our men from town?" Laura asked.

Doc Simms turned to Olivia. "Bunney, how are they at that other camp?"

"Already lost one. There's several sick."

"I suppose I need to visit them while I'm here."

"I've already treated them as best I can. Mr. Findley was boiling more water as I left. Laura promised to bring them some fresh food. So, only time will tell if they pull through."

Sheriff Ellison dismounted. "Seeing that Doctor Bunney has visited the other camp, would you head back and check on the Baker boy?"

"I suppose you are right, Sheriff. My guess is this is some form of influenza."

"Do you need our help?" asked Pastor West.

"You folks just need to watch over these here. Those men in town might change their mind."

"Kenneth, I could use you and Pastor West in town."

"But Doc thought we should stay here," Kenneth replied.

Sheriff Ellison shook his head. "No. The job I have for you is more urgent."

"And dangerous, I suppose?" Kenneth reached for his reins.

"Might be."

"Are you gonna let us in on it?" Pastor West asked, staring at them.

"Yes, on the way back to Santa Fe." The sheriff spurred his horse toward town, and the others rode beside him.

Chapter 48

S heriff Ellison had decided to stand on his word and jail the men who rode to the camps. He handed Kenneth a shotgun.

"A Greener?"

"I'm hoping the sight of it will change some minds when they tell me they ain't coming."

"Pastor, are you sure you want to go with us? The men may hold it against you and never come to your church."

"What kind of church do I have if the townspeople can take the law into its hands and burn people out?"

"Alright then. Put these badges on. I'm deputizing you both."

"Brass jewelry. I never had any," Kenneth said, smiling.

"Let's go."

Pastor West, Kenneth, and the sheriff's two deputies, Elijah Ellison and Yancy Bean, marched toward the saloon.

Sheriff Ellison peered over the swinging doors as the other men waited behind him. Then he pushed through the double-hinged passageway, adjusted his eyes to the low interior lighting, and searched the room.

Four deputies followed him and spread wide next to him.

"I told you men what would happen if you visited that camp. Cooper, Reeves, Weldon Bailey, Verner. Gus, you knew better than this. So do you, Weldon."

"We have our town to think of," Weldon replied.

"Morton, Shep, and you others toss back the last of those drinks and come with us. Where's Irvin?"

The bartender peered at Sheriff Ellison. "I ain't seen him, Sheriff."

"I'll find him in a bit, Sheriff," Kenneth said.

"Sheriff, you have no legal right to lock us up," Weldon said. "I demand you leave us alone, or I may see that *you're* arrested for false imprisonment."

"Weldon, there were plenty of witnesses that you men rode to that camp intending to harm men, women, and children. That's all I need."

Weldon raised his drink and swallowed as he mulled his options. "Men, we better do as the sheriff says, or he may shoot us."

They walked the men toward the jail as townsfolk gathered, hovering around them.

"Back up, everyone. Nothing here to see," Sheriff Ellison said.

"What'd they do, Sheriff?" asked Gordon Andrews.

"Do I have to explain?"

"Yes, you do, since they were minding their business drinking at the saloon."

"I'm arresting them for disturbing the peace and stirring up contention."

"That's not right, Ellison, and you know it."

"What's not right is burning out innocent folks."

"Those people are diseased."

"You know nothing about it, Gordon."

Laura had ridden in and stood nearby, listening as the crowd shouted their disagreements. *I must write a story to clarify.*

She turned and started for the newspaper office when Pastor West called out. "Laura, hold up."

She knew his voice and turned, smiling. "Hello, Steven."

"Will you have lunch with me? They don't need me now."

"I thought I'd write a story regarding this, but I suppose I can have lunch first."

"Great."

***

Gloria stood watching out the window when they arrived. "Hello, Pastor. What is going on across the street?"

"The sheriff arrested those men who went to the camps to cause trouble. I figure he'll hold them until the camp folks get well and move on."

Gloria stood, staring out the window.

"Don't worry, Gloria, typhoid is not contagious," Laura said.

"That's good."

Steven and Laura sat down.

"Gloria, what's the special today?" asked Pastor West.

"We have mashed potatoes and meatloaf with cornbread."

"That sounds delicious. I'll have it and sweet tea."

"Me too," Laura said.

"Alright, I'll be right out with it."

"I suppose any talk of disease scares people," Laura said.

"You can't blame them. These folks have families to think of."

"Those men don't have to act like idiots, though."

Pastor West laughed. "We all act like idiots when we fear something."

Laura chuckled. "I suppose you're right, and I would find myself the same way if something happened to Kenneth."

"Laura, you worry too much about him. Kenneth can take care of himself."

"Did you know it's been less than a year since I learned about him? Seems longer."

"That's something to think about. Um, you mentioned you were on the way to the newspaper office. So, what story are you working on?"

"Well, I wondered if I gave the people some information about typhoid that might lessen the concern. What do you think?"

"I suppose it can't hurt. But, of course, people will make up their own minds about such things. And if they are as hardheaded as I think, some will believe it, others won't."

"I figured as much, but I must try before someone gets hurt."

"What does Olivia say about typhoid? Didn't you see her at the other camp?"

"Yes, she believes the same as Doc Simms, which is surprising, though she thinks he will administer a different treatment besides boiling the water."

"Oh?"

"She's afraid he'll use quinine, which she said is poison if given too large a dose. But she hopes that offering fresh water will help against the disease."

"Yes, maybe so."

"I'm glad you stopped me on the street."

"I am too, and I always enjoy visiting with you, Laura."

"Yes, but I meant I should wait to write the story until I've spoken with Doc Simms."

"I see. But you have Olivia's views already, so why do you need to speak with him?"

"Because this town is far from trusting her. So, if I can

convince Doc Simms to give me a quote, I think that should calm the situation."

"That sounds like an excellent idea."

Other patrons entered the restaurant as Gloria brought their food. "Here you go. I'll bring more tea when you need it."

"Thank you, Gloria," Pastor West commented.

Laura peered at it. "This looks wonderful."

"Please enjoy." Gloria turned and walked to another table.

They ate their food while discussing the newcomers outside of town. Pastor West wondered if they would struggle to reach Oregon. "I don't think they have enough food or clothing, and I'm not sure they understand what lies ahead in those mountains."

"Is there anyone here who has been to Oregon?" Laura asked.

"Ota Moury and his wife Betsy have. Ota once told me they didn't like it there. Said the people were stuffy."

"Everyone has their opinion, I suppose. Another may love it there."

"I know you're right, but Ota also said those mountains almost killed them. If it wasn't for a warm-up along the trail, he said they would have frozen."

"Oh my. Maybe we should speak with them."

"I can do that. You should write your story. You said the people of Santa Fe needed someone to educate them about the disease. Maybe once you do, they won't be so prone to hurt outsiders."

"Do you know where Ota and Betsy live?"

"I don't, but Doc Simms can tell us. Betsy has had several babies, so the Doc should know. I'll walk with you to find him."

"Alright, as soon as we finish eating."

Chapter 49

*D*oc Simms was not in his office when Laura and Pastor West arrived.

"I'll wait and watch from the newspaper office," Laura said as they strolled toward the Santa Fe Journal.

"I should find Ota and Betsy's place," Pastor West said.

"Sure. Maybe Doc Simms will be here soon."

Orland Flack stood behind Laura as she watched Pastor West walk away. "You should marry that man."

"Maybe I should. But *you* have an ulterior motive for suggesting it, don't you?"

"What do you mean?"

"You believe if I marry Steven, I'll live in town, and that would give me easier access to the Journal."

"The thought has crossed my mind, but lay that aside for a moment. You two are perfect for each other. Oh, I know you're a career woman. But you can't deny that the older you get, the harder it is to start a family."

Family? She had thought little about having a family. Was she missing out on this experience, she wondered? She loved

281

the children from church and had seen how their parents cared for them.

Her plans had never involved family life. She had wanted to be a journalist since she first entered Boston College. She thought something was extraordinary about a woman who dove into everyday stories and delivered what others could not. Or was that prideful? What did God think about a career woman? Was there no proper way to include a career in marriage?

"West is a wonderful man, Mr. Flack, but he must find a means to accept what I love to do. Or at least offer a compromise. That's all I've ever asked."

"Well, he's crazy if he doesn't. I hear it all over town, mostly the men, saying Laura is a real find."

"Aw, thank you."

"Now, *I* didn't say that. That's what I hear."

Laura smiled as she watched the sheriff's office. "Looks like Steven, I mean Pastor West, has directions to the Mourys'."

"Oh, it's not too far. Just past your place, I think."

"I wish I'd known that."

"What's he going there for, anyway?"

"Pastor thinks the people in the wagons will have difficulty on their trip to Oregon. He doesn't believe they've prepared well for their journey."

"He may be right. I read stories all the time about folks dying along that trail. Those folks never bring enough food for the winters they face. What a shame."

Laura peered out again and saw Kenneth. "I thought he would have ridden to the ranch by now."

"Who?"

"Kenneth."

Orland walked to the doorway and looked out. "And there's the sheriff and Elijah. Hmm. Something must be wrong."

"I thought things would settle since they locked those men in jail," Laura said.

"Maybe something else *is* happening. Laura, you might want to see if there's another story."

"I'd like to know what Kenneth is up to. He put a shotgun and a box of shells on his horse. I'll see you later."

Laura pulled her dress high and hurried across the street and to the sheriff's office.

Kenneth spotted her as he peered over the saddle. "Sis, we've got trouble."

"Trouble?"

"There were others in the saloon when we arrested those men. We heard they are gathering weapons and plan to finish what the first bunch didn't."

"You don't mean the settlers?"

"Yes."

"Does Steven know?"

"This happened after he left."

"Do you have enough men?"

"Only the four. Yancy, Elijah, the sheriff, and myself." He pointed to the horses hitched in front.

"Who is watching the prisoners?"

"No one."

Sheriff Ellison spotted Laura talking to Kenneth. "Hey, lady, could you help us?"

"What do you need, Sheriff?"

"Follow me." As Laura trailed behind him, he turned and walked through the office door.

"I'm asking that you watch over the jail while we're gone because I know you can shoot a gun."

"Sure, I can do that."

Ellison reached and unlocked a cabinet and pulled out

another Greener shotgun and a box of shells. "Keep this handy and loaded. Some men may come and try to take the prisoners, but I can't be here. It may take all of us to get ahead of this."

"I can watch."

"Laura, it's the whiskey that has them stirred. Do not trust them."

"I'll keep that gun in my hands. Those prisoners will be fine with me. You go and watch over the newcomers."

Ellison nodded. "Thank you." He walked outside and mounted his horse. "Men, watch yourselves. We don't know what we're going up against."

"I'm hoping they're too drunk to ride," Elijah said.

"Don't count on it."

Ellison turned his horse and spurred it, and it started walking. Laura watched as they pulled away, with Kenneth trailing behind.

"Kenneth, be safe, brother."

He tipped his hat at her. "You too."

Laura closed her eyes. "Lord, keep our friends and Kenneth safe from this unruly bunch. And watch over our visitors. These folks only want to travel to Oregon."

As she sat on the front porch, watching folks walking about the town, her mind slipped to a time as a child when she had come to town with her father. Everything seemed normal until two men burst from the saloon, fistfighting. The whiskey had caused two who were friends to fight against each other. Both came away bruised and injured.

Laura peered down the street at the saloon and noticed three men standing on the porch, looking her way. *What do they want?*

Moments later, they started walking toward her. One giggled. They were no doubt drunk, which was bad for them and her.

She did not know them, but their hats and sidearms told her they were ranch hands from nearby.

"Where's the sheriff?" asked one man, who bore an unshaven beard and a patch over one eye.

"The sheriff is busy. What do you want?" Laura replied.

"Well, if Ellison ain't around, then you can let our friends go."

"Go on, mister. You're drunk."

"Nah, you're wrong. I've not drunk anything." He laughed, and the other two joined him. "Missy, you need to let them go now, or we'll shoot you." He giggled.

"If I let them go, the sheriff will shoot me."

His friend on his right hand nodded. "Yeah but, yeah, but—"

"Yeah, but what, Sparks?" said the first man.

"Well, I don't think I can remember."

They laughed in unison.

A horse rode in behind them and stopped at the hitching rail. Pastor West dismounted and rushed to the porch. "Fellows, what's up?"

The man with the patch said, "Hey, you're that pastor." He pointed at West.

"Yeah, that's me," Pastor West said, turning toward Laura and whispering, "Is there another open cell?"

"I'll check." She rose from the chair and walked inside.

"Hey, where's Missy going?" the man asked. "I'd rather talk to her."

"She's checking on the prisoners."

"Yeah, the prisoners. We want you to release them."

Laura returned and whispered to him.

"Well, Mister," Pastor West said, "I think we can all go together and check on them."

"Hey, Sparks, that's a good idea. They gonna let us check on the prisoners."

"Okay."

"Follow me, men," West said.

Laura led the way, grabbing the keys from the wall to unlock a cell.

Pastor West followed behind her and then turned toward the prisoners sitting in two cells on one side of the hallway. "Okay, men, here they are."

As the three drunks turned to see them, Pastor West reached from behind and took their guns, handing them to Laura. Then he shoved each one into a cell on the opposite side, closing the door. "Now, you keep an eye on the prisoners for us, okay?"

The man with the patch over his eye said, "Sure. We won't let nothing happen to them, Sheriff." He smiled, peering through the bars to the prisoners across the aisle. "Hello, fellows."

"West, who are these men, and what do they want?" asked Weldon Bailey.

"We thought they were your friends."

"Ain't no friends of mine."

"But they came to break you out."

"Of all the good it did. Where's Sheriff Ellison?"

"The sheriff ain't here right now. You got Laura and me."

"Hmph, that ain't no help."

"Just sit tight, Weldon. This will all be over in a few days."

"Oh no, it won't. Procedures will just begin against all of you who put us here under false imprisonment."

"False? Who rode to the pioneers' camp intending to burn them out? Who was that claimed what they had was spreading all over town?"

"And when it does, Pastor West, you'll eat crow like the rest of you no-goods."

"Weldon, don't you know God is against outright murder?"

286

"We were only trying to stop the spread."

"By killing those folks? Doesn't sound like you've learned anything. Maybe a few more weeks inside will help."

"Shut up, Weldon," said Verner Givens. "I'm in this mess because I listened to you."

"Now, there's one man with ears to hear," Pastor West said, walking toward the exit. "You should listen to Verner."

Laura laid the shotgun on the desk. "I never imagined so many would cause trouble in this town."

"That's what happens when men drink."

"And I'm thankful my friends stay clear of it."

"I am too. But now, will you explain to me why you are the one watching over the jail?"

"There's another bunch planning to run the pioneers from their camp. So the sheriff and his deputies, along with Kenneth, rode to stop it."

"If only these men would control their drink."

"And you've preached so many times how sin is the real culprit. You'd think some would understand."

"I know, but the drink blinds good men."

Laura nodded, agreeing with him. "Steven, do you mind watching over the jail until the sheriff returns? I still have to find Doc Simms and write my story."

"Sure. I believe I saw Doc Simms' buggy in front of his office."

"Thank you. I'll see you later."

Chapter 50

K enneth, Sheriff Ellison, and his deputies arrived at the first pioneer camp minutes before the riders appeared.

"Do you know any of these boys, Sheriff?" Kenneth asked.

"I don't know their names, but they work at nearby ranches."

"You gonna try to talk to them?"

"I'll try, but Kenneth, watch my back. Anything is possible with them juiced up on whiskey."

"You got it."

Five riders stopped at the road's edge when they saw the sheriff. As they considered their plan, the man in charge gestured with his hand as if giving orders.

"Hey there," called out Sheriff Ellison. "You riders get on back to town."

"This ain't none of your business, Sheriff," said the one in charge.

"What business is it of yours?"

"That don't matter. We got a job to do."

"You may lose your job at those ranches when I arrest

you."

A large vein on the side of the man's head throbbed. "I told you, Sheriff, that this was none of your business!"

"Well, I'd like to know why you're here. These folks have done nothing to you."

"Well, some of your townsfolk don't like them around and offered us money to get rid of them."

"Who paid you? Can you tell me that?"

"Sorry Sheriff, can't cut off the hand that feeds. Now, are you going to move out of the way, or do we have to make you move?"

"Nope, but I'll take those guns. Lay 'em on the ground and come down from there, and no one will get hurt."

The riders with him laughed.

Behind the Sheriff, Paul Albrecht and his son David, Amos Miller, Abner Bawell, Isaac Brandenberger, and his son Jacob eased closer, brandishing shotguns and rifles.

The leader of the riders pulled his sidearm first and fired, missing the sheriff. His friends followed suit, pulling out their handguns and firing erratically.

Kenneth and Elijah backed behind pine trees. Yancy Bean dove to the ground behind a small hill. They each returned fire at the riders.

During the first assault, a bullet grazed Sheriff Ellison, and he ran for cover behind a large oak.

Two riders fell from their horses. One held a shoulder wound, the other a leg injury as they scurried for cover.

Elijah aimed and fired at another rider, and he fell from his horse dead.

The two remaining riders drilled bullets at Kenneth and Sheriff Ellison.

The pioneers had crouched behind a wagon but had fired no rounds.

The leader of the riders let a bullet loose, catching

Kenneth in the chest and knocking him to the ground. He rolled and aimed for the man striking him in the head, and he fell to the ground, where he died.

The last rider raised his hands high. "I surrender."

"Toss that weapon," Sheriff Ellison said.

He dropped the handgun to the ground as Elijah ran to him and tied his hands to the saddle.

Sheriff Ellison hurried to Kenneth, who lay holding his chest. "Kenneth, where'd he hit you?"

Kenneth moved his hands. "Don't know how that missed your heart, but it may have hit a lung. Do you think you can ride?"

"Maybe," Kenneth said, gasping for air.

"Elijah, take Kenneth on to Doc Simms. Yancy and I will take the bodies back."

Elijah found the horse, and with Sheriff Ellison's help, Kenneth mounted it. He then straddled his horse, took the reins for Kenneth's black, and started for town.

✳ ✳ ✳

Laura sat writing her story when Benson Rupel, a young man who delivered the papers, ran through the door. "Miss Stone, come quickly. They said for you to come."

She rose from the chair and walked toward Benson. "Who asked for me?"

"Elijah Ellison, ma'am. He said you should come to Doc Simm's office at once."

Uneasiness settled on Laura's face as she stepped out the door. She knew something must have happened when the men rode to help the newcomers, but what could it be?

Laura walked into Simms' office and heard voices in the back room. "Doc, are you in there?"

"Laura, is that you?"

"Yes."

"Come in here."

As she entered the examination room, she knew it was Kenneth lying on the table. The doctor and Elijah Ellison stood over him.

Elijah backed away when he heard her come in, exposing her brother as Doc Simms worked.

Frustrated, Doc Simms tossed a scalpel into a metal dish, causing it to sing. "I can't get the bullet out. Elijah, find Olivia Bunney."

"The woman doctor?"

"Yes, Elijah. She has experience with this type of surgery."

Elijah ran out the door as Doc Simms turned to Laura. "I'm sorry, Laura. The bullet went through the lung and lodged into the inner spinal cavity. I've no experience removing bullets like this, though I've read that it's possible."

"Thank you for trying."

Pastor West had heard about the shooting and hurried through the door. "Laura, are you alright? I'm so sorry." He pulled her close and hugged her.

Laura wept on his shoulder.

Pastor West peered down at Kenneth. "Is he dead?"

"No," Doc Simms replied. "I gave him something to knock him out so we can remove the bullet. I'm waiting for Doctor Bunney to assist."

Moments later, Olivia walked in. "How can I help?"

"Doctor, this bullet is mighty deep," Doc Simms said. "I've not the experience to remove it."

"Allow me to look." Olivia peered down into the open wound. "Okay, do you have more clothing and gloves?"

"Sure, right behind you."

"Will he be alright, Olivia?" Laura asked.

Laura peered at Doc Simms. "The doctor and I will do everything we can for Kenneth."

"Laura, why don't you and I go into the other room and give them more space to work?" Pastor West asked.

"Yes, I can't watch."

* * *

Olivia took a closer look at the wound and realized the depth of the bullet. "Doctor Simms, we must open the wound wider to reach the spine from this side."

An hour later, Olivia walked through the door to the waiting section. "Kenneth is sleeping, and we believe he'll be fine. The bullet lodged in his spine, and we retrieved it after some strenuous work. He also had a large tear where the bullet passed through a lung. We drained the fluid and sewed it up."

"Thank God," Laura said. "I was so worried. To lose Kenneth now after only recently finding out he was my brother would be tragic."

"He'll pull through, Laura, but he will need lots of care, which is why I'm subscribing my place for him to stay."

"Kenneth is not good at following doctor's orders. But maybe you can keep him off that horse long enough to heal."

"Now look who is talking about those who won't follow the doctor's orders. You were the worst I've seen."

Laura chuckled. "I know. So, I suppose it's up to me to watch over the ranch until he's well."

"You don't have to take that on alone," Pastor West said. "I will help you."

"Thank you. What would I do without my friends?"

"You know we can be more than friends, Laura."

"Yes, you keep tempting me. Maybe one of these days, life will align so we can." She stared into his eyes, and he knew what she meant.

"You are right. Maybe one day it will."

"So, has anyone checked on the wagon train?" Olivia asked.

"Sheriff Ellison did," Pastor West replied. "After caring for those prisoners and the dead, he returned to the camps. Those folks were packing to leave. Said they were well enough to move on and thought they had caused enough trouble."

"As long as they do what I've prescribed, they should be fine," Olivia said.

"I'll pray they find what they are looking for," Laura said.

"We should all pray that prayer," replied Pastor West.

Laura smiled, wondering if he had directed the statement at her.

MICHAEL J SPANHANKS

My French Bride

Chapter 51

*L*aura sat to write a small story for the Santa Fe Journal, turned it in, then strolled to the telegraph office inside the mercantile.

"How can I help you, Miss Stone?" Jerry Compton asked.

"Do you have a piece of paper? I'm sorry, I should have prepared better."

"Happens all the time." Jerry reached beneath the counter, gathered a thin manila sheet, and slid it to her. "Here you go."

Laura fetched the pencil from the counter. "I'll just borrow this for a moment."

"Sure."

She scribbled several words and handed the paper back to Jerry. "I think that will do it."

Jerry took hold and read it. "A book? I knew you wrote for the Journal but didn't know you were an author. My, my, my."

Laura tilted her head a bit and shrugged. "I don't consider myself an author yet."

"But maybe it will work out for you. Okay, let's see." Jerry tapped the transmitter keys a letter at a time until her message went through. "That should do it. I'll bring your response when it arrives."

"Okay, thank you." Laura paid him and left.

A short distance from the telegraph office, some men talked and laughed. *I wonder what this is about.* As she drew closer, she could hear them plainly.

"You're too old for a bride, Harley," said Samuel Spence.

"Now, I don't care what you say. She's ordered, and I have proof."

"You're making it all up," Calvin Cook declared.

Harley Richards shook his head. "Now, why would I make it up?"

"Maybe because you're too ugly for a wife," Lester Farley chuckled.

"Maybe you should look this here writ over," Harley said. He shook the paper high in front of Lester's face.

"Let me see that." Lester read the heading: *Match-Making Service, New York City, New York.* "Looky here, Calvin, Match-Making Service, it says."

Calvin Cook had no comeback. He took the paper, read the words, and returned it to Harley. "When? When is she coming, Harley?"

"In a few days."

"I'm glad for you," Lester said.

Calvin put his hand on Harley's chest. "You got to clean up. You got to make yourself decent."

"I do?"

Laura wondered if Harley's romance would make a good story. "Calvin's right, Harley."

The three turned, shocked that Laura had overheard them.

"Miss Stone, this is sort of private," Harley said.

"But he's right, Harley. If you have someone arriving soon who is a potential candidate for marriage, you must prepare yourself. I'll help you if you'd like." What better way to grab a story than to get involved, she thought.

Harley smiled, pulled off his hat, and held it close before him. "You'd help me?"

"Sure, I will. Calvin is right. You must clean up for a woman. You wouldn't want to disappoint her, would you?"

"No, I wouldn't."

"How long before she arrives?"

"Two days."

"Two days. That's good." Laura pondered if Harley even had money to buy a new suit of clothes.

Harley lost his smile and peered at the ground.

"What's wrong?"

"I ain't sure two days is enough to make me presentable."

"Harley, do you have money?"

"I have a little, but I paid three hundred dollars before they would send me a bride. Why you asking?"

"Because you need a new set of clothes and maybe some new shoes."

"But that'll cost a lot."

"A fair amount, but your bride-to-be will love you because you've cleaned up and bought new clothes just for her."

"Harley, you better do it," Calvin said.

Lester nodded. "You got to. Miss Stone knows what a woman likes."

Harley turned to her with a huge grin. "Alright, what do I do?"

Laura nodded and grinned. "Good. We will go to Belcher Garments and find you something nice to wear."

"Belcher. I don't know I—"

"Do you have a proper suit, Harley?"

"Ma'am, you're seeing what I have and just one more set like it."

"Then we should get you some new clothes."

"Alright."

Laura placed her hand on his shoulders, and they walked away.

Calvin and Lester stood watching.

"Lester, what if Harley *does* find a wife?" Calvin asked.

"Then he'll be a lucky man."

"I wish I had me a wife."

"Oh, hush, Calvin. Ain't no woman in America would have you."

* * *

Laura stopped halfway to Belcher Garments.

Harley halted behind her. "Are we changing our minds?"

"I wondered, Harley, would you mind if I interviewed you?"

"You mean like for a story?"

"Yes. What do you think?"

"I don't mind a story."

Laura glanced around town, wondering if folks would make something out of her speaking with this man. *Too bad.* "That's great, Harley. How about we do this at the hotel restaurant?"

"The Queen? Ain't never been inside."

"Well, you can today, and it's my treat."

"Are you sure, Miss Stone?"

"Yes, I'm sure." She leaned and took Harley's arm, and they marched for the door.

Gloria spotted them and offered Laura a curious, wide-eyed look.

"We'll have a table, please. Harley is preparing for an adventure."

"Come this way."

Gloria took them to a table beside the front window. "How is this, ma'am?"

"Yes, thank you, Gloria. What do you have special today?" Laura asked.

"We have fried chicken, mashed potatoes, and gravy."

"That sounds great to me."

"Oh, and me too, ma'am," Harley said. "Only chicken I get is a wild one or pheasant I take from hunting."

"And bring us a couple of glasses of tea," Laura said.

Gloria nodded. "I won't be long with your drinks." She turned and hurried away.

"Now, Harley, where did you find out about this woman who is coming?" Laura asked.

"You see, I picked up a few things at the mercantile a while back. Old Gordon had my stuff in a box and wrapped it with newspapers. Those newspapers were out of date, but I don't have much around to read these days. So one night, I was eating some beans and looking at one of those old papers, and there was an ad telling about French Brides from New York. The ad said *Match-Making Service*. I thought, now that's a good way to get me a wife."

"So, did you telegraph them?"

"Oh, no. I saved my money to buy my Dollie."

"Dollie?"

"Dollie York is her name. I got a letter about two months ago telling me how things work. I mailed them three hundred dollars. Over a week ago, I got another letter saying she was leaving a few days later and I should expect her on the fourteenth. That's the day after tomorrow, right?"

"So we must hurry to get you ready. But tell me, what do you know about Dollie? Is she your age? Is Dollie pretty? Does she come from a good background?"

"She *is* pretty. I have a photo the Match-Making company sent with the first letter." He reached inside his vest, pulled out a crinkled paper of a black and white tin type, and raised it for her to see.

Laura wondered if Harley could tell anything from the tattered photo. "Oh, yes, nice."

"Don't you think she's pretty?"

Not wanting to hurt him, she chose her words with care. "From what I can tell, I'm sure she is. But what you think matters most, right?"

"Yes, that's right. And I know what I bought."

Laura hoped this was not a con. How easy it was for a company to prey on men who lacked companionship, offering to provide women for marriage. While living in Boston, she had heard horror stories about companies saying they needed long-term help, but workers soon realized the job was only for a week.

"What are your expectations of Dollie?" Laura asked.

"What does that mean?"

Maybe this was not the best direction, but surely Dollie wanted to know the character of the man she planned to marry. "Do you expect her to be a home keeper? A cook? Someone to keep your clothes clean?"

"Sure, all of those things."

"Harley, forgive me. I shouldn't ask these things."

"No, it's alright. Am I expecting too much?"

"Maybe you should remember that some women love to please their husbands and will do everything for them. But Dollie may be one of those women who would rather see balance in such things as house chores and cooking. And keep in mind that some women love to work, like me."

"I haven't thought of that."

Gloria arrived with their meals and set them down. "Can I get anything else for you?"

Laura shook her head. "I think we are fine."

"So, when do we start the interview?" Harley asked as the

waitress stepped away.

"Do you remember all the questions I asked?"

"Sure do?"

"That's an interview."

"Wow. I never knew that."

Chapter 52

L aura looked over the finances and realized she had never been so low on funds. The Boston job had provided well, but the Santa Fe Journal filled a mere portion in comparison. What was she to do?

Horace had left her with the ranch, but she knew little about it. She had thought giving Kenneth half was the answer and that he would soon make a go of it, but the cattle market had struggled, leaving the ranch somewhat surviving.

Kenneth talked her into adding horses because the army offered a fair price for those already broken, but they had only begun the undertaking. Time would tell if the horse market was even a viable investment.

In the West, many women suffered from a lack of paying jobs. Some yielded to saloon work. Others took their chances in the life of a soiled dove. Her mom, Naomi, warned her of this, insisting that she finish her schooling in Boston and avoid the way of life. She had followed her wishes. Traveling to Santa Fe after her father's death was unavoidable, though learning she had a brother made the journey worthwhile.

Kenneth? She should get back to the ranch.

A dog barked as Laura rode Copper up to the house. She dismounted and turned to see a black and brown dog standing behind her, growling.

"Wait a minute. I'm a friend."

"Hey, Jack. Settle down, boy. Don't worry about him, Laura." Kenneth called from the barn as he walked to the dog.

Jack calmed and stretched on the ground.

"You're safe now," Kenneth said.

Laura tied Copper to the fence. "When did you get a dog?"

"About a week ago. Jack's great with the cattle, which I need right now."

"I hope he doesn't bite anyone."

"He won't. But Jack has a lot of grit, and the cows know it."

She peered at the dog lying on the ground. "I guess."

"Did you come to help?"

"I can help. I'm sure you can use me since you're still healing from the gunshot. How are you getting on Ace and working cattle?

"You know me. I find a way when it's needed."

"Please be careful. Now, I must speak with you before we get to work."

"Sure. What about?"

Laura drew a deep breath and let it slowly escape. "Money."

"I knew this was coming." He turned and walked toward the ranch house door. "Let's have some coffee."

Laura watched the dog and followed close behind Kenneth.

Inside the large room, Kenneth stirred the fire on the potbelly stove and placed a coffee kettle on top. "So, am I spending too much money?"

"I don't know, are you?"

"I know I have little money for food these days."

"My job at the Journal is not paying much either. You should have told me, Kenneth. Are you getting your part of the cattle sale?"

"That wasn't much."

"I know."

Kenneth washed his hands in the water basin on the cabinet and grabbed a towel. "The price is still down on cattle."

"Well, that's what I wanted to talk to you about. You've added the horses, which could take several years to pan out. We are small compared to other ranches, and calves are slow coming."

"Laura, the only thing left is selling everything."

"I don't want to do that. But what do you think about raising sheep?"

"Sheep, in cattle country? Oh, you're talking trouble."

"How hard can it be?"

"I know nothing about sheep, not to mention how these other cattle ranchers will think about it."

"I don't care about them, only about us."

"Then you best figure out how to do it right."

"There are people who know. Maybe you can hire someone to help tend to the sheep."

"Oh Laura, don't do this."

"Listen to me, Kenneth, we must gain revenue with this ranch, or we will lose it. The ranch is all we have left of our father. I can't lose it."

A quiet moment settled in the room.

Persuading Kenneth to go against the norm for this territory and raise sheep could only materialize if he understood the value. "I've been studying sheep, and I know we can shear them once a year. There is almost always good money from selling their fleece."

"I'll think about it, but I've never sheared a sheep and don't know if I can."

"Yes, it will be a learning process, but I'll work with you. I'll send a few telegraphs to the east to gather more information. Before buying a herd, we'll need an outlet in place for selling the fleece. Once established, we'll find the sheep."

"Well, the ranch is half yours, and you are the smart one, but I'll warn you, we may have trouble with cattle folks if we bring in sheep."

"Why? This land belongs to us. We are not hurting any farm or ranch taking sheep on."

"They may not see it that way. I only know I've heard stories, and they all laugh about sheep farming."

"Kenneth, while they are laughing, we'll put money in the bank, and they will break even with cattle. We'll do this not for popularity but for profit."

"I'll go along with it. But we should determine how many sheep fit our land, and I don't want to give up the cattle and horses. Right now, we have forty-seven cows and some heavy with calves. We have six horses with two carrying colts."

"I'll figure out how many sheep we can handle. There is plenty of good land here, and we have planted new grass, so there must be a number that fits."

"I'm sure there is." Kenneth rose and poured coffee for them. "Someone told me about a man named Noble, and they thought he had sheep. Some men from town gave him a hard time once. I thought they had hurt him, but learned they were funning him. I'll ask about him at the mercantile. Gordon called him Noble and said he was a sheep farmer. I thought no more about him until now."

"Gordon may know where he lives."

"I'll take a ride and find out tomorrow."

"When you find him, you can let me know. And find out where he got his sheep."

"I will."

"The train is scheduled to arrive at eleven o'clock the day after tomorrow."

"What about the train?"

"You don't know? Harley Richard has ordered a bride."

"Harley bought a bride?"

"She is due to arrive on the train."

"I suppose you are writing a story about this."

"The entire town will gather for it. Harley worries that she won't like him, so I'm helping him prepare."

"Now, how are you going to do that?"

"I helped him buy a new suit. Then tomorrow, I'll make sure he gets a bath."

"Harley may need two baths."

Laura chuckled. "I know. Harley has a long way to go, but we don't know the bride-to-be. We can only hope she likes what she sees when she steps from the train, and he is the same."

"This might be the best entertainment Santa Fe has seen in years, and I can see a crowd gathering for it."

"Oh, Kenneth."

"What are you going to do when she arrives?"

"Depending on Harley's reaction, I'll welcome her and lead her to the hotel."

"The whole thing is interesting, and I gotta come to see."

"What about Olivia, Kenneth? How are things going between you two?"

"Great, I suppose. But I haven't seen Olivia in two weeks."

"Two weeks? Kenneth, a relationship won't last this way."

"I don't know what else to do. I'm busy on the ranch, and Olivia has so many patients now that she can't see them all."

"I see, but there has to be a way for you to see each other more often."

"If there is, I don't know it."

"Let me think about it. So, what do you have in mind today while I'm here?"

"Hey, I'm sorry staying here and writing stories didn't work out."

"I was just afraid Orval would fire me. When I'm here, I get caught up in the farm. In town, I find things to write about, though I know I should ride out and help more."

"I'm making it fine, but since you're here. The cattle have pulled down the grass in the north pasture. Can you help me move them?"

Laura raised from the chair. "Let's go."

They mounted their horses and rode to find the herd.

Chapter 53

S anta Fe was the busiest Kenneth had seen it in a long time as he rode in. *Surely, this is not all because of Harley Richards.*

He dismounted at the sheriff's office, tying his horse to the rail, and peered across the road, where Harley's friends had gathered outside the saloon. He shook his head as he entered the sheriff's office.

"I see the circus even brought you to town," commented Sheriff Ellison.

"Yeah, I thought it would take a fire to bring in so many."

"All these people mean for me is more drinking and gambling and more bodies to toss in jail."

"But that's what you get paid for."

"Paid for? *Phew!* I don't get paid enough for this."

Kenneth laughed. "Say, have you seen Pastor West?"

"Yes, I just left the Queen, and he was there having coffee and waiting on Laura."

"And where is she?"

"Her and your friend Olivia are so-called tutoring Harley before his fiancée arrives."

"Fiancée? I didn't think he'd proposed yet."

"That's what I said, but folks around town say the letter's enough to make it so. I talked until I was blue in the face."

"I suppose I'll join Pastor, then."

"You're not going to leave me, are you?"

"Well, you seem a bit fussy today."

"Oh, don't leave me," Sheriff Ellison said, leaning back in his chair. "I only got Elijah here to fuss at."

"I heard that, Ellison," Elijah called from a jail cell.

Sheriff Ellison grinned and pointed to the back. "Taking a nap. Said he stayed away from thinking about mail-order brides."

Kenneth laughed. "Yeah, it seems contagious."

"What would you know?"

Kenneth reached the door and opened it. Stepping through as Ellison called out, "When are you ordering one, cowboy?"

Kenneth closed the door behind him, smiling. Then he walked a few buildings away and crossed the street. Noticing the filled seats through the window at the Queen Restaurant, he started that way. *Wow, what a day.*

He entered the hotel and turned into the restaurant entrance, spotting Pastor West sitting alone near a window, peering out into the street.

"That's a lot of work out there for a man of the cloth," Kenneth said. "So many sinners he might not know where to start."

"There is, but a good cup of coffee can help him get going. And I could use a good man to help me witness to them."

Kenneth sat across from Pastor West. "I would, but I have work to do and can spend only so much time in town."

"We all have a time problem, don't we?"

Kenneth grinned. "So what does the Bible say about these mail-ordered brides?"

"Nothing, so far as I can tell."

"Do you believe this is a good way to meet someone? A man like Harley may never find a bride unless he does."

"If they are happy together, it's a positive endeavor," West said. "The difficulty comes when things don't work out. Of course, they may ask for my opinion in both instances."

"Makes it tough, I'm sure."

"Yes, it does."

"I heard you were waiting for Laura."

"I am, but I'm enjoying the coffee, too. She said she would come if she could work it in. I'm of the impression that I'm low on the list of priorities today."

"Now, don't take it so hard, Pastor. I'm sure Laura got herself involved with Harley only for a story."

"You think so?"

"I know Laura. Finances have been low for her of late, and she doesn't want to lose her job. And Orland Flack keeps pushing her for stories."

"I didn't know she was struggling so much."

"Don't say you heard it from me."

"I wish she'd marry me, Kenneth. I'd take care of her."

"Maybe you should try again."

"Maybe I will."

* * *

The sound of the whistle signaled everyone to move toward the depot. Harley walked in front of the crowd that moved like a swarm of bees toward the drop-off.

The train let loose a roar, and steam rolled from the sides as the conductor opened a back door. One by one, people stepped down, toting their baggage and purses. One man in a fancy vest and white hat lugged a saddle on his hip.

A gent in a dark hat and suit with a thick mustache peered

across the crowd. "A greeting party of sorts, I presume."

Kenneth and Pastor West saw Laura and worked their way through to her.

"There's a lot of people today," Pastor West said as they reached her.

Laura turned to them. "I hope it's good for Harley."

"And the woman."

"Dollie is her name."

"Okay, has Harley picked her out yet?"

Harley stood on the other side of Laura, looking over the new arrivals. "I don't know, Miss Stone. Which is she?"

Most women were too young, Laura thought, nothing like the woman in the photo; the others were men. Then a woman about sixty years old stood watching, waiting for someone. "Harley, the woman in the blue dress looks lost. I believe that's her."

"You think so?"

"Walk to her and see."

Harley turned to Laura, wide-eyed. "Okay, but I hope this works out."

As Harley strode away, Kenneth tapped Laura on the shoulder. "Do you think that's her? She's way older than Harley."

"Harley had a photo. Wasn't a good one, but that woman matches."

Harley stepped toward the boardwalk, his eyes dead on her. The woman in the blue dress bore a light-colored hat. Powder and rouge could not hide the years of wrinkles life had tendered. Still, Harley seemed pleased.

She gave a slight grin as he stood on the ground below. Her foot tapped, giving way to the anxiety as Harley smiled back.

"Are you Dollie?" Harley asked.

"Yes, I am," she replied in broken English.

Many in the crowd started giggling, realizing the woman in blue was Harley's bride-to-be.

"Why they laugh?" Dollie asked.

"I don't know." Harley turned to the crowd. "Stop, stop!" But they continued.

When others joined in, Laura could tell it was Harley's friends instigating the laughter, betraying him. "I have to get to her."

"Help her, Laura," Pastor West said.

"She's not that pretty, but I never expected our folks to treat her like this," Kenneth said.

Before Laura reached the depot's boardwalk, Dollie had turned to leave. Down the walk she strolled, carrying her suitcase. Harley's friends and others followed alongside her, still laughing. Dollie tossed the suitcase toward them, kicked off her shoes, lifted her dress, and ran down the boardwalk.

Laura pursued her, but it was too late. Dollie found a horse tied at the rail, mounted it and rode away.

Oh, no.

Pushing through the people, Laura reached the other side of the road, mounted another horse, and rode after Dollie.

Kenneth slapped Pastor West on the back. "Yep, this is why I came. The best entertainment in years."

* * *

Laura kicked the paint horse, but it didn't respond like Copper. She spotted the bay horse Dollie rode from town when she reached a curve. *Where is Dollie?*

Dismounting, Laura tied the paint to a tree. "Dollie, where are you?"

Dense woods covered both sides of the road. She saw a hill near a sparse section, but no Dollie. Then she heard someone crying and hurried from the road, stepping over limbs and large trees blown down by the storms. At last, she spotted the blue dress.

A limb cracked, and Dollie peered up as Laura came closer. Tears covered her face, and she reached for a damp sleeve to dry it. "You shouldn't have followed. I will lay here and die."

"Oh, no. You'll not die out here for a long time. The night may be cold, and you will suffer."

"I *can't* go back."

"Sure you can. You have to ignore those people. They only laughed to make fun of Harley, not you."

"Is Harley a good man?"

"I've not heard any bad about him, and he's a hard worker."

"I don't know," Dollie said, still crying. "Maybe wrong for me to be here."

"Maybe it is, but why don't you come with me to the hotel for now? We'll get you settled in. You'll have time to think it over. No trains are leaving for a few days, anyway."

"Thank you for coming. I'm too much trouble, aren't I?"

"You're not, Dollie."

"I go with you now."

Laura smiled, then reached for her arms to pull her from the ground. "Let's find those horses."

Chapter 54

$\mathcal{G}$ ordon Andrews carried a sack of feed outside and set it in the wagon. "Now that's a lot of feed, Laura."

"We may only have to do this for a short while. The sellers suggested we feed them well for a few weeks after the train ride, then grass only."

"When are these sheep supposed to be here?"

"They are coming on the next train."

"Well, I hope you know what you're doing."

"Yeah, so do I."

Pastor West walked toward them. "Can I help?"

"You're too late, Pastor," replied Gordon, heading inside. "That was the last bag."

"Hello, Steven," Laura said.

"Um, I saw you here and thought I'd ask if you'd like to have lunch with me."

"Sorry, I have to take this feed to the ranch. Can we make it supper? My horse is there, and I can ride back later."

"Sure. I'll drop by your place around six to see if you are ready."

"Sure." Laura climbed into the wagon as Pastor West offered a hand.

"So what's with all the feed, anyway?"

"That's a long story. Maybe I'll fill you in tonight?"

"See you then."

Sheriff Ellison walked by as Laura pulled away, making his morning rounds. "Pastor West, you should marry that woman."

"Believe me. I've tried," West replied, observing as Laura's wagon left town.

"What's her problem? Don't want to marry a preacher?"

"No, the problem's all me. I suppose I have crazy ideas about a woman's place and have messed things up between us."

"What do you mean, you have some crazy ideas? Aren't most women the crazy ones?"

West laughed. "I'll put it this way. A good woman can cause a man of *God* to dig deeper into his word."

"And did you find what you're looking for?"

"Well, I'll know tonight."

Ellison grinned and nodded. "Wish I could hear that conversation."

* * *

"Thanks for bringing the wagon home, Laura," Kenneth said as he approached, riding Ace. "How did everything go in town?"

Laura smiled. "Well, it was a long day, but we got the supplies we needed. That's a lot of feed in the back of the wagon."

She backed the team into an opening at the barn until Kenneth raised a hand for her to stop. "That will work."

She shoved forward the break. "Do you think there is

enough feed?"

"I hope so because I'm not sure we can afford more."

"This should give those sheep a head start."

"Laura, I still don't understand why we need it. Our grass is as good as it gets, especially the new fields."

Laura stepped down from the wagon. "I know you're right, Kenneth. But let me remind you that the man said to offer them some feed for a while because traveling is hard on them. And he said we still might lose some."

"I remember, and it will be a waste if we lose any."

"The farmer worried because this trip is further than he's ever sent his sheep."

"So, we are guinea pigs?"

Kenneth had agreed to take on the venture, but Laura knew it was only because he still felt the ranch mostly belonged to her. She hoped that in the first year, they would see a profit following the shearing. Any profit should change Kenneth's outlook on it. "Maybe we are guinea pigs. But it will be good knowing how sheep handle the trip should an instance arise that we have to ship."

"I hadn't thought of that."

"Let's get unloaded. I have to get back."

"What's the rush?"

"I have a date."

"West?"

She smiled.

Kenneth grabbed the first sack of feed. "Why you two aren't married is a genuine mystery."

"Well, he has asked me."

Wiping the sweat away from his forehead, he nodded. "Yeah, I remember. I also remember that you backed out."

She sat on the edge of the sideboards. "Well, maybe there's still hope for us. But what about you and Olivia? Do you have any plans for marriage?" She knew enough to know

Olivia would make him a wonderful wife for Kenneth.

He laid down another bag. "We've talked some about it, but with our lives so crazy, I don't see how it can work."

Laura shoved the last bag to the edge of the wagon. "Your story is as gloomy as mine, brother, but you shouldn't give up."

"I guess we're the sad siblings," Kenneth replied, picking up the bag and tossing it on the pile. "Though I'm not giving up. But I don't have faith it can happen."

Laura pulled herself around to the seat. "Then I will pray for you. Help me unhitch the team so I can hurry back."

"You're not even gonna drink coffee?"

"Not today."

Kenneth released the traces and pulled the collars from the team.

Laura offered Copper water and then tossed the saddle on him. "Don't forget the sheep are coming on Thursday." She kicked the horse forward.

Kenneth waved. "I won't forget."

* * *

After putting on her dress, Laura took out the curlers from her hair and arranged it. *What if this is the time? What if, today, West says the right things?*

"Lord, I've asked you this before. Am I to marry Steven West? I've read through your word and prayed for a sign, yet I've no answer. How am I supposed to know?"

She examined herself in the mirror, questioning what Steven saw in her. Some said she was pretty, but Laura viewed herself simply as a resilient woman with a pleasing complexion. Steven West was handsome and may be the most attractive of men in Santa Fe.

That first day she brought the wagon to town came to mind. Moving behind the wagon, she had tried to avoid him.

But he sought her out like a man on a mission. She could only stand and stare at Steven's beautiful blue eyes in his dark suit and tie. She never imagined a minister wearing a Western hat. Marriage may have worked, except for certain issues she discovered about Steven's beliefs and prayed they got resolved before he or she found matrimony with someone else.

"Lord, Steven may ask again for my hand. If it's a mistake to unite with him, please let me know. But if he's your choice, allow our time together to be as relaxing and peaceful as light rain on a spring day."

She sat and strapped on her shoes and then raised for another glance into the mirror. A knock sounded at the door as she preened for the last time. *He's here.*

She opened it and saw him standing. "Now that's a fine suit you have on there, sir, and a fine black tie."

"I purchased this a while back when we first—"

"—talked of marriage."

He turned his eyes downward. "That's right."

"Well, it suits you just fine."

"Have I seen that dress you're wearing?"

"Oh, it's not new."

"Well, you look lovely tonight. Shall we make our way there?"

Laura stepped outside and walked with him to the buggy, and they got in.

The driver clicked his tongue, and the horse pulled away, halting when they reached the Queen Hotel.

"Is this alright?" asked Ishmael Pepper.

"Yes, it's perfect."

Laura stepped down, examining the driver. "Steven, how did you manage Ishmael?"

"Oh, he borrowed the buggy from the mayor for the evening at my request."

"I could get used to this arrangement," Laura said as she stepped to the ground.

Steven held her arm, pleased with himself, and led her to the door.

Gloria appeared, escorting them to a table with candlelight. English ivy draped across one side.

"Thank you, Gloria," Steven uttered. "Give us a few moments before our meal."

When Gloria had departed, West drew back a chair for Laura, and together they sat.

Laura looked at him with suspicious eyes. "You've been busy since I left for the ranch today."

"Um, I hope I didn't overdo it."

"Not at all."

"I trust you like broiled fish with peas and corn."

"Sounds wonderful."

He turned and gestured to Gloria, who dispensed a young fiddle player who set in on an Irish ballad called *Danny Boy*.

Gloria brought glasses of sweet tea as they listened to the masterful musician.

When Laura had sipped the tea, she turned to Steven. "That song is so beautiful."

"Yes, it is one of my favorites."

The fiddler reached the song's end, and the waitress set down their plates of food before stepping away.

"How did we manage the restaurant for ourselves?" Laura asked.

"I suppose it's a slow night. Shall we pray?"

"Yes."

After the prayer, they sat enjoying their meal until West thought of something from earlier. "I didn't realize you fed your cows grain."

"We only feed grain whenever we're preparing some for the market, but you're wondering why we carried so much to the ranch earlier."

"Yes, it seemed odd."

Laura chewed a bite of food and set the fork on her plate. "We are starting a new adventure."

"With cows?"

"No, with sheep."

"Oh, sheep. I would never have guessed."

"I know we are in cattle country. Kenneth has reminded me a hundred times. But I did some research and felt sheep might help fill the gaps. We've found the cattle market often unpredictable."

"I've heard the same story from other ranchers. Some say another war would turn things."

"I hope war doesn't happen only to encourage the cattle market. Too many men lost their lives in the War Between the States."

"I am well aware."

They soon finished the meal and sat looking at each other. West motioned for Gloria, who sent the fiddle player for more tunes.

As the soft music played, West reached for Laura's hand. She felt him trembling as they touched. "You know how much I care for you, Laura. And tonight, I hope to ease some fears you've held about me."

"What do you mean?"

He swallowed, struggling to look at her. "Er, I know you want to continue working at the Journal. I've prayed for hours about our situation and have studied God's word more than ever. I admit that my views before were primitive. Maybe they filtered into my life from my past. I don't know. But now, I have taken another assessment of our lives or what they can be. Honestly, I can say my views will not hinder you."

West rose and moved to the other side of the table. Kneeling beside Laura, he took her hand. "Laura Stone. I may not be the best man for the job. I know you can find other options more suitable than I, though my heart doesn't believe that. I confess I am a changed man and ask for your hand. Laura Stone, will you marry me?"

Laura smiled and gazed into his eyes. "I wondered if you could change. Do you remember when I said before that I will not be the one to stand in the way of your beliefs and that any change must come from God?"

"I have a greater understanding of God's ways than before."

"Maybe you do. So, with your confession and willingness to make such far-reaching alterations for God and me, why wouldn't I marry you?"

Pastor West's eyes grew large. "So, that's a yes?"

"Yes!"

He reached and hugged her, and then they kissed her for a while. "Tonight, Santa Fe has a more confident pastor who will soon have a beautiful wife. I promise I will help at the ranch, and you'll have more writing time."

The fiddler plucked the strings with a finger and then took off on a speedy celebration song as Gloria appeared to congratulate them.

Chapter 55

*D*ollie York stood at the bed inside the hotel room, staring into the open luggage. She had not expected to leave for New York so soon and could not help but imagine Harley Richards' surprise when he saw her, an old maid.

The sight of the other girls leaving and not returning filled her with hope, but what was she thinking coming here, that it was her turn? Those girls were much younger and prettier. The best thing she could do now was find another job. Maybe she could spend her days waiting on some wealthy gentleman and his wife.

She folded the dress and laid it inside the trunk. "You old fool. You made a long trip for nothing. Maybe Martha May will find a job for you—something more permanent?"

A light knock sounded at the door. Who might that be? Not Harley Richards, I hope.

She strolled towards the door and opened it. Standing there was the young woman she had encountered the previous day in the woods. "Hello."

"May I come in?" Laura asked.

Dollie marched toward the bed where her belongings lay. Being pressed for time, she held uncertainty about conversing. She must soon board the train to New York.

Laura followed behind her, noticing her clothes and suitcases. "Leaving already? I must share something before you go."

Dollie inhaled air deep into her lungs and released it. "I suppose it can't hurt." She flopped on the bed, and Laura drew near and sat in a chair.

"Those men upset and mistreated you, and I understand," Laura alleged. "Though I think leaving may not be the best solution."

"Yah, the best solution is to get back to New York as fast as I can. I'll find a suitable job there."

"Don't you think you're being unfair to Harley? He spent a lot of money to have you come."

"I know about men like him. They'll have a good laugh at my expense. Whatever Harley paid doesn't come close to what he cost me."

"But that's where you're wrong."

Dollie lifted her chin, her pulse pounding. "And how am I wrong?"

Laura reached to the bed and touched Dollie's arm. "Harley spent days preparing for your arrival. He showed me the photo that you sent, and oh, how he loved looking at that photo. Dollie, Harley wasn't the one laughing. Those other men did, but not Harley."

Dollie's expression shifted to one of surprise. "Are you sure?"

"I am very sure because I was there."

"You're not saying that because you are Harley's friend?"

"I knew Harley, but then I learned of his intentions to bring in a bride."

Dollie stood from the bed and paced the floor, lost in

thought. "I don't know if I can ever live here. Won't I see those men around town?"

"That is possible, but none of that should matter if you love Harley."

Dollie spun to Laura. "I must clarify my intentions. Coming here was to meet with Harley. I do not have any contractual obligation to enter marriage. Martha May never conveyed that to me."

Laura stood and walked toward Dollie. "Who is Martha May?"

"Martha runs the Festival House where I worked the past two years."

When she heard they offered women as brides, Laura realized the implications. How could they encourage these women to become brides? But as soon as she thought about it, she knew it was wrong of her to take this attitude. The women were slaves to these establishments and did not choose this life. Despite their circumstances, they had every right to escape and start anew. "You have yet to meet Harley. Give him a chance. Meet with him alone and find out if you like him."

"But I have a train ticket purchased, and it leaves at one o'clock."

"There's still time."

"I don't know. How can I get past those men?"

"The best way is to meet them. Before you marry, have Harley bring you to meet his friends. I assure you they only laughed to embarrass Harley."

Dollie turned to the window. "They embarrassed *me*."

Laura could sense Dollie's discomfort. "I know they did, sweety. But sometimes, you must look straight into the face of those who desire to harm you."

"Not where I come from. If you try that, you'll get knocked to the floor."

Laura shook her head, realizing what she must have meant. What men did to women in that business was often brutal, and only Dollie and God knew the extent. If only she would stay. Perhaps life in Santa Fe with Harley would turn out differently. "Moving to this town may not guarantee a perfect life, but it has the potential to offer a better one than you have experienced."

Dollie peered at her, pondering what she said. Could it work? Or will my hopes vanish again? Leaving New York was a dream. An opportunity to escape that life filled her mind with happiness not known in years. But if she didn't try, she would return and soon find herself with these awful men. Persuading Martha May to find her a job with the wealthy was not a reality. "I'll do it. Please set up a time with Harley. I will ask him to meet with his friends. If this works out, I'll stay."

Laura smiled. "I believe you'll stay."

"But you must set this up now, for I have little time."

"I'll find Harley and hurry back." Laura walked toward the door. "Dollie, this is the right thing to do." She opened the door, gazing back at Dollie, whose face seemed unconvinced.

Chapter 56

Olivia had worked non-stop since the clinic opened. Her body ached, and she needed to recuperate. So today, she would take some well-deserved time off. Ishmael prepared a horse and buggy, and she set off towards Kenneth and Laura's ranch.

The dusty road was bumpy as the sun beat down on her back. But drawing closer to the ranch, she felt a sense of peace. The sprawling green fields and the sight of cows grazing in the distance were a welcome change from the chaos of running a physician's clinic.

Kenneth rode in near the barn and dismounted.

"Are you in a hurry?" Olivia asked.

"I'm here for medicine. A calf is sick on the other side of the gulley."

"Is there anything I can do?"

He pondered the question. "Yes, maybe so. I'll saddle a horse for you."

"So, what did you come for just now?" Olivia asked.

"Liniment. That's all I have."

Olivia followed him toward the barn. "Does it have a muscle problem?"

He paused and spun to her. "Well, liniment is all the medicine we have at the ranch, except for stuff to drench them with."

"Get the horse's saddle, and we'll look. But I don't know if I can tell you what's wrong."

Olivia watched as Kenneth saddled the paint mare, wondering what life would be like if they were married and living here. Although it would mean more time with Kenneth, the amount of work at a ranch made her question if it was feasible. But what if she treated her patients from here? *What a thought.* At least they could see more of each other.

He led the paint from the barn. "I'll ride Splash. She's green, and I don't want you getting hurt."

"Splash?"

"That's what I named her."

Olivia laughed. "Okay. So I will ride your horse." She started for the black gelding. "Are you sure he won't hurt me?"

"Don't act like you're scared, and Ace will be great."

"What if I'm not acting?"

Kenneth smiled as he mounted the horse. "Let's go."

They rode through the pasture, examining the other cattle along the way.

"What are you doing out this way, Olivia?" Kenneth asked. "Shouldn't you be working?"

"I took the day off. I felt like I'd been in a race since the clinic opened and needed to breathe."

"You can breathe here, and I'm sorry you're not resting."

"Getting my mind off the clinic for a day is refreshing. Being with you is like a tonic."

He smiled. "That means a lot. I've missed you so much."

"And I've missed you. We've some things to discuss after we check the calf."

"Okay."

Olivia saw a cow and a calf together as they pulled out of the gully. "Is that the one?"

"Yes."

The calf bellowed, and its momma did the same. They dismounted and walked closer.

"Kenneth, the calf is in pain."

"Yes, but why?"

"That's the question. Its voice sounds muffled."

"I thought so."

Olivia moved closer. "I wish I had my stethoscope, though it may be useless with cattle." She rubbed his neck, and it flinched. "Hmm."

"What are you thinking?"

"Something may have lodged in its throat."

"I have not thought of that."

Olivia shrugged. "Remember, I told you I've not treated cattle, so that may be wrong. But his voice sounds off."

"No, I trust you. So what do we do?"

"Can you hold open his mouth?"

Kenneth stared at her. "Are you sure about this?"

"No, but we should find out why his voice sounds this way."

He narrowed his eyes and gave a nod. "Okay."

Placing a leg behind the calf's rump, he held it across the back. Then, with one hand on the upper jaw and the other on the bottom, he forced its mouth open. "I can't hold this long."

Olivia peered into the calf's throat but saw nothing. "Hold it open." She reached her hand inside and pushed it deep to induce vomiting. "That should help. Let go, Kenneth."

The calf coughed and then regurgitated a pile of chewed grass mixed with milk to the ground.

"Oh wow," Kenneth said. "Is that a wooden stick?"

"I believe it is."

"That's the first time I've seen this."

"He got a little carried away foraging."

"Olivia, you saved that calf's life. I didn't know what to do."

"Yeah, the liniment thing would never help this." She giggled.

"You're laughing," he said. "At least I was trying."

"I'm only kidding. Can we ride back to the house now? We have things to discuss."

"Am I in trouble?"

She mounted the black horse, smiling. "You'll find out."

* * *

When they reached the house, Kenneth unsaddled the horses and led them to the barn. He provided them with hay as Olivia waited on the porch.

"This is a beautiful place you and Laura have," Olivia said as he approached.

Kenneth gave a slight smile. "I think of it as more of Laura's than mine."

"Laura doesn't see it that way. Half is yours."

"Well, her father owned it all the time she lived at home. She only learned of me less than a year ago."

Why was he saying this? "Horace was your father, too."

"But I didn't know that all these years, and sometimes it feels like I'm butting into Laura's life."

"How can that be? She was no more aware of it than you. But you know now she's your sister, and Laura knows you're her brother. That's all you need."

"So, why do I feel I'm working for her rather than partnering with her?"

"Time will change that."

"I hope you're right."

329

Olivia opened the door, and they went inside. Then she took a chair at the table. "Has Laura made any comments that would cause you to question that you are her brother?"

"No," he said, pouring a cup of coffee.

"You must settle this in your mind, Kenneth, or you will be miserable."

"I realized that."

"Then promise me you'll speak with Laura." She stared at him as he turned to walk away. "Look at me."

He leaned back toward her. "There."

"Promise me, Kenneth."

He tipped his head to one side and nodded. "Alright, I'll speak with her. So, is that what you wanted to talk about today? Maybe you came out to thrash me."

She laughed. "I did not. I came to spend time with you."

"But you sound quarrelsome."

"I'm sorry. I don't mean to." She turned her face downward, saying no more.

He walked to the buffet and dipped sugar into his coffee. "Okay then, let's hear what else you have to say."

Olivia sighed. "Nothing ever comes out right."

"What doesn't?"

She paused a moment, then turned to him. "When I arrived in Santa Fe, I expected to hate this place, but I didn't. My life in Boston had undergone significant changes. And when I realized Laura had stayed in Santa Fe—. Oh, you know all of that."

"But go on. You're telling this story for a reason," Kenneth said, now seated at the table.

"When I found out there was a doctor here already, all my hopes of establishing myself as a surgeon and practitioner vanished. But Laura has a way of helping people discover who they are."

"She does at that," Kenneth said.

"Most people don't know this, but after learning about my trouble in Boston, Laura put the idea in my head about opening my clinic. She suggested the house where I now reside and then helped me locate the owners."

"And I'm glad you are here."

"I am too, but my patients take more time than I envisioned, affecting our time together."

Kenneth sensed her anguish, got up from the chair, and walked closer. Olivia rose and reached her arms around him.

"Olivia, I understand you must see your patients. That's what you trained to do." He looked into her eyes and then kissed her. "Yes, things would be better if we could spend more time together, but that doesn't mean I don't love you."

"I'm glad because I love you, too, which brings me to what I must say. Do you think we can ever marry?"

He peered into her brown eyes. "I was hoping to be the one who asked that."

"Well then, ask it," she said.

He removed his hat and tossed it. "Olivia Bunney, will you marry me?"

She bounced on her toes and then settled to the floor, smiling. "I will. But will we ever see each other?"

He pulled her close again. "The thought of being away from you after we marry is something I can't bear. I'm willing to do whatever it takes, even if it means giving up my share of the ranch."

"No, you shouldn't have to do that." Olivia pulled away from him and sat again. "I have an idea."

"I see the wheels in your head turning."

"Those wheels were turning well before I came today."

"Maybe you should tell me."

She grinned. "Okay, I will."

Chapter 57

*L*aura informed Kenneth of her need to stay in town for Harley and Dollie, and he wished her well. She believed the couple would be perfect for each other if they could overcome their obstacles.

Thinking of them caused her to reflect on her upcoming marriage to Steven. She questioned if she had made the right decision and if he was ready for her to balance work and being his wife. Had she made the right choice? Was Steven prepared for her to work and be his wife?

She slapped the side of her face. "Steven said he was ready, and I believe him. So, stop doubting. You're getting married this time."

She crossed the street to the hotel and knocked on Dollie's door, half expecting the older woman to back out, but when Dollie opened the door, she met her with a smile and welcomed her inside.

"Harley should be here soon," Laura said. "He was so excited when you agreed."

"I hope I'm doing the right thing."

"Even if this doesn't work out, Dollie, you don't have to leave."

"Oh, I doubt there are jobs in this town for a woman with my background."

"You never know. I would be happy to help you."

"Laura, you've already done so much, which brings me to why? You don't know me."

Laura sat in the same chair as before. "I suppose I'm the kind of person who sticks my nose into people's business."

Dollie slid a suitcase to the side and sat on the bed. "Someone downstairs said you are a journalist."

"Yes. A journalist must be inquisitive, and I have no difficulty in that area."

"So you write stories for the newspaper."

"Lots of them. I may write one about you and Harley."

"What on earth about us makes a story?"

"People here would love to read about how a couple who lived miles apart came together."

Dollie tipped her head, peering beneath her brows. "We're not together yet."

A knock at the door paused the conversation.

"That may be Harley," Laura said. "I'll get it."

When the door opened, Harley stood wearing a fine suit and shirt. He was clean-shaven except for a mustache, with salt and pepper hair beneath a brown felt hat.

Harley smiled, peering across the room and seeing her on the bed.

"Come in, Harley," Laura said, holding to the doorknob. "I'll leave so you have privacy."

"No, please stay," Dollie uttered.

Harley stood inside as Laura closed the door.

"Yes, stay," Harley stated. "I want you to stay."

"I will stay quiet unless needed," Laura said.

They nodded in agreement.

Harley rubbed his hands, blinking. Laura sensed his uncertainty. "Harley, sit in the chair. Dollie, move closer so you can talk."

He paused, shifting his gaze from Laura to the empty chair. Doubt crept in as he contemplated his decision to come. Frozen in place, he waited, unsure of what to do next.

"Harley, what's wrong?" Laura asked.

"I don't know. I thought this would be easier."

"This is difficult for me, too," Dollie said.

A soft smile came on his face. "I like your accent. I never knew a French woman before."

"Yes, my mum brought me from France."

"I see," he said. "New things are always difficult, ain't they?"

"Yes, they are. Please sit. We'll get through the meeting, and you can decide if I'm right for you."

He made his way to the chair and sat. "I already know you are right for me. That's why I sent for you."

Dollie lifted herself from a slump. "But you don't know me."

"I know you are a fine-looking woman. We can figure out the rest."

Smiling, she looked at Laura and then at Harley. "Can you tell me about yourself?"

"Well, I ain't afraid to work. I help at the railroad and the sawmill. What sort of work do you do?"

Laura's throat tightened, reviewing in her mind Dollie's next words. The revelation that the woman had worked at a brothel could spoil the moment. She couldn't help but wonder if this information would alter Harley's perception.

Dollie turned her face to the window, gathering her thoughts. "I did some work as a maid. Is that possible here?"

Harley turned to Laura. "What do you think?"

"There are some homes around that require help. I can ask."

Harley smiled and took Dollie's hand, reassuring her he would work and that she should never feel obligated to unless she wanted to.

Dollie smiled, her aging teeth exposed. Harley's hard work and dedication to supporting them comforted her. "Thank you, Harley. I appreciate it, but I want to contribute to our life together. If you think it's alright, I can help us build a happy future."

"It's more than alright," he said, "if that's what you want."

"I think it is."

"So, Dollie, you're not catching the train back?" Laura asked.

"I will stay and see what happens. But what about those men?"

Harley looked on with curiosity. "Men, what men?"

"Those men at the train depot."

"Harley, she means your friends," Laura said. "They laughed and embarrassed her. If she could meet them, they could see how wonderful Dollie is."

He turned to Dollie. "They embarrassed me too. They were friends, but I've been angry with them since you came, and they laughed."

Laura walked closer. "Harley, Dollie needs to feel welcomed, and those men did their best to stir up folks against her."

"The town did nothin' wrong. That was all Lester, Calvin, and Samuel."

Dollie took his hand. "Harley, I want to stay, but I must feel welcomed. If your friends don't like me, they may laugh whenever I see them."

Harley rubbed his forehead. "I know where they are, and I'll speak with them right away. Those men will apologize." He

MICHAEL J SPANHANKS
rose from his chair. "I'll be back in a while with my friends."

Chapter 58

$\mathcal{H}$arley stepped in behind Lester Farley and Samuel Spence as they leaned against the hitching rail. "I still can't believe, after all the laughing you men did, you ordered brides."

"Well, Harley, we can't let you have all the enjoyment," replied Lester.

"I reckon. So, did you get them from New York? I never asked."

"No, from St. Louis. The outfit advertised in one of those dime novels with the gunfighters."

"Hmm, I wondered how you got them here so fast. Took me two months."

"They liked our money better," Lester said, laughing.

"Where's Calvin?" Harley asked. "Didn't he order one?"

"Yes, but Calvin was last getting a bath and wouldn't take one in dirty water," Samuel said. "Had to wait for the bathhouse to warm more."

"Thanks for meeting with Dollie and me. That means a lot."

"Sure, Harley. We didn't mean nothin' by it," Lester said.

"Hey, there's the train," Harley said, peering down the tracks.

They watched it roll in, screeching, sounding its horn. People gathered at the depot when they heard about the brides for Harley's friends.

Pastor West and Laura stepped up close by.

"Hello, gentlemen," Pastor West uttered. "This is a great day for some of you, though I thought there were three."

"I'm right here, Pastor," said Calvin Cook, walking up behind them. "My friends made me clean up last."

"No, you were late," Lester replied.

"So Laura, is Dollie finding Santa Fe to her liking?" asked Pastor West.

"She is. There were some hiccups at first, as you know, but these men helped, and we worked things out." She looked at Lester, smiling. "Isn't that right, Lester?"

"Yes, ma'am, it is."

"What's taking the women so long?" Samuel asked. "The train has stopped."

"I'm sure they are refreshing themselves after the long trip," Laura replied.

"What's that sound?" Calvin asked.

"I believe they call that bleating," Pastor West replied.

"Ble—what?" Lester asked.

"Bleating, as in sheep."

"Sheep!" Calvin said. "This country can't stand no sheep. Who brought in those stinking things to Santa Fe?"

"I did."

They turned, gazing at Laura.

Kenneth walked up behind them.

"And my brother," Laura added.

"I'll never live it down either," Kenneth said.

"Kenneth, don't you know this is cattle country?" Samuel said.

"Well, maybe it's time this country changed. Men, these are only a test run to see if there's any profit in them."

Lester slapped the hitching rail with his hand. "I hope you know what you're doing."

"Well, it's us doing it, and it will be us who may lose our pants."

"Don't be so negative, Kenneth," Laura said. "We're only getting started. We have a long way to go."

"That's what worries me."

"Hey, Lester," Calvin said. "Look what I see."

"That's our women," Lester replied.

Laura turned to Lester. "Don't you men think you should walk closer and meet them?"

"I reckon," Samuel answered. "Let's go, Calvin and Lester."

They marched toward the depot, where the women waited beside the ticket window. They looked at their future brides, who stood wearing Victoria Rocco Renaissance and Mary Antoinette layered dresses in lavender, wine, and blue colors, over petticoats and wire bustles. They each held a handbag in one hand and a matching parasol in the other.

"Now, ain't that something?" Calvin said. "Which one is mine?"

"Whichever you want, I guess," Lester replied.

"Well, I'll take the one in the blue dress. I think she's a might pretty. I like her yellow hair." He walked closer. "What's your name, ma'am?"

"I'm Claudia. What's your name?"

"Mine is Calvin. Calvin Cook and I paid for you."

Harley rejoiced to watch his friends meet with their new brides.

* * *

339

Laura and Kenneth went to examine the sheep stock as the workers set up the ramps for removal.

Kenneth climbed the side of the box car and peered inside. "I don't see any dead unless they are farther back."

"That's good. I hope we can keep them *all* alive and see them soon put on weight. The train trip had to be difficult."

"They look in fair shape, considering. The railroad watered them, or we'd have lost some."

Several ranchers stood outside the fence, mumbling between themselves.

"They don't like that we brought sheep in," Kenneth said.

"I don't care," Laura replied. "And they can mutter all they want. They aren't out money on this project."

"They don't have to like it."

"Maybe in a year, we will change some minds."

"If it works."

Burney Cutts, a bronc rider for the ranchers around, overheard them. "Mr. Speers and Mr. Barto will not appreciate this. You can count on that."

Kenneth pulled off his hat and wiped a hand through his hair. "Our ranch is five miles out and on the other side of town from those two. So there's no way we can cause problems for them."

"They may not see it that way."

"Well, it's too late to change it, Burney. The sheep are here, and we're taking them to *our* ranch."

"You know I have to mention this to Mr. Barto."

"I knew you would, but that doesn't change our plans."

"We're not hurting anyone with our sheep," Laura said. "We have plenty of land and will keep them away from everyone else's cattle."

"Well, I've been around those cattle ranchers and heard them talk bad about sheep farmers. I'm not saying I'm against it, but they will fight you over it."

Kenneth jumped from the box car and climbed over the fence beside Burney. "Then I hope you will stay out of it. We've been friends a long while, and I wouldn't want to see you get hurt."

Burney grinned as he stepped away. "I'll be fine. Better worry about yourselves."

"What are we going to do, Kenneth?" Laura asked.

"You mean now that *you've* gotten us into this mess?"

"You agreed."

"Sometimes I'm just blind!" He punched the fence with a fist. "I should have realized those other ranchers might cause trouble."

Laura stepped back from him. "What do you think they will do?"

"Anything is possible with them. I'll speak with them. 'Cause maybe I should tell them before they hear it from some old ranch hand."

"Tell them we are experimenting with this batch to see if we can profit."

"Yeah, if there's one thing they understand, it's money. The cattle business has hurt them as much as it has us. I'll ride out there as soon as we get the sheep home. Right now, I should round up Pastor West and some others we trust and get the sheep home. If there's any trouble before we get there, we need folks who can shoot."

"Alright. How long before we leave?"

"An hour if I can find help."

"I'm staying with the sheep until you return."

"That's a good idea."

Chapter 59

S heriff Ellison stepped onto the porch of the barbershop as Harley exited. "Hey, Harley. I hear it's the big day for you."

A broad smile came to Harley's face. "Yes, I'll be getting married."

"I thought for a while your woman was going back to New York."

"We worked it all out, Dollie and me. Was just a misunderstanding."

"So, what time is the wedding?"

"Eleven o'clock at the church. Going to be a biggun."

"What do you mean?"

"All my friends are marrying at the same time."

"Lester, Samuel, and Calvin, too?"

"Yeah, they didn't want to wait, so Pastor West agreed to hitch us all at the same time."

"Well, blow me down. That's a lot of weddings for one day."

Harley put on his hat. "Well, Sheriff, I have got things to

do. You go on inside and get a trim."

"Yeah, I bet you do. See you around."

Sheriff Ellison walked inside and spotted Irvin Speers sitting under the cutting hand of Roscoe Fry, barber and owner. "Hey, Irvin. How's the cattle business?"

"Not as good the last year. Beef prices have fallen across the board."

"But are you making out?" Ellison asked as he sat.

"Like I said, not as good. But my question to you, Sheriff, is what are you doing about those stinking sheep Kenneth Barlow and his sister brought to this country?"

"There's nothing I can do, Irvin. Kenneth and Laura have broken no laws."

"Now listen here, Ellison, this is cattle country in these parts. We can't have someone bringing sheep in and messing up things."

Sheriff Ellison saw Roscoe had completed Irvin's haircut and removed the cape. He stood up and placed his hat on the hat rack. "Too late for that. Irvin, have you ever wondered why they are doing it? I *don't* believe it's so they can fight against the cattle ranchers. But if you're telling me the cattle business is not what it used to be, then maybe it's the same for them. Perhaps they are trying something new to cover their losses, fill the gaps."

"I don't see how sheep can make them any profit. There's not enough meat there."

"The *money* is not in the meat."

"What do you mean?"

"No, the money is in the wool. I hear you shear the sheep about once a year and sell the wool in bundles back east. Didn't Kenneth talk to you about it? Laura said he was riding out your way."

"The boys said Kenneth came by, but I was deep in the canyon at the time."

Sheriff Ellison sat down in the barber chair, and Roscoe pulled the cape around him and started cutting. "I'll tell you what Laura told me. They brought in forty sheep to test the market. The idea is to keep them healthy, and when the time comes for shearing, they'll ship the wool to New York. But after the sale, they will run the numbers and see how things pan out."

"Well, I still don't like it. And we can't all raise sheep."

"How do you know, Irvin?"

"I don't, but I only want to raise cattle."

Ellison pointed his finger at Irvin, and Roscoe pulled back the scissors. "Irvin, I'll say this to you once. Leave Kenneth and Laura alone and their sheep. If I hear of any cowboy interfering, I'll run 'em in."

Irvin waved him off and turned toward the door. "You're taking sides, Sheriff."

"I'd do the same for you." Ellison watched as Irvin walked out and closed the door.

"Roscoe, changes are hard for old people."

"I suppose so," Roscoe replied. "Now, what changes do you think are coming for Harley and his friends?"

"The worst kind. Those men are taking on wives today. But they'll make changes for me. I expect they'll celebrate later, and you know what that means."

"Yep, means your jail will be full tonight."

"I just hope those grooms aren't some of them."

When Roscoe had finished cutting Ellison's hair, the sheriff left to finish his morning rounds. While passing by the mercantile, he noticed Kenneth and Gordon Andrews inside.

Gordon raised from behind the counter. "Hey, Sheriff. Making rounds, I suppose?"

"Yep, but I need a word with Kenneth."

"I didn't do it, whatever it is," replied Kenneth.

The sheriff laughed. "You did, in fact."

"How's that?"

"You brought those stinky sheep to Santa Fe. At least, that's what Irvin Speers thinks."

"Guilty as charged."

"The point is, Kenneth, I spoke to Irvin at the barbershop just now. Told him what Laura said yesterday."

"And what did he say?"

Ellison picked up a handful of peanuts from a barrel and cracked one open. "Just as you'd figure, not happy, but he listened. I told him you only intend to test the market and not go full-force with sheep. Maybe my speaking with him will calm the trouble for a while. Did you ever talk with Barto?"

Kenneth grabbed a sack of feed and walked toward the door with it. "Yes. Said he will keep his men in check until we learn more, but wants first dibs on our findings. I sensed Arche might invest in them later, depending on our results. He said he was tired of losing money in cattle."

The sheriff stepped closer. "Then Irvin is the one I'll look to if trouble comes. Are you going to the weddings?"

"Yes, I'm about to head toward the church. Laura has me helping."

Ellison turned back toward the counter. "I'm moving that way."

"I'll meet you there. Gotta set the wagon behind the church."

"Sure. Gordon, I got a bag," Ellison said. "Put about a half pound of peanuts on my tab." He reached into the tub for another handful.

"You got it, Sheriff."

＊ ＊ ＊

Sheriff Ellison and Kenneth walked inside the church. Pastor West addressed the men taking vowels later that day. When West had finished speaking, he stepped away from the grooms. "One wedding is hard enough. I never imagined I'd marry four couples in one day."

"You have your hands full, Pastor," Sheriff Ellison said. "And I'm glad it's not me."

"But you'll be busy later, don't you know?"

"Don't remind me."

West stepped out of the way as Laura, Olivia, and Lurline Willcock passed. "Lurline agreed to help. She is great with weddings. Kenneth, have you heard from Irvin?"

"I did," Sheriff Ellison answered. "Just moments ago at the barbershop. I told Irvin about their plans, but who knows if that will keep the trouble at bay? Time will tell." He looked at Kenneth. "I'm glad your ranch is miles away on the other side of the town. Irvin has men working for him who love to tangle and need no asking."

"I'll pray that Irvin keeps them busy," Pastor West said. "Well, gentlemen, folks will arrive soon, and I must prepare myself. I have a few weddings to perform."

Ellison reached and grabbed West's shirt sleeve. "So, Pastor, you and Laura are not getting married today?"

"Not today, but soon."

"So, who will marry you since you're the pastor?" Kenneth asked.

"I've sent a wire to a friend. We'll marry when he arrives."

* * *

The church filled up with folks who came to see Harley and his friends marry their mail-ordered brides. To make room, Pastor West aligned the couples down the main aisle: Harley and Dollie, Lester and Bessie, Samuel and Vella, Calvin and Claudia.

The organist started playing the wedding march, and the couples, understanding their places, marched down the aisle.

"Laura, it's wonderful how you worked things out for

Harley and Dollie after they embarrassed her," whispered Olivia.

"They did it all themselves."

"But you got them together."

"I may have had a small hand in it, though I had a motive. I wanted a story."

"I know it may have started that way, but you have a compassionate heart. God made you that way."

"I'm glad he did."

"If only that compassion leads to your wedding."

"Soon. That's all I know. Why don't you and Kenneth join us?"

Olivia smiled. "That's a great idea. We'll talk about it."

The music stopped, and Pastor West rose from a chair and walked to the front. "Today, I'm privileged to join not one couple." He pointed to Harley and Dollie, who smiled back at him. "Today, with God's help, I will join four couples in matrimony."

Sheriff Ellison watched from the back of the church. *I see trouble coming.*

Chapter 60

The town whirled with a flurry of activity as people bustled about, going back and forth on the street, shopping. Cowboys haggled over the price of horses as others sat gossiping outside the saloon.

A gray horse pulling a buggy appeared in the street, carrying a man dressed in a dark suit and hat with medium-length hair and a neat beard.

Pastor West waved as the driver brought the buggy to a halt. "Jess, you're earlier than I expected."

"Well, you know, funerals are not long at all. But I need to get back soon. So, could I marry you today?"

"Today?"

"Yes, I must leave in the morning."

"I wish you had wired again to say you're coming. Our women may not have prepared for such urgency."

"Did you say *women*?"

"There will be two couples marrying."

Jess grimaced, stepping down from the buggy. "I know I should have sent a telegraph, but knowing you, I thought you'd be ready."

West removed his hat to tap the sweat from his brow. "We expected your arrival but not the suddenness. In your telegraph, you said maybe three to four weeks out. But I can ask Laura and Olivia if it's a problem. I'll go now."

"Sure. But before you leave, tell me, where can I get a meal?"

"At the hotel. They will have what you need. I'll find you soon."

While searching for Laura, West spotted Kenneth driving the buckboard and walked over to him. "Kenneth, do you know where I can find Laura?"

"She is at the boarding house or Olivia's."

"My preacher friend is here in town to marry us."

"He's here now?"

"Yes, Jess During, and he wants to marry us today."

"That's rushing things."

"And are you and Olivia still getting married?"

"That was the plan, but now—"

"I know. I'll find Laura and see what she says."

* * *

Kenneth drove the team to Gordon's mercantile, stopped, and jumped down.

"Barlow!" came a loud voice.

Turning to find who was shouting his name, Kenneth spotted Burney Cutts standing outside the saloon, a cigarette in one hand and a bottle of whiskey in the other.

Kenneth waved, and Burney laughed.

"Barlow, you got to get those sheep out of this country!"

Burney and Kenneth once worked as bronc riders for Irvin Speers and others. Now, Burney divided his time between working for Irvin and Arche Barto. Kenneth had known Burney to struggle with whiskey's effects and thought the best thing to do was to walk over and try to calm him down.

As he neared the saloon, Burney pushed up his hat. "Kenneth, you want a drink?" He held up the bottle.

"You know I don't drink."

The townsfolk started gathering on the opposite side of the street.

Burney put the cigarette in the edge of his mouth, pointing his hand toward Kenneth to imitate a weapon. "Well, if you're not going to drink with me, then I guess you got to move those sheep."

"Where do you suggest I move them to?"

The drunk cowboy chuckled. "I hadn't figured that." But a thought came to him. "Oh, oh—back on the train, Barlow. You got to move them back on the train."

Kenneth stepped onto the porch. "Burney, how about giving me the gun? You know how you get with whiskey under your belt."

Cooper Tillman stood behind the swinging saloon doors. "I told him that, but he got to thinking about those sheep, and they riled him. Then he kept a drinkin'."

"I've seen him this way before, Coop. Burney will be okay."

Sheriff Ellison watched from across the street before strolling their way. Laura, Olivia, and Pastor West had gathered near a crowd that watched.

"Hey Burn, there's a bench behind us. Why don't we rest for a while? I'm exhausted."

Burney looked at Kenneth and nodded. "Sure, I'll sit with you, Kenneth." Then he paused. "But what about the sheep?"

Kenneth could do nothing about the sheep and knew only one way to help Burney. He put his hand on his pistol. "I'm sorry for this, my friend." He raised his gun from the holster, grabbed the barrel, and smacked Burney over the head.

Burney dropped the whiskey bottle and crumbled, gazing at Kenneth with glassy eyes. "That hurt." Then he passed out.

Sheriff Ellison rounded up several men to carry Burney to jail. "Yeah, I thought a four couples' wedding would challenge me, but then you pulled that pistol, Kenneth. I sure thought you might fire it."

"Nah, I've seen Burney this way before."

Laura, Pastor West, and Olivia rushed to Kenneth.

"I'm sorry you had to see that, folks," Kenneth said. "I didn't want to hit Burney, but he needed it."

"We know," Pastor West replied. "But the weddings—" West held a suit in his hands. Laura and Olivia waited in their Sunday outfits for Kenneth to respond.

"The weddings? Are we doing this now?"

"It looks that way."

Kenneth turned to Olivia. "Is this what you want? We could wait."

"That pastor came all this way to marry us. I think we should."

"Alright then, if everyone else is ready, I'll borrow that suit, Pastor." He grabbed the suit by the hanger and marched toward the jail.

"Kenneth," Laura said. "Meet us at the church."

He nodded and walked on.

* * *

The news of the two weddings circulated throughout the town. Folks filled the church, and others stood outside.

Pastor Jess During stood near the podium, waiting with a Bible in his hand as the organist played. Kenneth and Pastor West stood to one side, awaiting their brides' arrival.

"I thought they had already dressed," Kenneth whispered.

"No, they had other apparel for this occasion." West

chuckled.

"But wedding dresses are expensive."

"Don't ask me. I was okay with what they were wearing."

Soon the organist switched to the wedding march, and everyone turned to look at the back doorway, expecting the brides' appearance.

Olivia progressed first down the aisle. Kenneth met her at the front pew and led her to the one side, where they waited together.

Laura embarked, wearing a beautiful white silk dress covered with lace in the front. Pastor West approached and ushered her to their designated place.

Pastor During smiled and nodded to the organist, and the music stopped. Then, peering at the audience, he began. "The union between a man and a woman is a significant event in the eyes of God. According to scripture, God made the woman so man would not have to be alone, and then he said—*It is good.*

"Scripture declares to us in Matthew chapter nineteen, For this cause shall a man leave father and mother, and shall cleave to his wife: and they twain shall be one flesh? Wherefore they are no more twain, but one flesh. What therefore God hath joined together, let not man put asunder.

"Today, we gather to join these couples, Pastor Steven West, Laura Stone, Kenneth Barlow, and Dr. Olivia Bunney, in holy matrimony and according to scripture."

As the minister continued, Laura reminisced about the day she first met Steven and how ashamed she felt when she could not take her eyes off him while standing at the mercantile. Steven's staunch beliefs about women in the workplace had divided them for a space, but through prayer, he reconciled his faith with God's word, and they grew close. Now they waited at the altar with joy in their hearts and souls to join in marriage.

She glanced at her brother Kenneth, another benefit of

returning home. The long journey from Boston to set things straight about her father and his belongings had led to the discovery of a brother she never knew.

The town of Santa Fe brought its trials since her return, but provided rich blessings for her life.

As her mind wheeled, Pastor Jess remarked, "You may kiss the bride."

Laura turned to look at Steven through the bridal veil. Joy burst inside as he reached to lift it, remembering the blessings—her faith in the Lord, a brother who was a good friend, and Steven West, the finest man she had ever met. The opportunity to be this good man's wife made her grateful.

Steven kissed her, though it was not the first time. But this kiss was with a greater passion. Their zealous devotion would celebrate a life together.

AUTHOR INFORMATION

If you enjoyed reading this book,
please leave a review at Amazon.

For more books by this author see
Website - http://www.michaelspanhanksbooks.com